THE ADVENT OF MURDER

THE ADVENT
OF MURDER

A FAITH MORGAN MYSTERY

MARTHA OCKLEY
WITH SPECIAL THANKS TO REBECCA JENKINS

LION FICTION

Published by Lion Fiction
an imprint of
Lion Hudson plc
Wilkinson House, Jordan Hill Road,
Oxford OX2 8DR, England
www.lionhudson.com/fiction

ISBN 978 178264 006 6
e-ISBN 978 178264 007 3

First edition 2013

Acknowledgments
Scripture quotations taken from International Standard Version, 2012
© 2012 The ISV Foundation.

A catalogue record for this book is available from the British Library

Printed and bound in the UK, June 2013, LH26

MARTHA OCKLEY'S

FAITH MORGAN MYSTERIES:

THE RELUCTANT DETECTIVE
THE ADVENT OF MURDER

CHAPTER

1

Faith wiped at the vomit stain on her skirt with a tissue, trying to keep her eyes on the road. It would need to be dry-cleaned – just one more job to do.

Despite the unfortunate incident with a three-year-old boy called Nathan, the visit to the nursery attached to Green Lane Primary had gone exactly to time. Monday task, no. 6: Check! And it was still only halfway through the morning.

Faith took a deep breath. Just two weeks to go before Christmas Day. Thanks to an operation of military precision (or so she told herself) involving well-maintained databases, computer labels and a printed circular, she finished feeding the Christmas cards into the postbox on the Green at 6:32 a.m. The Christmas pageant script was in the hands of Clarisse and Sue, the stalwarts in charge of rehearsals and marshalling the angels and shepherds, and she – Faith Morgan, vicar of St James's, Little Worthy (it still gave her a thrill to think of her official designation) – was on her way to see Oliver Markham, aka her Joseph. She sang along to the haunting melody of her favourite carol on the Advent CD:

Tomorrow shall be my dancing day,
I would my true love did so chance
For to see the legend of my play,
To call my true love to my dance.

Oliver Markham and his wife were newcomers to St James's. As a relative newcomer herself, having taken up the "cure of souls" – as they used to say – of St James's parish just a few months previously, Faith found it particularly pleasing to be making someone else welcome to where she now belonged: *her* parish, *her* home.

The Markhams had arrived with their two daughters last summer, moving into a property down by the River Itchen. Julie Markham worked away quite a bit – as a lawyer or something high-powered in London. Oliver, a master carpenter, made bespoke furniture. Their teenage girls had taken to rural life immediately, but Faith sensed some tension between the couple. Perhaps their escape to the country might have seemed a little rushed – in one partner's eyes at least?

To be honest, Markham's ready agreement to play Joseph in the Christmas pageant surprised Faith, because she usually had a struggle to get the fathers involved in any sort of performance. She smiled as she pictured Oliver Markham, so exactly right for the part. Tall and steady-looking, good with animals too…

Task no. 1 flashed in red neon from the back of her mind. *Oh dear! The blessed donkey!*

Faith refocused on her driving. Council funds never stretched to gritting side roads, and last night's plummeting temperatures had frozen surface water from a weekend's heavy rainfall into a skin of ice. Sparkling frost this morning transformed the countryside into a magical scene, and the roads into a death-trap. Faith tasted spicy mincemeat and something else in the back of her throat. The nursery children had made their own mince pies and she hadn't had the heart to refuse their festive treats, offered with such pride and jauntily trimmed with a holly sprig; besides, she'd missed breakfast. Baked with more enthusiasm than skill, the half-cooked pastry now lay like lead in her stomach. Evidently little Nathan had sampled one too many.

The car slid around a mild bend. She *really* didn't like driving on ice. *Not too much brake or accelerator. Find an optimum speed and try to ride the road, not confront it.* That's what Dad used to say. He had taught her to drive in just such a winter as this.

For an instant, missing him engulfed her, as raw and intense as the day she lost him. The sensation passed quickly. A full-grown, self-sufficient woman now, Faith had learned to find refuge from sadness in professional purpose and pressing responsibilities…

One of which was to book the donkey for her pageant. Pat Montesque would never forgive her if Little Worthy's Joseph and Mary didn't parade with a real-life donkey this year. She hadn't meant to leave things so late. The task had sunk out of sight in the Advent rush. She'd managed to do some ringing round over the weekend, only to find the better-known local donkeys were all booked. She knew Pat suspected. The churchwarden had been mentioning with increasing frequency how Faith's predecessor-but-one, Pat's favourite vicar of all time (who had only left Little Worthy because he'd been called to higher office as an archdeacon in Wales) *always* made the Christmas pageant the highlight of the year. It was *the* moment when every inhabitant of Little Worthy, churchgoer or not, could watch Joseph and Mary make their way down the aisle of their ancient Saxon church and feel Christmas truly beginning.

"*Not*" – and here Pat would look at Faith severely down her small nose, the rolling of her Rs betraying her Scottish origins and the depth of her emotion – "*not* an oppo*rrr*tunity to be squande*rrrr*ed lightly."

The car swung sideways on a patch of black ice. Faith's stomach lurched sickeningly in response. Thank goodness there was nothing coming the other way. A close call. She slowed her speed and the tyres settled to the road again. Not far now. The Markham farm was just around that bend. Her fingers felt stiff from gripping the steering wheel so hard, so Faith wiggled her shoulders, willing herself to relax.

Around the next bend she saw a red post van canted into the ditch. It must have slid on the ice. No obvious broken glass. She hoped the driver was all right. It didn't look too bad – but why all the police cars?

Vehicles jammed the space in front of Markham's farm. A couple of uniformed constables stood unrolling blue-and-white police tape. At the back of a van, scene-of-crime officers were pulling on white body suits. A green Vauxhall Astra had pulled off the road at an angle. A pair of plain clothes officers stood by it, both tall and very familiar – one with gingery hair and an open face, Sergeant Peter Gray; the other dark and saturnine.

She hadn't seen Ben for eight weeks or more. They'd last met in the aftermath of the terrible tragedy that had engulfed Bishop Anthony's family. The scandal had disjointed everything and the bishop and his wife retired soon after, leaving the diocese still waiting for his successor's appointment.

As Faith parked to one side of the lane, Detective Inspector Ben Shorter acknowledged her presence with a glance that lingered for barely a second. She pressed the switch and the sheet of glass between them slid down into the window casing, letting in the freezing air.

Faith glimpsed the figure in the back seat of the green car behind him. A man in the uniform of the Royal Mail; he looked pale and distressed.

"What's happened?" she asked, glancing back over her shoulder at the red van in the ditch. Then she caught sight of the forensic tent being carried across the field stretching down toward the river.

"What brings you here?" Ben asked.

"Are the family all right?" she said.

Ben's expression gave nothing away. "I asked you a question first," he said.

Faith could have told him that wasn't quite the case, but nothing would be gained from arguing. "I'm on church business to visit Oliver Markham," she said. "He's a parishioner."

"Of course he is!" Ben rolled his eyes. "Well, Mr Markham is not in a position to receive visitors at this time."

Faith's hand went to her mouth in an involuntary action she'd seen many times herself. "He's not dead?"

Ben's expression softened. "The family are all safe," he said, "but…" He turned to one of his juniors, hovering nearby.

"What?" he asked.

"The pathologist is just wondering…"

"I am on my way." The junior was dismissed. Ben walked over to the back of the van and began pulling on a pair of white overalls.

Sergeant Peter Gray smiled at Faith apologetically. He and his wife, Sandra, had become friends since Faith met them over that first case. They were regulars now at St James's with their two boys.

"We've found a boy's body by the river on Markham's land."

"A boy?"

"Well, a teenager."

"Doesn't anybody know who he is?"

"Not yet. We only got the call forty minutes ago."

"Sergeant! When you're ready." Ben walked back over to them, fastening the tabs on his forensic suit.

"Sorry, boss," Peter responded cheerfully. *He must be getting Ben's measure*, Faith thought. There was a time when he would have jumped at Ben's chivvying. Now he responded in his own time.

Ben leaned his hand on the car roof and bent his head toward hers. His bulk filled the window.

"Want to come take a peek?" His face wore his insufferable *I-know-what-you're-thinking* expression. She struggled with her demon curiosity for a moment. He watched her lose the fight. He tapped the roof of the car. "Of course you do. Park up over there and join us. You'll have to suit up." He walked off without waiting for a reply.

CHAPTER

2

Ben crossed the field at a rapid stride. Peter followed with Faith at a more reasonable pace.

"Do you have an ID?" Faith asked.

"Not yet. I don't recognize him. I somehow doubt he's a churchgoer." Peter blushed. "Sorry, that's uncharitable of me. See what you think."

Faith avoided a patch of mud with an ungainly skip. "You don't think Markham's involved?"

Peter's flat tone as he reeled off his answer took her by surprise. He was in professional mode – it felt strange to see him like that. She found him so open and approachable as a friend.

"He's got some explaining to do. He says he's on his tractor clearing debris brought down the river by the rain at the weekend. The postman has an accident and ends up in the ditch. He sees Markham on his tractor; goes over to ask him if he'll give him a pull out so he can get back on his rounds – Christmas rush and all that."

"And?" Faith prompted. She couldn't see anything so bad so far.

"The postman sees the body down there by the river just yards away from where Markham's sitting high up on his tractor. It's the postman who calls it in. Markham claims he never saw it."

"Perhaps he didn't," said Faith.

"Hm," said Peter. *He sounds like Ben*, she thought. "There's the history too, though."

"History?"

Peter stopped, and blew out his cheeks. "Seven weeks ago, we got a call that Markham threatened some kids with a shotgun. We investigated – he said he thought it was someone stealing his oil, but his wife had complained a few times about youngsters hanging around on their land. The kid who called didn't want to take it any further. Still, there's paperwork, y'know."

"Oh!" said Faith. That didn't sound so good, but she wasn't surprised Oliver hadn't mentioned it to her. She thought of Oliver Markham as she had seen him, a craftsman who could be absent in his own world among his beloved timbers; a man who cared about making beautiful things. She thought of the family at the village fete that August – Markham clowning around with his daughters and throwing beanbags at coconuts to win prizes for them. "Sounds like he lost his temper a bit," she said.

"Doesn't do him any favours in the boss's eyes," said Peter. He glanced down at her, less formal for a moment. "Do you know him well?"

Better than Ben, she was about to say. Thinking about it, though, how well did she really know Oliver Markham? She compromised. "The Markhams only moved here in the summer. But I've seen quite a bit of them – they seem a nice family." Or at least, he seemed a fond father to his girls. Faith suddenly realized that his wife didn't feature in any of her memories of the Markhams. The gossips said Mrs Markham didn't spend more time at home than she had to.

The field dropped gently down to the river. The farm sat in a long bend of the waters' course. The landscape here was quite flat. The river ran like a horizon along the margins of the frozen soil. The recent heavy rain that had caused the river to flood was receding, the water level dropping back to leave a blurred margin of mud and debris, now solidified and laced with frost only just beginning to thaw as the sun rose higher. A circle of white-suited figures grouped around a sodden mass near the river's edge. Ben stood over a woman with red hair, vivid against the frosted grass and white forensic suits. She was crouching down by the body, but with her face lifted toward him, his concentration full on her as she talked. They broke off as Peter and Faith approached. The woman nodded to Peter and introduced herself to Faith: "Harriet Sims, pathologist."

Faith glimpsed shrewd speculation in her eyes. "Ben tells me you're the vicar – but you were in the force with him once? I'd better not shake hands." She had pulled the forensic gloves on carefully; not a wrinkle to mar the elegant outline of the hands she held up in illustration. She readdressed them to their task of picking delicately through the victim's clothes.

He was a teenager – maybe sixteen, seventeen, thought Faith. A stud decorated his left eyebrow. The metal protruded, a jarring addition on that half-childish face. His hair was dyed dead black and styled in a long fringe cut to cover his face to the chin, except that someone had pushed it back – leaving three-quarters of his vulnerable features bare to the bright winter light. A wave of compassion and sour sorrow washed through Faith, almost overwhelming her.

"So – is he one of yours?" Ben's question carried an edge of anger. Faith recognized his disgust. Her congregation at Little Worthy was comfortably off, for the most part. He knew it wasn't likely to contain a boy such as this. She felt acutely guilty. Ben always said that she was running away from reality, playing at being a vicar in such a picture-perfect place. To her own ears, at least, she managed to keep the emotion out of her voice as she answered.

"No. I've never seen him before – as far as I know."

Ben ignored her words. "You're formal for a Monday." He jerked his chin, indicating the dog collar that could be glimpsed under her winter wrappings. "Where've you been?"

"Telling the Christmas story to five-year-olds," Faith answered absently, her eyes still on the corpse.

The dead boy's hair was fine. In life it must have obscured half his face all the time; irritating, you would have thought. Now river mud had mixed with oozing blood, tangling it into matted streaks around the lad's temple.

The team junior finished his phone call and turned expectantly to his boss.

"Anything?" Ben asked him.

"Not local, sir. They're running the national database to see if anything sparks."

"No ID on him, just keys and maybe £15 in cash.' Harriet held up an evidence bag containing a battered mobile phone. It oozed river water, puddling the sides of the plastic. "There's this phone. It was in his hip pocket – but the case is cracked. It must have taken quite a knock."

Peter took it from her – holding the bag up against the light to examine it. Faith could see that the casing had come away, exposing the inner workings of the phone.

"We might get something off it," Peter said dubiously. Ben joined him for a closer look.

"After it's been in the river? Waste of time – but we'll process it anyway."

Harriet Sims was examining the boy's arms.

"No needle-marks, but…"

"… he might have been on something," Ben cut in. Their eyes met.

He finished her sentences for her. Was there something between them? *None of my business*, Faith scolded herself. She focused her attention back on the victim. Somebody's son.

The clothes were soaked, but once you looked past the mud, they weren't heavily worn or tattered, like the garments of street kids she'd come across in the past. He wore a padded jacket over a dark T-shirt, and jeans. His trainers would cost a lot, even second-hand. The exposed skin on his hands and face, and a bared patch of thin midriff, bore scratches of the kind that might be inflicted from branches or twigs. When he was alive, he had chewed his nails.

Traces of silt covered every bit of him.

"He's been washed down the river – some way I would have thought," she said out loud. For a moment she had forgotten she wasn't part of the investigating team – that wasn't her job any more. Ben flicked her a glance of recognition – just like him to notice her slips.

"Maybe." Harriet got to her feet. "He's a mess," she said briskly. "I'll have to get him back and cleaned up before I can tell you more." The direction of her gaze shifted to a point just beyond Faith. Faith saw her eyes widen and turned to see a large Dobermann a couple of yards away, slavering copiously. She took an involuntary step back, bashing into Ben.

"Damn it!" he snapped, apparently not alarmed by the

dog's belligerent appearance. "You'd have thought we could be spared rubberneckers way out here. Get that dog away from the crime scene!"

A petite woman accompanied by a second large Dobermann had come down the path from upriver. A well-preserved forty-something wearing a new tweed jacket of fashionable cut and matching tweed skirt, she strode toward them swinging a bright blond wood walking stick.

"Go on, sergeant – get rid of her. We don't want her blasted dogs trampling evidence." After a split second's understandable hesitation, Peter set off. "Why don't you go with him?" Ben continued to Faith. "Now *that* looks like a potential member of your flock. Make yourself useful." Faith narrowed her eyes at him. This provocation was starting to annoy her. His gaze met hers in mocking challenge. Faith liked dogs but she wasn't keen on breeds created to guard and attack. Ben knew that. Refusing to give him the satisfaction of admitting her apprehension, she turned resolutely to go.

The dog hadn't moved. It stood square, ears pricked, its bright eyes fixed on her. She set out to follow Peter, giving the beast a wide berth. As if pulled by an invisible thread, the soft side of the dog's pointed muzzle curled up, exposing a flash of impressive teeth. The well-muscled barrel chest emitted a low hum.

Still some yards away, the woman slapped her walking stick against her booted calf in a flash of irritation.

"Jam! Shush!"

The dog dropped its ears and lowered its head. The Dobermann joined its partner at its mistress's heel.

The woman turned her stare toward Peter and lifted her chin. "What's going on here?" she asked, exposing perfect white teeth. Bonded, thought Faith. Her jaw line was sharp –

not a trace of softening, even though Faith thought she might have turned fifty, now she could see her up close.

"There's a police investigation in progress, ma'am," said Peter. "I must ask you to move on with your dogs, please."

The newcomer didn't move. "Has there been a death?" She turned her attention from Peter to examine Faith. She noted the dog collar. "Have you come to arrange the funeral?"

"I am here only by chance," Faith explained. "I am vicar at St James's."

The woman tossed her head. "Of course. The new one. I attend the cathedral – although I have no problem with women vicars myself. We haven't been introduced." She pulled off her glove and reached into the inside pocket of her jacket for a laminated business card depicting an artful shot of some exotic bloom. "Mavis Granger – I have a florist shop in town." As she talked she craned her neck to look past Peter to see what she could of the activity around the water's edge. The body was concealed behind a patch of reeds and the forensic team were erecting the tent over it.

"Faith Morgan," said Faith, taking the card. A brooch pinned the turquoise blue pashmina scarf around Mrs Granger's neck – a stylish Swedish-looking piece in platinum and gold. Ostentatious for a country walk, she thought.

"You've probably heard of my husband – Neil Granger," said Mavis. "He's well known in the community; his family have farmed in the area for at least three generations. We live at the Old Mill, over that way." Mrs Granger nodded upriver, then treated Peter to a rather fierce glare. "I often walk Jam and Marmalade down here," she told him. "You are a policeman?"

"Sergeant Peter Gray. And when were you last here, Mrs Granger? Did you walk this way over the weekend?"

"Oh, not since last week sometime," she said. "Last Wednesday, maybe?"

"And when you've come this way before, you've never noticed any teenagers hanging out in the area – they don't make a habit of using any spots along here?"

Mavis looked at him sharply. "What for?"

"Well, you know – the usual; to meet up, hang out, the things teenagers do."

"Take drugs you mean? Disgraceful! I wouldn't know about that."

Faith could see Peter had categorized the conversation as fruitless and was losing interest, and Ben stood deep in conversation with Harriet Sims. Very close, she thought. Almost touching.

"I am afraid I must ask you to move on, Mrs Granger," Peter said. "Back the way you came, if you don't mind." He offered her the direction she had come from with an outstretched arm and a conciliatory expression. Mrs Granger's mouth and chin took on a stubborn expression.

"But we haven't finished our walk."

"If you don't mind, ma'am," Peter repeated. "This path is closed until further notice."

Mrs Granger looked to Faith.

"It's procedure, I understand," Faith commiserated. "It is a bore to have to turn back, I know, but I am sure the police will be clearing the path just as soon as possible." Mrs Granger stared straight at her. Faith could almost see the cogs whirring behind her eyes. Something clicked into place.

"Of course. We must support the police. Good boys!" (This last addressed to her dogs.) The Dobermanns moved neatly synchronized to heel as Peter accompanied Mrs Granger back up the path. As she went, Faith heard her confiding,

"Though I will say, sergeant, as a long-time resident of this neighbourhood, it's hard to feel safe any more. Only this summer, while my husband was away, we were broken into at the Old Mill. If I didn't have the boys for company, I don't know what I would do. You people still haven't caught anyone for that!"

Peter exercised enough self-discipline to thank her for her help, then returned to Faith's side. Together they watched as Mrs Granger and her dogs grew miniature in the distance. She never once looked back.

"Could this be connected to burglary?" Faith asked Peter. "Have there been many break-ins round here lately? I vaguely remember something in the local rag, but I haven't had time to follow the news much."

"Not as many as the press like to make out," he replied. "You always get a few more in the run-up to Christmas. It's mostly young offenders – other people's Christmas presents. All laid out in plain view from the front window and ready to go."

"Sergeant!" Ben called across from the crime scene. "Do join me inside, if you've got the time."

"On my way, sir. Sorry, Faith – got to go…"

"Don't worry, I'll walk with you," Faith said quickly, skipping a couple of steps to catch up with him. She wondered if she'd be allowed to speak with Oliver before they took him away. They strode back toward the house.

"Do you remember the burglary at the Old Mill this summer?" she asked, puffing slightly.

"Not our department," said Peter, a little defensively. "But you know the statistics on theft. Hampshire's clear-up rate is less than 20 per cent."

"Not a conviction score to brag about."

"No. But like I said, not our department."

The Markham house was a 1930s building with a modern extension. To one side stood the barn that Oliver Markham had converted into his joinery workshop. Ben had shed his white boiler suit and was waiting for them outside.

"There hasn't been a recent break-in here, has there?" Faith asked Peter, as they stood side by side, wrestling their way out of the nylon fabric.

"None reported," Peter replied, curtly. His attention was fixed on freeing his lower leg from the clinging forensic suit, but she could tell her question had hooked his attention. They joined Ben.

"You took your time getting rid of her."

"Recognize who that was?" Peter asked. "Mrs Neil Granger."

"Ah…" Ben snorted.

"Who is Mrs Granger?" queried Faith.

"Mrs *Neil* Granger? Put herself up to be a magistrate not so long ago. Likes to speak out on behalf of her community."

"She told me her husband was very well known," said Faith.

"Even if he's heard of more than seen," Peter said, rather naughtily, Faith thought.

"Piling up the dosh keeps him away from home," Ben added. "Mr Neil Granger does a lot of business over in Scandinavia, so they say. I was thinking, sergeant, we should invite Mr Markham down to the station for a chat. He's in the kitchen with young Eagles." Peter nodded and went in.

"You can't be serious," Faith said. "You can't think Oliver Markham is responsible for that boy."

Ben looked down at her fondly – or maybe it was just condescension. "You know about the shotgun incident?"

Faith sighed. "Peter told me. It's a jump from that to murder, isn't it?"

"I thought you were keen on leaps of faith," said Ben. He was definitely smiling now.

Peter came out of the house with Markham, holding him loosely by the arm. She glanced at his profile and tried to see the carpenter objectively. He was a big man, with strong shoulders and forearms, and broad hands. Right now he had them clenched as if he might hit out. But did Oliver Markham really look like a man who had murdered on impulse and then been caught red-handed trying to dispose of the body? Faith hurried over.

"Oliver! What a wretched business." She pulled back her outstretched hand before it touched him, repelled by the electricity of his suppressed emotion. It took him a moment to recognize her.

"Faith!" he greeted her jerkily. "I forgot. Sorry – can't offer you coffee."

"Where are Julie and the girls? Is there anything I can do to help?" she asked.

Oliver blinked. "Gone to London for a few days; Christmas shopping. No need to bother about them." He lowered his head and gave Ben a bull-like stare. "Are we going, or what?"

Faith sat in her car, waiting for the heaters to breathe life into her hands. Down the lane, the postman was chatting to the man from the AA. At least some Christmas cards would be delivered late that day. Her phone beeped officiously. She needed to leave for her next appointment at the cathedral. She watched Ben execute a neat three-point turn and drive off with Peter and Oliver not talking to one another in the back.

Surely all this with Oliver Markham would sort itself out soon enough. She prayed that it would.

As Faith attempted to turn in the lane (less successfully than Ben), an additional thought stole into her mind unbidden, though it seemed trivial in the circumstances. If Ben's ridiculous suspicions had any foundation, Little Worthy's Christmas pageant had just lost their Joseph. And they still had no donkey.

CHAPTER

3

A light snow began to fall, and the road into Winchester soon clogged with slow-moving vehicles. After crawling in traffic for longer than seemed worth it, Faith finally found a space in a car park not too far from the cathedral. She felt glad of her padded winter boots. Whirling snowflakes filled the air, veiling everything in white as she made her way to the high street.

She might have mailed her cards, but she still had nothing to give to her mother. Her sister offered no problems – Ruth liked to know she was getting a refill of her favourite perfume – and Sean, her nephew, had been considerate about letting her know a couple of things he would be happy to receive. But Mother – she must find something nice. She hadn't been able to get over to Birmingham to see her for a couple of weeks now because of the Advent rush. Ruth had been dropping dark hints that they "needed to talk" about their mother. She must schedule some time to find out what that was about.

Medieval and Tudor timbered buildings looked on benignly through the falling snow. "Rudolph the Red-nosed Reindeer" played from a sound system somewhere. Along the high street, crowds of serious shoppers, bulky with bags, mixed with rushed mothers hoping to pick up some Christmas presents in the last hour before the school run. Such a fuss surrounded this winter holiday – it was as if the whole street pulsed with illuminated anticipation of the one day in the year when happy families would exchange the perfect gifts and enjoy the perfect day.

Faith made for the shelter of the porticoed shops of the Pentice, just the sort of place she was bound to find a suitable present. On the way, she spied a nifty calendar clock in an electrical store's display. That would be useful for the kitchen – never again need she forget what day of the week it was. The clock could tell her the day, the date and the time as she made the morning coffee. The thought of herself standing in her kitchen brought her up with a start. Christmas food. Oh dear! She hadn't got back to Ruth about that either. The problem with being a vicar at this time of year, Faith meditated, gazing at an incongruous pink teddy bear in a Santa's outfit, is that there just isn't enough time to organize Christmas with your own family.

Ruth usually had Mother over since Dad died, and nephew Sean would be back from uni for Christmas at least (New Year was another matter). Ruth would be expecting Faith to join them. Faith's elder sister was a born hostess. She liked cooking and laying out feasts for other people. Ruth even found time to maintain Mother's old tradition of constructing elaborate Christmas table decorations. As a child, Faith's favourite had been a cardboard boat with painted sides and aluminium foil sails, chocolate coins covered in gilt paper concealed in its hold. That one had lasted for years (minus the chocolate, of course). It was probably still in Mother's attic somewhere.

She drifted closer to a shop window framing an enticing Christmas scene. The sight of all those perfectly wrapped boxes surrounding the silver gilt tree brought to her mind Peter's words about young offenders stealing other people's Christmas presents. The atmosphere curdled around her as the horror of the morning returned. The black and white of the dead boy's face came between her and the glow. He'd never see another Christmas.

Flakes of snow found their way inside her collar and dripped cold on her skin. Faith tried to move toward the shelter of an awning, but she found herself elbowed out of the way by a group of excited young people, absorbed in their conversation. Suddenly the glut of festivity seemed terribly shallow, feverish and misplaced.

She shook herself, physically and mentally. The boy's death was a tragedy, but she had to get on with her day. Others were relying on her. She ventured inside the shop and selected a beautifully carved bird table for her mother's garden.

Having paid, she looked at her watch. Mr Postlethwaite had said he would be rehearsing until three. She still had time to visit her avenue.

Its parallel lines of graceful trees always took her breath away – and today the sparkle of frost and snow had transformed them to a fairyland. The cathedral's west front, snow-dusted, soared like an intricate ice palace against violet cloud-banks heavy with snow still unshed.

She savoured every moment of walking through her avenue of winter trees in stately rank, turning back as she reached the steps of the cathedral to appreciate its loveliness from another angle.

Faith had never met the junior choirmaster, and wondered what he would be like. Postlethwaite – wasn't that a northern name? She imagined a small, portly Yorkshireman with a balding head. Mr Postlethwaite, it seemed, had had some success running youth choirs locally, but the collaboration with the cathedral was a new venture entirely. George Casey, the diocesan press officer, had been circumspect about the appointment, which in Faith's eyes was as good an endorsement as any. Pat too, and that added a further naughty satisfaction.

She crossed the threshold into the chill, lofty space, looking up at the medieval builders' attempt to encapsulate eternity. They had certainly captured peace. At this time of day a hush fell over the cathedral, its few visitors dwarfed in the vastness. Her rubber-soled boots padded silently across the stone. Her white breath suspended in space for a moment as she exhaled.

From a side chapel she heard voices singing with energy and without accompaniment. Captivated by the joyous energy of song, she followed the sound.

A blast of hot air basted her as she passed a garden-style heater. Beyond, the choir ran through rehearsals with its back to her – maybe twenty or more young people, teenagers mostly; early twenties at the most. Their attention was focused on someone invisible from where Faith stood. She slipped into a pew to listen. A young man's voice came in a beat late. He broke off with an exclamation of frustration.

"That's just slightly off..." The choirmaster's voice was calm. "But we're getting there." Voices dropped and Faith heard a murmured altercation with the soloist. Two girls in the back row noticed her sitting behind them, then several other heads turned.

"OK. We've run out of time. Thank you, one and all." Chairs scraped back and a rising hum of young voices drifted over as the group before her fragmented. The junior choirmaster's voice rose a notch. "Wednesday, 6 p.m.; meet in the choir room. Text alerts will follow."

Faith was conscious of the stares examining her as the group passed – especially from the girls. She rose from her seat and saw the conductor for the first time. Neither short nor bald – mid-thirties, Faith guessed. He rose a comfortable two or three inches taller than her, with close cropped fair-ish hair. He hailed her.

"You must be Faith?" He had guarded, worldly, hazel eyes. "Jim Postlethwaite."

"Faith Morgan," she responded. His hand gripped hers.

Without warning, Faith suddenly felt a little faint. She reached for the support of the nearest pew-back. The choirmaster slipped a steadying hand under her elbow. He bore her weight easily.

"You all right?"

"So sorry! Festive stress. I've been running on empty since first thing."

"Really? I thought this time of year was supposed to be joyous," he said ironically. She was grateful for the lack of fuss. His tone made her feel a little less of a fool.

"And it is," she replied, "but less so when you are short of a donkey for the nativity pageant. You try booking a donkey this close to Christmas." The dizziness passed and she straightened up.

"It's freezing in here," he said. "I don't know about you, but I'm gasping for a cuppa. How about we transfer to my lodgings? I might even have a stale mince pie sitting around."

"Now you're talking," said Faith. "Lead on."

They left the cathedral by the south door. The snow had ceased, leaving a glimmering in the dusk.

"So tell me about your choir," Faith said. "How many should I expect for our Midnight Mass?"

"Probably fifteen or so. They won't all turn up, but I'll bring those that do in the minibus, so you'll be sure of a quorum."

They made their way cautiously down the icy paths crossing the Close toward the ancient King's Gate.

"How did you come to be here?" asked Faith.

"You think I don't look the part?" Jim gestured back at the historic magnificence of the Close behind them. He grimaced self-deprecatingly. "You're probably right. I came to Winchester on an Arts grant this summer – *Bringing harmony to troubled lives…*" Faith looked at him sideways.

"Really?"

He grinned – an endearingly open and boyish grin.

"Well, that was the pitch. The dean came to one of the concerts. He thought it might be something we could replicate with the cathedral's backing. I help out with the main choir as well, of course." Jim stopped before a painted mews house. "Here we are."

They climbed a polished oak staircase and he unlocked the door to a suite. What had once been gracious proportions had been divided into more modern spaces by plasterboard partitions – a bedroom, bathroom and a truncated sitting room dominated by a startlingly lofty window. The space was furnished with chairs and a sofa bed covered in an easy-clean fabric in a dull red. On the short wall, a drinks fridge and a mini microwave gave the appearance of a galley kitchen. An electric kettle sat on a narrow worktop beneath a cupboard too small to hold much more than a few mugs.

"Take a seat," he said. She peeled off her outer layers and sat on the uncomfortably geometric sofa while Jim flicked the kettle on.

"They're a good bunch," he was saying, as he deposited three mince pies on a chipped floral plate. "The numbers fluctuate, but we have maybe twenty to thirty regulars, aged between sixteen and twenty-one." He nodded over his shoulder to a pile of leaflets lying on the coffee table. "Some of the kids came from the summer choir; others are newbies. You might be interested in those. Publicity leaflets. St James's is in the list. Take a bunch to hand out at your pageant. Might pull in a few more punters for Midnight Mass – you never know."

The flyers were eye-catching – candid shots of choir members against lozenges of colour. Faith's eyes stopped on a youth with his head tilted to one side against the weight of a fringe like a black wing.

The dead boy's eyes were striking – they looked straight out at her.

"You don't take sugar?" Jim was leaning in front of her, placing the mince pies on the table. She shook her head in a rapid negative, startled by the warmth spreading over her skin as he looked down at her. She dropped his flyer on the table and took a mince pie.

"That boy with the black fringe down the bottom there…" she said. "The picture against the yellow…"

He leaned over her to look and then converted the movement, twisting his body gracefully to sit down, lounging, relaxed, opposite her. The flyer lay on the table between them.

"Lucas Bagshaw. Pity," he grimaced, regretfully. "He had a really good voice."

"Had?"

"He walked out on me," Jim said wryly. He smiled at her, unguarded, as if they were old friends. "These kids aren't always reliable. Lucas left us in the lurch; didn't turn up for Sunday's performance." For a moment his hazel eyes reflected annoyance. "Didn't even bother to text to give me the heads-up. He had a solo, too – you heard us trying his replacement. He is a good lad, but like most of them, he lacks confidence."

"Lucas?" Faith asked, confused. Jim frowned, puzzled a moment. Then his face cleared.

"I meant the substitute. No. Now you mention it, Lucas is pretty mature for his age."

He got up, and poured boiling water into two mugs. Faith let her teeth sink into the pastry of the mince pie. She couldn't be sure – could she? She swallowed without chewing properly.

"I don't suppose I could use your facilities?"

"Feel free," he replied. "It's just down the hall. First on the right."

She locked the bathroom door behind her and fumbled in the depths of her bag for her phone. It barely rang twice before Ben picked up.

"Shorter." *He's in a mood*, she thought. There was no use beating about the bush when he was like that. Faith took a deep breath.

"Lucas Bagshaw – he could be the…"

"The victim at the river?" Ben cut across her. No small talk. No preamble. Just straight in, the way it always used to be.

"His face is on a flyer for a choir. I think. He is – was – a member of a youth choir performing around the diocese." There was a pause at the other end of the line.

"Where are you calling from?" She had a sudden vision of herself sitting on the covered toilet in the bathroom of an attractive man she had only just met. She felt the heat rise up her cheeks.

"The cathedral," she answered. Bother! That sounded defensive. What was she – sixteen? Faith screwed up her face, waiting.

"Where*abouts* in the cathedral?" Ben's voice asked in her ear.

There was a gentle tap at the door.

"Are you all right in there?" Jim asked.

Faith muffled the phone in the towel hanging by the sink.

"Fine!" she called out, cheerily. "Be out in a minute." She heard him retreat down the corridor.

"Got to go," she said hurriedly in to the phone, and rang off. She depressed the toilet handle and washed her hands, drying them carefully to buy herself some time. Until Ben confirmed the ID, she'd keep this to herself. "Bluff," she told her reflection. "Just bluff."

"Anything wrong?" Jim asked as she reappeared. There was a steaming mug beside the mince pies.

"Had to take a phone call," she said breezily. "Mobiles are convenient, but so *inconvenient* sometimes – don't you think?" She smiled at him, picking up her tea and taking a sip while she sat back down. "Tell me more about your choir," she resumed. "Where do you draw the kids from?"

"They come from all sorts of places."

"But all from Winchester and hereabouts?" She paused to drink more tea. "Do you not worry about them, these kids, when they fail to turn up or drop out all of a sudden?"

"I'm not a social worker. If they join my choir, they do so as individuals, not children. I don't need them to account for their lives or their families. It's the secret of my success," he said, with a lopsided smile. "So long as they show commitment to the choir – that's good enough for me." He apparently read the doubt in her face. A pulse of energy bent him toward her, his forearms on his knees. "Some of these kids – they don't have good relationships with adults." She liked the conviction in the way he spoke. "If I want their trust, I don't pry. They talk to me about non-choir stuff only if and when they want to."

"But you care about them."

He sat back in his chair. "What I do is about building their confidence. But I can't pretend to take responsibility for them," he stated with unexpected emphasis, as if he held a long-running argument with himself. "That would be a lie. They've had enough people letting them down."

Faith looked down at the flyer lying on the table between them. She remembered this feeling from the interrogation rooms, back in the old days – the feigned ignorance, playing the innocent. She shouldn't be using the ploy now, but she couldn't help it. She told herself it was wrong to tell Jim until she could confirm her suspicions. She pointed to the black-haired boy.

"This boy, he looks familiar – Lucas, you said? Is he local? I wondered if I'd seen him somewhere…"

"Lucas Bagshaw. You might have seen him about town. He's a Winchester lad."

"He's not sleeping rough?" Her question caught Jim mid-swallow. He gulped down his tea and shook his head.

"No. Lucas has a home. I think someone said his parents are dead. He lives with a relative. He joined the choir with a couple of friends."

If Lucas had a home and friends, Faith thought to herself, *why would no one report him missing; especially when he failed to turn up for a performance over the weekend?*

"Is there some trouble with Lucas?" Jim's steady gaze challenged her. She took a deep breath.

"No," she said, guilt sitting heavily in her gut. "Just curious."

CHAPTER

4

Faith tried to maintain her concentration on the Midnight Mass, but in truth the boy's face on the flyer was distracting. She gulped her tea too fast and left in something of a hurry. As she reached her car her phone trilled, shrill and urgent from its nest in the top of her open bag.

Perhaps it was Ben with confirmation.

"Faith Morgan?" A familiar voice, and unwelcome. George Casey, the bishop's press officer. Not one of her favourite people. "Thank goodness I've found you!" The exclamation had an accusatory edge. "What is this about another body you've turned up? After the mess last time, you could have had the decency to ring me to warn me. I've had the police on to me. Apparently the victim was a member of the wretched youth choir."

The wretched youth choir! Faith struggled to find suitable words. George Casey hardly paused to draw breath.

"It *would* be connected to the youth choir," he lamented. "I always thought it a risk bringing in urban youth. And in the run-up to Christmas! The time of the year when we are most in the public eye."

Faith wondered if there might be steam coming out of her ears.

"I realize that tragedy is inconvenient…" she began icily. She heard an intake of breath at the other end of the line and then a brief pause.

"Of course, of course, it is a tragedy," Casey fussed impatiently in her ear. "But a death of a boy like this – well, sudden death, press-wise, takes a lot of handling, as you well know," he ended, resentfully.

Faith bristled at the injustice. It wasn't her fault that her arrival in the diocese had coincided with the notorious case of the murdered vicar. She'd grown increasingly sure that George Casey blamed her personally for those weeks of lurid headlines in the papers.

"I am not sure what I can do for you, apart from sympathize," she said, keeping her voice level.

"That is why I am ringing. Apparently the police need to interview the youth choir. They are calling people in tomorrow morning at the cathedral."

Faith frowned. What did this have to do with her? "As it happens, I was just with Mr Postlethwaite, the choir director – you should let him know."

"Oh!" At least she'd startled him. "Yes. Of course. But as I was saying. The dean asks if you can be present at the interviews tomorrow."

"Me?" Her first thought – an uncharitable one, she quickly acknowledged – was that she simply didn't have the time. "I'm not sure how I can—"

"10:30 start in the Lady Chapel,' interrupted George. "We think there should be a female on hand, as chaperone, you know. Underaged girls, and all that."

"Really?" Faith could feel her sixth sense tingling.

"This was the dean's idea?"

"Well, not entirely. The police suggested it."

"They did?"

"Yes. The fellow in charge – Detective Inspector Shorter," said Casey, pompously. "An old friend of yours, isn't he?"

It was a clear, icy night. In a bundle of winter clothing, warmed in the middle by the glow of the microwaved pasta bake she had just consumed, Faith crunched down the path to the church hall. Someone had gritted it, bless them! The phone in her pocket beeped. On time to the very minute. Not bad.

Between Ben and George Casey, she had felt powerless to refuse tomorrow's appointment at the cathedral.

The porch light illuminated the iron-banded door. Her mittened hands gripped the ring. It gave way, protesting. Fresh muddy traces on the tiled floor inside told her the others had already arrived. The lobby still felt cold and a bit dank, but they had got rid of the unfortunate pea-green colour that had covered the walls when she first arrived. It had been replaced by a delicate lilac in a flurry of communal hard work that summer – a cold shade for winter, but it made the space lighter. A chilly draught touched her face. The door ahead stood open, the hall in darkness beyond. The stars offered distant radiance through the high windows. Beyond, the door leading to the back room spilled warm light.

"Rice Krispie stars…" It was Sue's voice, loaded with humour as she exaggerated her tale. "I had to use so much sugar to keep their shape, I tell you – they set like iron. The edges were sharp enough to put someone's eye out."

"Did you spray them with gold paint? Then you could

keep them as tree ornaments," Clarisse's calm voice responded.

"I found Benji trying to use them as martial arts throwing stars; they ended up in the bin."

Faith entered the room. Four familiar faces were laughing at Sue who was holding up her thumb and finger an inch apart, her dark eyes full of life. "Honest! He missed the neighbour's cat by so much…"

Clarisse Johnston, Sue's best friend, was by the tea tray handing round mugs. She wore a simple roll-neck over a mid-length skirt and still managed to look like an off-duty model. Delicate, grey-haired Elsie Lively sat at the table with her sister, Grace, and their friend Marjorie Davis.

"We've been discussing Christmas crafts," said Clarisse, handing Faith a steaming mug.

"Hello, vicar," Sue greeted Faith with a twinkle. "Have one of Elsie's festive lemon curd tarts – they're fab." She loaded a piece into her wide mouth.

"Please do," Elsie contributed in her breathy voice; she pushed the plate toward Faith. "Grace and I have never got on with mince pies." Faith helped herself.

"Fred sends his apologies," Sue said. "The Hare and Hounds' darts team needed him tonight, but you'll notice he gritted the paths before he left."

"Dear Fred." The tart spread lemony gorgeousness in her mouth. Faith reflected just how lucky she'd been with her churchwarden; Fred Partridge was one in a million. She realized the other churchwarden, Pat Montesque, was missing. And it was Pat who had called the meeting. Clarisse saw her look at the clock.

"Pat's not here yet," she said, with an impish look in her dark eyes.

"I think it is a poo*rr* show," said Sue in a fair imitation of

Pat, "when she called the meeting herself. After all, we are but here at her command."

"The Christmas pageant and carol service is very dear to Pat's heart," Faith said diplomatically.

"Then why isn't she on time? She always makes a frightful fuss when one of us is late," Sue complained.

"Pat rang me to say she would be a few minutes late," Elsie said quickly. "I believe she is bringing someone else to join us." Elsie hated dissent. Sue was immediately contrite at the old lady's concern.

"Don't worry, Elsie, I was only joking."

"How are things on the pageant front?" Faith asked. Sue and Clarisse were managing that part of the grand Christmas event. Sue had been directing the local amateur dramatics for years.

"All on schedule," replied Sue.

"Fingers crossed…" said Clarisse, with a fond look at her optimistic friend. "Amanda Knight got into a stew because her boys told her they were cast as a camel and she doesn't sew; she thought she had to produce the costume, poor girl. She was too shy to say anything. We only worked out what was up when she cut Sue dead in the supermarket."

"Silly sausage! Believing those boys of hers," Sue said, reaching for another tart. "She's the only one they take in. They're a handful, those Knight boys. I told her – never mind how Lucy Taylor goes on about the magical life-sized puppets in *The Lion King*, the only animals in the Little Worthy Christmas pageant are real ones. By the way, you do have the donkey booked, Faith, don't you?"

Business-like heels clicked across the wooden floor of the hall. The door swung open. Pat stood there, holding an old leather zipped folder to her chest, her eyes like bright buttons.

There was another woman standing in her wake.

"Ladies, vicar! Thank you all for waiting," she greeted them as she swept into the room. "We are very fortunate that Mrs Neil Granger has agreed to join us. Some of you will know Mavis already as chair of our Women's Institute." Pat surveyed the older ladies present with a benign look. Clarisse looked a little uncomfortable. She and Sue had avoided joining the WI. Sue licked lemon curd off her forefinger, immune to Pat's hints. Pat continued: "She's most kindly agreed to help us out with the carol service catering and flower arrangements – welcome to our little group, Mavis."

Mavis Granger had changed her clothes. Without her dogs, her walking stick and tweed she was less conspicuous, but she still carried herself with an air of authority. Faith was so startled to see her standing there on her own home ground, she didn't know quite what to say. How do you bring a boy's dead body into this homely circle?

Mavis Granger met her eyes, and Faith fancied she saw acknowledgment of the predicament.

"Mavis – have you met our vicar, Faith Morgan?" Pat made her introduction. Faith waited to see how their visitor would play it.

"We've met," Mrs Granger said simply, and shook Faith's hand. Her fingers felt stick-thin in Faith's palm. Her nails were perfectly manicured.

They arranged themselves around the table. Three small electric heaters, aimed under the table, blasted hot air at ankle height. Faith was glad of the protection of her winter boots. She manoeuvred the one closest to her into a slightly different angle with her foot so it blew between her and Sue. As she did so, she watched Pat surreptitiously. She'd surely heard about Markham, and would soon begin a wearing discourse on how she, Pat, had always warned against the dangers of giving an untried newcomer the vital role of Joseph, and how such things would never have happened in the Reverend Alistair's time. And then conversation would surely come round to the donkey…

Pat was definitely simmering. The churchwarden's little mouth had pursed up tight against the pressure of something she was determined to share. She barely waited until they were all settled.

"Mavis has had a terrible shock," she declared. "She was walking her dogs this morning and came across the police. They have found a youth dead down by the river – and it's Lucas Bagshaw."

"Lucas Bagshaw – dead?" said Grace Lively.

"Oh no," Marjorie exhaled as if the wind had been knocked out of her. The old lady turned quite white.

"Not poor Trish Bagshaw's son!" Sue exclaimed. "That's just too unfair. Another tragedy in that poor family."

Faith looked from one to the other in confusion. First, how on earth did Pat know who the boy was? The forensic tent had been erected over the body when Mavis Granger came by; she was almost sure of it. And Faith's conversation with Ben about the boy's identity had taken place barely four hours ago. And then again – how did everyone in the room seem to know Lucas Bagshaw personally? Across the table from her, Elsie and her sister and their friend Marjorie all looked deeply upset. Faith turned to Sue, who sat next to her.

"Who is Trish Bagshaw?" she asked, quietly. "And – why *another* tragedy?"

"You remember – Trish…" Sue began.

"No, she won't – Faith came after Trish died," Clarisse interrupted.

"But it was only at the beginning of the year…" Sue stopped. "Of course, I forgot. You haven't been here a year yet, have you?" She wrinkled her nose. "Weird. I feel as if we've known each other for ages."

Faith was momentarily diverted by a warm rush of pleasure at the compliment. She pulled herself together sternly. *This isn't about me.*

"Trish?" she prompted.

"Trisha Bagshaw – a lovely woman," said Sue.

"Single mother," Pat sniffed.

Elsie looked straight at the churchwarden, which was as near as she came to censure.

"Trisha was a hard-working, good-hearted woman," said Grace Lively. "Her boy was always kept clean and tidy, and he never missed a day of school."

"Not while she was alive," Pat added, darkly.

"She died earlier this year – February, I think it was," Clarisse explained, addressing Faith. "Poor soul. A brain aneurism or something similar. Very sudden."

"How awful," said Faith.

"She used to come and help Marjorie out, didn't she, dear?" said Grace. "A lovely girl." Marjorie had tears in her eyes. Grace patted her friend's hand. "I know, I know. We were all very fond of Trisha."

"Trisha earned her living as a carer," Sue explained. "She had a real gift with people. I think she was your mother-in-law's carer for years, isn't that right, Mavis? I remember Trish bringing old Mrs Granger to the Wednesday service sometimes."

So that was the connection. Mrs Granger inclined her head slightly in acknowledgment. She seemed to find Sue's question too intimate – as if she did not appreciate strangers knowing her private family business.

"Mother did like her ten o'clock Eucharist," she responded stiffly. "She found it more manageable than the Sunday service."

"Is the elder Mrs Granger no longer with us?" Faith asked, arranging her face sympathetically. Mavis had disconcerting eyes, like flat pieces of sky. They looked at her distantly.

"No," Mavis answered, after a beat. "She lives at the Mount now."

"The nursing home," Grace supplied.

"The very best in the area," added Pat effusively, her eyes on Mrs Granger. Faith wondered what she was up to. Pat hardly welcomed strangers with open arms normally. Mavis Granger's eyes flicked toward the churchwarden momentarily, as if she felt Pat's eager support superfluous.

"She became too immobile to manage at home," she said.

"And was Lucas Trisha's only child?" Faith asked, aiming to change the subject. "What happened to him after his mother's death?"

"His uncle – Trisha's younger brother – he's lived with them for years, so at least Lucas could stay in his own home," Sue said. "After Trisha died, it was just the two of them."

Pat looked over her spectacles. "That *man*!" she pronounced.

Grace Lively leaned toward Faith. "Drink," she confided.

"Come, come, Mrs Montesque," Marjorie Davis challenged Pat. "Trisha was very fond of her brother, Adam. They were a close family."

"Came to live with them when Lucas was growing up," Grace added. "He came to help out, seeing Trisha had no man about."

"You've met him – Lucas's uncle?" Faith asked.

It was Marjorie who answered. "Trish would bring him

43

round when I needed something fixing. He mended my kitchen cupboard door. It never closed properly for years. I was always catching myself on it. But Trish's Adam, he fixed it, just like that." Lucas's uncle had clearly made an impression. The old lady wore a fond expression. "He was so very kind. He and Trisha were always cheerful and helpful," she reminisced. "He fixed my bath leak, too."

Pat's eyes sharpened; she was no doubt about to say something cutting. Faith intervened to head her off.

"So – Lucas's father is dead, too?" she asked, in a rush. The trio of old ladies opposite her greeted the question with comically similar looks of startled embarrassment.

"No one ever knew who Lucas's father was," Clarisse explained.

"Trisha never said," Sue agreed. "He never seemed to figure in their lives."

"Walked out before the baby was born," Pat got her word in at last. "No wonder the boy strayed off the path so young."

"Being dead can hardly be the boy's fault," Sue responded, sharply.

Pat wrinkled her neat nose. "It is a tragedy, of course – but young Lucas had gone off the rails since his mother died. He stopped going to school." Pat shot a challenging look at Sue. "You know he did, Sue. Your Emily said so."

"My Em attends the same school," Sue clarified for Faith's benefit. "She is a couple of years younger, of course."

"What was he – sixteen?" Faith asked. "It must have been devastating to lose his mother like that." A sliver of guilt twisted in her. What had Ben said earlier – "one of yours?" As it turned out, he could well have been. Why hadn't she known about this tragic family? She felt the force of Ben's disgust. She had given him up, and so much else – her career in the police, her "normal" life, for her belief in her vocation as a priest. She thought she had followed that vocation here to St James's, Little Worthy, and its people. It hurt that she had been found wanting. If she had been more aware, more in touch with the community around her as vicar, might she have been able to help this orphaned boy?

You and your saint complex! She heard Ben's voice mocking her. *Who made you responsible for everything?* He had a point. Just because a person believed they might be called to a vocation, that didn't give you superpowers. You did what you could.

The conversation had moved into argument and Pat showed signs of being under siege.

"Trisha did work hard. You have to give her that, Pat," Sue said.

"And how did she afford some of those things she gave the boy on a carer's salary?" Pat demanded.

"He never seemed short of money." Mavis Granger spoke low.

Pat leaned forward to give her an approving look. "Those break-ins?" she lifted her sandy eyebrows.

"Pat!" said Sue. "Let's not speculate."

"How did that boy afford that brand new bike he's been riding around?" Pat defended herself. "Where else would he get the money?"

"You think Lucas Bagshaw was stealing?" asked Faith.

"More often than not it is the youngsters these days. Stealing or something worse."

"Drugs?" said Elsie, speaking up for the first time in ages.

"Well, I would hardly know about that!" Pat bridled.

Faith thought of standing by Peter down at the river's edge that morning and the burglary Mavis Granger had referred to when they had met earlier. Mrs Granger's face was hard to read. Caught in an unguarded moment, she was looking down at her hands. She appeared tired. *A long day*, Faith thought, sympathetically. She'd come to volunteer her charitable services and now she had to sit through this. Perhaps they should get on to business. But Pat wasn't finished yet. She had the tenacity of a small Scottish terrier. She turned her glare on Mavis.

"What about your break-in this summer?"

Mrs Granger's head lifted, startled. "In June, wasn't it?" Pat said, for the rest of circle.

"It was more damage than anything," Mavis Granger said vaguely, as if to brush the topic away.

Pat was never good at picking up hints. "Now Mavis – I remember how it upset you," she said, touching her friend's arm. "Some stranger coming in, trampling through your home and touching your private things." The churchwarden's cheeks were pink with sympathy. "It's a violation."

Mrs Granger looked acutely uncomfortable.

"Oh, look at the time!" Faith exclaimed. "Don't you think we had better get on with our meeting, Pat? It's a cold night, and I am sure everyone would like to get home."

Pat widened her eyes at her, pursed her lips and unzipped her leather folder. The leather was a rubbed claret colour, with the initials GMM embossed in gold leaf in the top left-hand corner. No doubt a relic of her husband, Gordon Mackenzie Montesque, now deceased. Faith wondered what kind of man Pat's husband had been. Another Scottish terrier, like her? He must have had some strength of character to have partnered Pat for forty years or more.

Pat took out a sheaf of paper typed on her old electric typewriter. You didn't often see print like that these days;

it reminded Faith of her childhood and the activity sheets Brown Owl would hand out at Brownies. Pat handed her sheets around the circle.

"I've broken down the assignments," she was saying. "Based on last year, we are looking at attendance of a hundred and sixty or so. Elsie and Grace – a hundred and fifty of your little cakes, I think. Remember: finger food! And do think of the carpet runners – nothing with cream or jam, if you please. It's bound to get trodden in, and we'll have to hire the cleaner to get it out."

Faith couldn't see her own name listed. She wondered whether to be relieved or put out. She looked over the page. Pat had divided out each person's task and responsibilities, down to the precise number of mince pies and fairy cakes they were to supply, along with times to the half hour when they were to be delivered to the church hall, and a detailed rota for setting up.

"Perhaps Pat was a quartermaster in another life," Sue murmured.

"It's certainly impressive," Faith agreed.

"Marjorie – your cheese straws are always popular," Pat was saying. Marjorie flushed with brief pleasure. "And Mavis has very kindly agreed to donate festive table arrangements," Pat moved on. "We are lucky! I do think we should offer Mavis a round of applause for her generosity." Pat raised her plump hands to chest height and patted one cupped palm brightly. After a startled moment, the rest of the company joined in.

"What is going on with Pat and Mrs Granger?" Faith whispered to Sue, under cover of the clapping.

"I heard that Pat wants to be the next chair of the Women's Institute," Sue whispered back. "The elections are coming up and the sitting president's endorsement usually makes for a shoo-in." Sue cleared her throat and said out loud, "Pat – are you sure about numbers? We wouldn't want to seem stingy in our hospitality. And don't forget the youth choir's coming to sing at Midnight Mass. Some of them are coming quite a way; what are we going to give them?"

Pat looked a little put out. "A pan of soup and some bread should be sufficient, if you really think it necessary," she said. "Myself, I never eat after 7 p.m. if I want to sleep at all." Suddenly, she checked herself. She turned to Mavis. "Do we know how many of these young people there are likely to be?" she asked, in honeyed tones.

Sue saw Faith's surprise at the direction of Pat's enquiry.

"Your boy's in the choir, isn't he?" she commented, helpfully. Mavis nodded.

"Yes." She glanced over at Faith with a touch of defiance. "My son joined in the summer with some friends. Well – a girl. I employ her in my shop," she ended curtly.

Faith couldn't quite work out whether Mrs Granger thought the youth choir inappropriate for a young man from a good family such as her son, or whether her distaste stemmed from her son's relationship with her employee. She was intrigued. Perhaps her son had been friendly with Lucas? That might account for some of her discomfort with the preceding conversation.

"I am a little concerned about welcoming this choir," Pat said dubiously. "I hear some of these young people have been gathered up from who knows where." Her face froze for one split second as she remembered her company. "Your son excepted, of course, Mavis. Beautiful manners; a lovely boy. You must be very proud of him."

"And we are very grateful to him," Faith interrupted, smoothly, "along with all the other young people who are giving their time and energy to come and sing for us at Midnight Mass. So – soup and bread for, let's say, twenty-five, for the visiting choir. And an extra batch of chocolate chip cookies for those with a sweet tooth. I can organize that." She made a note. "Now," she smiled efficiently at Pat, "is there anything else you need? I don't see my tasks on this list." She hoped her offer sounded sincere.

Her churchwarden gave her a firm look.

"I thought it hardly fair to burden you, vicar," she said, with a thin, sceptical smile. "I know how little time you have during this season." It was patently clear Pat did not think much of her vicar's organizational skills. "We can manage the practicalities."

"Pat – that's hardly fair," Sue protested. "Faith is already doing her fair share and more. She's written the pageant script and cast the leads, and that's on top of all the extra sermons and services at this time of year…"

"Of course, of course." Pat shuffled her papers. Here it comes, thought Faith. *And what about the nativity? What about the donkey?* "Although I have to say, I am concerned about that girl you've cast as Mary, vicar. The pageant is the highlight of our year at Little Worthy. Of course, being a newcomer, you are not to know, but Alice Peabody from the Hare and Hounds is flighty. She is bound to let you down at the last minute."

Faith allowed herself a smile. Either Pat hadn't appreciated the Joseph predicament, or she had chosen not to bring it up. For either, Faith was grateful.

They had all left with their chorus of goodbyes. Faith locked the door of the church hall. Poor Lucas Bagshaw and his broken life filled her thoughts. In this season of Advent, God called you to face up to the sin in the world. In the crumpled remains of that dead boy she felt faced with an acute and actual example.

And what are you going to do about it?

The voice came from both within her and without.

The snow glittered around her in the frozen silence. She pulled her scarf up against the icy wind and buried her nose in the soft wool. She hadn't forgotten her superiors' concern over her getting mixed up in the last police investigation. The outcome of that had been painful, of course. But looking back on it, she believed she had been of some use to everyone caught up in it. And George Casey might protest, but he had used her connection to Ben and the Winchester police more than once. She knew she wasn't in the police force any more but, she protested silently, you didn't confront sin by ignoring it. If indeed she had the care of souls in St James's parish, she needed to understand how Lucas Bagshaw's young life had come to its end in that muddy river.

"You can't change who you are," she sighed into her scarf. "And the truth is, you are a nosy parker by nature."

CHAPTER

5

The little robin on the bird table was a picture postcard of winter cheer against the backdrop of her frozen garden, a flash of red and a charming chubby outline. It caught Faith's attention as she sat at her desk struggling with the bones of her next sermon. *Make ready for the coming of the Lord…* And instead she was watching a bird pecking at the scatter of icy seeds she had put out the day before. The delicate Edwardian dial of the vicarage's enamelled clock read thirty-five minutes after eight. She'd left her phone in the kitchen.

The robin paused, head up, alert, then flew off in a blur of brown and red. She stood up and saw the Beast, a handsome silver and grey shorthaired tabby with a charming face and a gift for murdering small mammals and birds. He looked up and opened his pink mouth to mew silently at her through the glass.

"Oh, very well," she told him and went into the kitchen, carrying her laptop with her. She opened the door to the garden a couple of inches, and took a sachet of cat food from the stash she kept in the cupboard by the sink. The door opened a fraction more and the Beast padded in. He chirruped at her with an expectant look. She put the dish of cat food down for him.

"Here you are. Eat this and keep away from my birds," she told him, crouching down to stroke his thick fur. The Beast had excellent manners. He expected conversation before he dined. He rubbed his head against her knee before focusing his full attention on the jellied meat in his bowl. She made herself a mug of tea and sat at the kitchen table to check her emails.

Another donkey potential ruled out. Heather at the RSPCA sanctuary regretted to inform Ms Morgan that the one possible donkey they had in their charge was otherwise engaged. Things were getting serious.

"I've prayed for guidance on this one," she informed the Beast. "The good Lord must have better things to worry about." The Beast sprang gracefully onto the table beside her. He sat, curled his tail around his feet, and gazed at her. Inspiration struck and she set to her sermon again.

The next time she looked up, it was nearly twenty past nine. She had to be at the cathedral by 10:30. The tabby mewed indignantly as she showed him the door. She rushed around making the bed, brushing her teeth and collecting her bag. A yard from the front door, the house phone rang. She hesitated. She was still officially in, standing there in the hall. She debated for a second whether to let the answer-phone get it, then picked up the receiver on the hall table under the mirror.

"*There* you are!" It was her sister. She saw the brief annoyance in her face reflected in the mirror and then felt the rush of accompanying shame. She looked down at the table: *Repeat after me: Family is important.*

"Good morning, Ruth – I am just on my way out…"

"Of course you are, but I need to talk to you."

"Right now?"

"It's about Mother. And Christmas." Despite the studied pause, Faith understood this was not simply a topic of conversation. Ruth was worked up about something.

"Of course – I'd love to talk about that, but I am running late…" She grimaced as she heard herself. The face in the mirror blushed. She could feel the phone glowing hot in her hand. She turned her back on the mirror and took a short step toward the door. "Really – I have to be at the cathedral in thirty minutes," she pleaded. "And you know what the traffic's like this time of day."

"Of course, your life is important," her sister said. She didn't have to say the rest out loud; they both knew Ruth believed she carried the burden of the family alone. "And I'm pretty busy, too." Ruth worked for the council. Faith visualized her sitting at her desk, everything neat and in order, with a fresh cup of coffee to hand. "But I need to know what we are going to do Christmas Day."

We… Faith felt an inner surge of rebellion. Why did Ruth have to assume her little sister had no life and commitments of her own? Instead, she said tentatively, "I sort of assumed it would be at yours…?"

"Of course you did," Ruth said coldly. Faith was confused. She always thought Ruth liked to have Christmas on her territory. She heard her sister's intake of breath down the line. "Well, *I* think we need to discuss it."

A pause stretched its electricity between them. Ruth's voice came back on, charged with a false sweetness. "So could we book in a time to talk?"

It was past ten o'clock. She had to go. Why did family have to be so unreasonable? Faith became aware of childish echoes infiltrating her reply.

"I am *so* sorry, sis, but I just have to go. I'm sooo late! I'll ring you tonight – promise."

A sign taped to the stanchion read "Interviews" with a square black arrow pointing authoritatively toward the Lady Chapel. The PC took her details and waved her in. Members of the youth choir clustered in the front pews, and beyond them Faith could see Ben's team interviewing one-on-one. Her entrance attracted attention from a trio of girls sitting between two boys, four rows from the front. They gave her hostile up and down stares then firmly turned their backs. She had been prepared for that: what young girl wanted a chaperone of any sort, these days?

The sounds of voices were hushed. No one seemed upset. Everything seemed calm and businesslike. Faith felt rather redundant. She slipped into a pew a few rows back to be on hand if needed.

Her mind drifted to Oliver Markham. Ben had seemed pretty interested in him, and Ben's instincts were usually good. She couldn't see Inspector Shorter from where she sat. She wondered whether he was elsewhere, interviewing Markham and building up a case against him.

Of course, Lucas's death could have been an accident. Or it could have been suicide. She turned the speculation around in her mind. An accident was terrible, but not as bad as murder. The barrier of her rational thought gave way to a wave of sadness. Lucas's life had been marked by such awful tragedy; not knowing his father and losing his mother so suddenly like that. At the meeting last night, Pat had referred to Lucas dropping out of school after his mother's death. Maybe he had given up hope and decided to end his misery. A verdict of suicide would be awful enough, but marginally better than having to accept Oliver Markham as a murderer… She wished she knew how the investigation was going.

Her eyes searched out the familiar profile and gingery hair of Peter Gray. She would rather pass what she'd learned to him than Ben. She had a feeling that Peter would hear her out rather than barking questions. But Ben's sergeant was collecting up another subject for interview. A young man wearing a long black coat and a woolly hat pulled down over curly brown hair stood up. He had been sitting by a girl with an abundance of golden hair. Her hand reached out toward him. He turned away and followed Peter over to a pair of chairs overlooked by a life-sized recumbent figure, carved in marble, of some ancient patron of the cathedral.

Something struck the panelled back of her pew, jolting her. She smelt soap and turned to find herself facing the freshly shaven cheek of George Casey, the press officer. She caught him leaning in to address her; their foreheads almost collided. They both recoiled.

George Casey blinked his pale blue eyes rapidly behind the round lenses of his wire-rimmed glasses. He pushed the frame more firmly onto his nose.

"Ah yes! Ms Morgan – Faith. Glad to see you could make it. I've just stopped by to say hello. Can't stay, I fear – very busy time."

"Yes. Advent is rather a busy time for all of us in the church," she agreed, solemnly.

Casey looked at her blankly. He went on, "Bishop Rodney, our suffragan, he's recording the Christmas message with the local BBC chaps in ten minutes. He's got a real way with him. You'll have heard him on *Thought for Today* on Radio 4?" He hardly gave her a chance to murmur a response. "Of course; a natural communicator." He agreed with himself. Then he ran out of words and goggled at her.

Faith felt sorry for him. He could be a bit obtuse, but the only time they'd had much to do with each other was over the business that led to the diocesan bishop, Anthony Beech – the bishop who brought her to Winchester – taking early retirement. The press officer had avoided Faith as much as possible after that. Her presence forced him to struggle with the correct way of referring to his previous employer. Not that Bishop Anthony had been anything other than a good man, but George Casey seemed to find the murder connection unspeakable. It was one of the reasons Faith didn't entirely approve of him.

"Do you think Bishop Rodney might be promoted?" she asked, trying to fill the silence and turn her train of thought into something less controversial. They were still waiting for Anthony Beech's successor to be appointed to the bishopric. George Casey grimaced, relieved to be on safer ground.

"Not here, I think," he said regretfully. "They rarely promote suffragans in their own diocese; it's just not the way things are done."

Faith thought it would be kind to keep the thread going. "Have you heard anything?" she asked conspiratorially. The press officer seemed to fill out as his confidence returned.

"Maybe a whisper," he said, with an arched eyebrow, "but nothing I could talk about just now." He smiled, letting her absorb his superiority. "I must be off. We have to get something in the can by midday."

The press officer hurried off with a slight frown, head held high and his leather folder clasped to his left breast. As she watched him leave, she realized that he probably wanted her here as much as Ben did. She was a spy in both camps.

As if summoned by thought, she felt the air shift beside her. Ben towered above her, wrapped in a heavy wool overcoat, his hands in his pockets and his collar turned up. He stepped over her and dropped into the seat beside her.

"It's damn freezing," he said.

"Don't swear in the house of God," she said, with a straight face.

He leaned his head back and gazed up into the stone vaults of heaven above them.

"Sorry," he said, unconvincingly.

The girls squirmed around in their pew. They were whispering to one another, throwing glances toward Ben. He tended to draw admiring looks from teenage girls. Probably due to the height, the intense blue eyes and dark hair. Faith glanced at his profile. His nose was a bit big and sharp, though, once you knew him. She wondered how she could distil the previous night's gossip into what Ben would term "intelligence".

"So where were you, precisely, yesterday, when you called?" Ben was looking at his team and their interviews. "You hung up in a hurry."

Faith struggled to subdue the memory of blushing on Jim's toilet seat the day before.

"What's it to you?" she said. "I'm not under caution, am I?"

Ben snorted, but he was smiling.

Time to take control of the conversation. "How's the investigation going?" she asked. "Have you charged Markham?"

Ben sank further into his upstanding collar. He flicked a glance at her, his eyes crinkling at the side. "What's it to you?"

"I am a curious person," Faith replied.

"Ain't that the truth."

She smiled. "So – you must have some prelims from the post-mortem?"

"Maybe."

Over by the marble statue, Peter had finished with his current interviewee. The young man in the beanie hat joined the blonde girl. Peter spotted Faith and came down the aisle toward them. He sat down in the row in front of them and, with a welcoming smile, stretched his hand over the pew back.

"Hello, Faith." They shook hands. "Has the boss been bringing you up to date?"

"He's was about to tell me about the PM," she replied, reflecting Peter's warmth in her own smile. "What's the latest news?"

Peter looked to Ben, and Ben shrugged. "May as well tell her."

"Death occurred more than twenty-four hours before the body was discovered," said Peter.

"And we know this because...?" she queried. For a moment she was back in the force, speaking as if Peter were her trainee. He didn't seem to mind.

"Condition of stomach contents – digested pepperoni pizza and black coffee," he responded, pleased with himself. Peter was still fresh enough to the investigating team to betray his excitement with his trade. "Probably died sometime in the afternoon or later on Saturday. Pathologist said it was hard to tell."

"Taking into account the frost affecting decomp?" Faith asked.

Peter nodded. "So that takes Oliver Markham out of the running," Faith commented, just resisting slipping a pleased glance in Ben's direction.

"Could be." Peter's expression didn't have the force of

agreement she was looking for. "Markham says he drove his family down to London on Friday night, and stayed with the family at their hotel through the weekend before driving back Sunday night."

"And you don't believe him?" Faith addressed her query to Ben. His face gave nothing away.

"We're checking." Peter's response seemed more intended to placate her than give the answer she wanted. She tried another tack.

"I suppose it could have been suicide," she mused.

"Bruise on the hip and two knocks to the head," countered Peter. Faith examined Ben's profile, trying to read him. He ignored her.

Inebriation made you reckless and clumsy. If the boy had been drunk or high… Lots of the young seemed to deal with emotion that way these days. Lucas might have had an accident. His phone had been in his hip pocket, and it had been hit hard enough to break the casing. She tried to imagine a scenario to explain such a bruise and the wounded head. She was conscious of Ben waiting for something – for what? For her to make a fool of herself?

"*Two* knocks to the head?" she repeated, slowly.

Peter nodded. Holding his palms flat, fingers stretched out, he pantomimed a blow with the flat of his hand up the right side of his face, bisecting the temple and then, with the opposite hand, tapped the front part of the crown of his head.

"Here and here."

Ben was watching her, his expression sober.

"So he was facing his attacker," she stated. Ben looked away again. He grunted, and she recognized it as his way of agreeing. Faith turned to Peter.

"Could either of the knocks have been post-mortem?" She knew as she said the words she was being silly.

"Official cause of death is drowning, but the pathologist is taking a second look – the theory is that the blows got him in the water."

Faith closed her eyes briefly. That poor boy, dazed and hurt, falling, and the water closing over him, pulling him down. He'd been falling most of his life, she reflected. Peter was still speaking. "Being carried down in flood water with all that debris knocked the body about a bit." Had she ever been used to this? "He *was* carried downstream." Peter concluded as if giving her a brownie point, "You were right. He didn't die where he was found."

Faith felt the thrill of vindication. Markham was looking more unlikely by the second. She tried not to let her voice betray her sense of triumph. "Any idea where he went in?"

Ben crooked an eyebrow at her. "Give us a chance," he said.

So they were still looking. Faith thought of Oliver Markham as she had last seen him, his fists clenched at his side.

"What about under the fingernails – was there anything?" If there had been a fight, the river water might not have washed all evidence away.

"No evidence of defensive wounds," Peter said. "Traces of his own blood around the nail beds on the right hand."

"Just his own blood." Faith saw Lucas, disorientated and putting his hand to his bloodied head…

"Any drugs in his system? Was he drunk?" she asked.

"Nothing in the blood tests. Clean and sober," Ben answered her, curtly.

"Really? Nothing?"

"Not a trace. And no signs of regular use. It seems Lucas was a *good* boy." Ben's expression was grim. Faith winced internally in sympathy. Ben had his faults, but what had first drawn her to him was his fierce feeling for the victims; she knew it was the reason he did the job, even if he would never admit it, even to himself.

Faith thought about the chronology. *If Lucas died on Saturday...* She considered the Sunday just past. Advent II. As she remembered, it had felt like a really long day – six times she had hurried down the muddy back way between the vicarage and church, as heavy rain swept across the county. The main service had been joyous, though. It was the yearly Toy Service. Her congregation had turned out in their wellington boots and umbrellas, clasping wrapped gifts for the Salvation Army collection. The slightly damp parcels with their garish paper covers still occupied her vestry. (The volunteer who was due to collect them had been felled by a bout of flu. She made a mental note – she really must work out a time to deliver those to the drop-in centre this week.)

So Lucas Bagshaw might already have been lying dead in the rain while her congregation praised God and brought their gifts for the poor and needy. That afternoon – Jim, the dishy choirmaster had said – Lucas had missed the Sunday concert in which he was due to sing a solo.

"Why on earth didn't his uncle report Lucas missing?" she asked. "For goodness' sake, the boy was due to sing a solo with the youth choir at the cathedral on Sunday. Why did no one respond when he failed to turn up?"

"Yes, the choir chap told us about the concert no-show," said Ben. "You might have mentioned it."

Faith felt herself blushing. She should have, really, but with everything else going on it had slipped her mind. "Actually, last night, I learned a few other things about Lucas's background. The lad had a hard time."

"We're up on the absent father bit," said Ben. He nodded toward where the girls in the fourth row were being invited up for interview. They were refusing to move without one another, tossing their heads and giving the PC lip. "Maybe you should go and do your thing," Ben continued.

At that moment, the girls seemed to acquiesce and one broke from the others, accompanying the officer. Faith was rather glad – she didn't think her presence would have been particularly welcome.

Peter stepped into the silence.

"The uncle's a piece of work. Adam Bagshaw. We tracked him down at the family home in The Hollies – after you'd given the boss the lead on Lucas's ID," Ben's sergeant mentioned, helpfully. "We called soon after 6 p.m. and, according to him, we'd just woken him up. Said he wasn't aware that his nephew had been missing for two days. Been unwell, he says."

"He's a drinker." Contempt dripped from Ben's words, and Faith's antennae quivered. Ben considered himself an impartial investigator, but she knew how he could be when a case summoned ghosts from his past. Ben hated addicts who neglected their kids. Lucas's uncle Adam had better watch out. He would get no breaks from Ben Shorter. But the fact he wasn't in custody suggested they had no lead to follow.

One of the investigating team came down the aisle, leaving the girl with the golden hair waiting behind him. She wasn't very tall. In the half-light shadow of a soaring column, she looked cherubic with her head of pre-Raphaelite curls.

"Boss!" the officer said. He indicated the girl with a tilt of his head and a significant lift of his eyebrows.

Ben stood up.

"You'll never make senior investigating officer," he told Peter. "You talk too much. Fay," he took leave of Faith with a nod. If Peter was surprised by his superior's use of a pet name for her, he didn't betray it.

Ben stepped past her. Faith closed her eyes momentarily as the rough wool of his coat brushed her face. *Terre* by Hermès; the aftershave she used to buy him. A clean, clear smell – and so familiar. She opened her eyes. Peter and Ben were walking away discussing something. They hadn't noticed. She breathed out.

Peter turned back. He retraced a step or two, catching her unawares.

"You're still on for supper Thursday?" he asked. Faith nodded, her lips pressed together in an overly bright smile. "Great!" he acknowledged. "Come early, if you can. The boys would love to see you before they're put to bed." He began backing away to catch up with his boss. "And Sandy told me to remind you to bring a plus one, if you fancy it."

An hour later, Faith was frustrated and itching to go. So far her services as chaperone had been predictably spurned. Even the investigating officers seemed unsure of what role they wanted her to play. She felt as if she had sneaked in from the street to watch a rehearsal before a play had opened to the public. It wasn't as if she didn't have other places to be.

Adam Bagshaw. Lucas's uncle. Ben's distaste worried her. Last night Marjorie Davis had said Adam Bagshaw was a good man. Of course, she wouldn't have known him very well, but the fond, grateful look on the old lady's face stuck in Faith's mind. Marjorie might be old, but she was no fool. She had been quite high up in the civil service before she retired. Faith's curiosity smouldered and took hold.

Peter had said the Bagshaws lived in The Hollies, one of a number of developments put up on the city outskirts during the property boom before the bottom fell out of the market. An upmarket address for someone on a carer's salary like Trish. Perhaps Adam owned the house outright, and had neither mortgage repayments nor rent to find. She found herself constructing a history for him – a good job, perhaps in IT or accounting, personal problems, then a break-up, divorce and drink. She had to tell herself to stop it. One thing she'd learned as a policewoman, which had only been reinforced in her recent role, was that human lives didn't always follow the neat course of cause and effect.

Bagshaw. Not a local name. There shouldn't be that many of them around. Unless the family were ex-directory, she could find the address online. Adam Bagshaw was, after all, doubly bereaved, she told herself. He might appreciate a pastoral visit. She got up to leave.

Jim Postlethwaite was standing in the shadows looking at her. How long had he been watching? He must be wondering about her connection to the police inspector and his sergeant. He might even think she had been spying on him on their behalf. She was surprised at how much she disliked the idea that the choirmaster might think her deceitful. She gave a friendly wave as he walked toward her.

"You're going?" he asked, his expression blank. The relaxed friendliness of yesterday had vanished.

"I'm not needed here."

Jim turned his face away from her toward the activity at the front of the chapel. "They say they're finished with me," he muttered.

Ben was standing by the marble statue, listening to a colleague. Faith felt the beam of his intense stare. Jim

Postlethwaite wasn't Ben's type. She could almost hear his thoughts; the look on his face said it all: *"Do-gooder" – what's he covering up?*

"Investigating officer seems a bit of a bulldog," said Jim. "Do you know him well?"

Faith hesitated, not knowing how to answer. Jim stepped back, widening the space between them. The hazel eyes looked down at her coldly.

"Don't worry," he said. "I appreciate the value of discretion." He started striding toward the exit. She followed after him.

"I'll walk out with you," she said. They marched side by side a few yards. Faith felt tongue-tied. She searched for something to say.

"So, how did you get involved in all this?" Jim asked. "Did you know before you accepted my offer of a mince pie and a cup of tea? Was the fainting an act too, to lure me in?"

"Please," said Faith. "It wasn't like that at all. I wasn't sure until you showed me the flyer. Not even completely sure then." She hurried on, determined to explain herself. "Lucas's body was found on a parishioner's land. I happened to call on the landowner to discuss some church business and ran into the police there."

Church business – a visit to talk about the costume and role of Joseph in a Christmas pageant. How trivial that sounded now! For a moment she was disorientated by the disconnect. But the Bible was full of human tragedy, and she had faith in a God who made a difference in the face of it all. She felt the ground under her feet again.

They had reached the parting of ways, and stood at the point of a triangle of light pushing in through the open door. She didn't usually find herself at a loss like this. There was something about Jim Postlethwaite; she sensed compassionate intelligence and guarded experience. He made her feel girlish in comparison, even though she must have been the older of the two.

"I can see you're telling the truth," he said. "I apologize for my suspicions."

"That's quite all right," said Faith. "Tragedy like this – it… confuses things."

He acknowledged the moment with his lopsided smile.

"Do you mind if I drop by at some point," he said, "to see your church? These kids aren't professionals; I find it useful to check the layout. You know, scope out any potential problems so all goes well on the night."

"That seems very sensible." No need for the "very", she edited herself crossly in her head. "Of course. You'd be very welcome." (Not again!) "Just let me know when – so I can be there to let you in." He turned his body to go, his eyes still on her face.

"So you'll let me know?" she said, by way of a farewell. His expression shifted into an "idiot me!" look, and he pulled something out of his pocket.

"I've got this for you." He held it out to her. It was a scrap of music paper with a name and address written on it in blue ink from a fountain pen. "One of the girls works at an animal sanctuary… The owner's a bit of an eccentric – an older lady; Ms Whittle. The Ms is important – don't 'Miss' her, or you'll rub her up the wrong way," he added with his sly twinkle. "Anyway, the animals are sort of her family, but apparently there's a donkey…"

"Thank you so much!" Faith felt herself blush pink with pleasure. She slipped the paper into her glove.

His smile lingered on her face as he walked away and she went out into the bright winter light, the paper crackling between her skin and glove.

CHAPTER

6

The Bagshaw house was number 5 in a cul-de-sac of modern brick houses with uPVC windows, single-width garages and pocket-handkerchief lawns. At lunchtime, it was a quiet place. These were family houses – the adults at work, the children at school. No. 5 had a stripped down, anonymous look. There were no signs of the Christmas lights and decorations of its neighbours. The snow in the driveway lay undisturbed. At the margins of the white covering, Faith could see that the garage door had old leaves and debris blown up against it, as if it hadn't been opened for a long time.

The front door had a panel of frosted glass in its upper half. A light was on in the hall behind. Faith stood under the fanciful little vestige of a porch and pressed the doorbell. She listened to the chimes die away. No answer. No other footprints than her own disturbed today's fresh fall of snow. The phone directory listed this address for Trisha Bagshaw. She pressed the bell again. She thought she saw something come between the door and the light in the hall. Silence. She stepped off the path and took a couple of steps around the front of the house. The curtains to the front room were drawn back. She glanced behind her. The black holes of her footprints spoiled the pristine snow and reproached her. What right had she to pester the poor man? So what if he didn't want to answer the door? She retraced her steps.

She had almost made up her mind to leave when she caught a strangled noise from inside. There was definitely someone in the hall behind the door. She knocked on the frosted glass.

"Mr Bagshaw? My name is Faith Morgan," she called. "I am vicar at St James's – I just wanted to see if you are all right." This time she heard a distinct sob. She crouched down and looked through the letterbox. A man was sitting on the stairs in his shirt, socks and blue gingham boxer shorts, head in hands. He was crying.

"Mr Bagshaw – Adam – please open the door." She couldn't just leave him. She could feel the misery radiating out toward her. He was alone in that house; floundering under the weight of such tragedy, his sister dead and now his nephew. From what she gathered, his whole family had gone. All at once he was left to cope alone. So what if he was a stranger to her?

"You shouldn't be alone like this – please let me in," she repeated. To her astonishment the figure on the stairs stood up. She straightened and took a step back. She heard the latch turn and the door opened halfway.

Adam Bagshaw was maybe an inch taller than her, with tousled hair – a short back and sides that had grown out. Above several days' worth of stubble, his skin was smooth with fine pores. Late thirties, she guessed. The hand holding the door trembled. He rubbed the other across his chin and face, his eyes fixed downwards.

"Don't know you, do I?" he mumbled. He stood there, swaying slightly. He didn't smell too good – unwashed, with a lingering under-note of stale alcohol – and the open door was letting the icy air in. Time to take charge. She put a hand on the door, and pushed lightly. He stood aside to let her in.

"My name's Faith Morgan," she said again. "I am vicar at St James's in Little Worthy. You go and sit down. I'll make you a cup of tea." She stepped into the hall and closed the door behind her. Her determination acted like a force field, shifting him before her into the front room, a plain, modern, open-plan rectangle. A brown leather sofa occupied one wall, with a matching armchair at an angle to it. It looked as if Adam had been sleeping on the couch. A pummelled pillow was jammed in the crook of one armrest and an unzipped sleeping bag flopped open, like a split fruit, its ruby inner lining contrasting with the military green outer quilting. The room was a mess. Faith removed an old newspaper from the chair and Adam Bagshaw collapsed into it, his bare legs smacking against the leather. She spotted a plaid blanket pooled on the floor by the couch. She scooped it up and draped it over his legs.

Kitchen units stood beyond the barrier of a breakfast bar at the top of the room. "When did you last have something to eat?" she asked. He murmured something she didn't catch. He had stopped crying. He just sat, his eyes cast down. "Not for ages, I'll bet," she answered herself. "I'll make some tea and find you something to eat." As she moved purposefully toward the kitchen, her foot knocked glass. A vodka bottle. In her head, she amended the tea order to coffee; strong coffee.

The instant coffee jar was empty, and she couldn't locate any tea bags. At first Faith thought she might have to resort to stale bags of ginger tea she found at the bottom of a tattered old box, then she discovered half a pack of ground coffee at the back of the bread bin. No milk in the fridge – just a pack of beer with three cans missing, and a foil container half-filled with what looked like Chinese takeaway. How long it had congealed there she didn't like to think. There seemed to be nothing else of substance to eat. The kitchen cupboards looked as if no one had done any proper shopping since Trisha Bagshaw died. In the main cupboard, in the margins by the door, a couple of dog-eared boxes of cereal shared a shelf with a stack of cup-a-soup packets. At the back she could see the neatly ordered supplies of someone who had enjoyed cooking – herbs, spices and curry mixes; a tin of asparagus spears.

Faith made the coffee double strength and loaded sugar into it.

"Drink this." Adam hadn't moved. She put the mug into his hand. It shook. He wrapped his other hand around the ceramic to steady it, and took a sip.

"Thanks."

A framed photograph of a younger Adam hung on the wall. Taken in bright foreign light, he wore a soldier's uniform, shading his eyes with one hand, smiling shyly into the lens. Yes, she might have guessed he had been a serviceman – he had that toughened look she often saw in Christmas-time soup kitchens. He looked sweet and uncertain in the photo, though.

"Were you getting up or going to bed?" she asked, conversationally.

"What?" He looked at her for the first time. Despite the swelling and red rims, his chocolate brown eyes had an appealing, lost puppy quality. She nodded down at his black-socked feet and bare calves protruding beneath the blanket on his lap.

"Were you getting up or on your way to bed?" she repeated.

"What time is it?"

"Late lunchtime. Nearly two o'clock."

He didn't seem to have the reserves to answer her question.

"You used to be in the army?" she asked. He nodded reflexively, but there was a residue of pride in the firmness of his answer.

"Signal Corps."

"My grandpa was in the artillery during the war. He used to say a shave was as good as a rest." He looked at her, bemused for a moment. "Why don't you go up and have a shower? Get dressed," she prompted. "I am sure it'll make you feel more like yourself. I'll tidy up down here while you do that, and then you can have something to eat."

He obeyed her. He got up and climbed the stairs. He seemed to be grateful to be told what to do. Trisha, his big sister, must have been the one in charge.

Faith looked around her, feeling a twinge of guilt. He had acquiesced to her so easily. She hadn't been planning to snoop. At least, not consciously.

She imagined the sceptical curl of Ben's lip. *Of course you hadn't, vicar.*

Someone else had made an attempt to tidy up in the not too distant past. They had gathered bits and pieces into a cardboard box and left it neatly flush with the wall. She wondered if that had been Lucas – had the bereaved boy been struggling all year to care for the only adult he had left? She used the box as a repository, piling up stray newspapers and magazines. Even though she'd heard plenty about Adam's problems with alcohol, the extent of his dependency became disturbingly apparent as she restored order in his home. Among the debris and takeaway wrappings she found another two vodka bottles. One still had a third of the clear alcohol left in it. She dumped the empties in the trash and stood undecided with the other bottle in her hands. Maybe they drank together – Lucas and his uncle – using the alcohol to dull their lost-ness. Except the forensic tests said Lucas had gone into the river sober. She placed the bottle in a cupboard and put the dirty dishes into the dishwasher. The chow mein, or whatever it was in the fridge, smelled all right. It would have to do. She emptied it into a bowl in the microwave, ready to reheat. On a bleached pine table by the window, she set a place with cutlery and added a glass of water for them both, so she could keep Adam company while he ate.

All in all it didn't take very long. The chaos was superficial, a bachelor wash over Trisha Bagshaw's shipshape home. She thought of Pat and Mavis Granger's speculations about Lucas and his lifestyle the night before. *He never seemed short of money… how could she afford it on a carer's salary?* There weren't that many luxuries about that Faith could see. The TV must have been relatively new and there was an Xbox with a small-ish pile of games – but nothing stood out to suggest anything other than a comfortable but low income home.

On the mantelpiece over the gas fire stood a skilfully carved white stone figure of a mother and child, six or seven inches tall. Its lines were tactile, flowing and deceptively simple. The style was reminiscent of blue Danish porcelain figures, but the stone held better definition. Faith picked it up, thinking it looked expensive. It had a lovely heft in her hand, smooth and cool. She turned it over to see if she might recognize the maker's mark. The monogram scratched into the base meant nothing to her – an N and a T crossed, or something like that. She replaced the figure carefully in the neat clean oval its presence had preserved in the dust.

She stood listening. Upstairs the shower was running. She had never known the dead woman, but she knew instinctively

Trisha Bagshaw would hate to see the dust cloaking her possessions. She might as well make herself useful while she waited. She found a clean duster in a kitchen drawer.

Faith made quick work of the mantelpiece and moved on to the whatnot standing in a safe corner by the window beyond the table. Sundry ornaments vied for space with numerous framed photographs. Trisha Bagshaw evidently had eclectic taste. A pretty silver engine-turned 1920s bedside clock sat beside a cheap and cheerful painted 1950s model of a Neapolitan horse and cart. A fairyland lustre bowl took pride of place on the top shelf. Faith had seen something similar in a recent episode of *Antiques Roadshow*. As she remembered, the one on the television programme had been quite valuable. She picked up photographs from the level below, dusting them thoughtfully. Pictures of Lucas at various stages of growth: in his mother's arms – one of those badly lit, amateur photographs that pull at the heart; the toddler with huge, long-lashed eyes, standing precariously in a romper suit printed with blue cars; a little boy giggling uncontrollably in the arms of his teenage uncle. And centre stage, the three of them together in a park somewhere – Trisha between her boys, hugging them fiercely; a small, strong woman between a man and a gangling youth. The pictures radiated love. Faith felt tears welling up.

She realized there was silence upstairs. How long ago had the shower stopped running? She went to the bottom of the stairs and stood still, listening, her hand gripping the painted balustrade. Could he have fallen asleep? Done something stupid? Should she have left him so long? She'd reached halfway up the stairs when a high, mechanical whine came from behind the door. He was brushing his teeth. Faith felt her shoulders drop as she let out her breath.

From her vantage point, a couple of steps from the top of the stairs, Trisha Bagshaw's home had an air of the Marie Celeste about it. The short upstairs hall was neat and blank, a runner of matting over boards and eggshell painted walls. Three doors, in addition to the bathroom, led off it. Two were closed. The one door still ajar was across from the bathroom. Beyond Faith saw an anonymous room – coconut matting on boards and the corner of a metal-framed bed illuminated in the natural light of a window. Someone had made the bed neatly and a laptop lay on a low table beside it. A single-width wardrobe with a mirrored front seemed to be the only other piece of furniture. Reflected in the glass, she could see a man's suit in dry-cleaner's plastic hanging on the back of the door. Adam Bagshaw might be a drinker, but it looked as if he hadn't lost the neatness of a soldier where his own quarters were concerned. At the head of the corridor, the master bedroom was sealed up against the absence of its occupant. On the final door, next to the bathroom, hung a gothic plaque, "By Invitation Only" painted in blood-red lettering on it. Obviously Lucas's room.

Her eyes fixed on the plaque. "By Invitation Only". Pat's dark hints that Lucas had been stealing itched at her. Of course, the police would have searched it already – or would soon do so. That thought pulled her up short. It would be awkward if some of Ben's team arrived and found her there. Would they accept the excuse of a pastoral visit? Ben Shorter surely wouldn't.

Faith heard the bathroom door being unlocked and retreated down the stairs on tiptoe, her cheeks hot like a naughty child's. She hurried over to the microwave and pushed the button to reheat.

The microwave pinged as Adam Bagshaw came down the stairs wearing slacks and a striped shirt. He looked surprisingly presentable. He wasn't a bad-looking man; just oddly anonymous. The impression of togetherness dissolved as he came nearer. He hesitated in the middle of the room as she put the reheated food on the table for him. She smiled at him warmly.

"It's all I could find, but I think you could do with it."

His answer was a tentative smile. He sat and stared at the noodles for a moment, then picked up his fork and, mechanically, began to eat. His acceptance of her intrusion into his home was surreal. At any moment Faith expected him to wake up from his torpor and demand to know what she was doing there. She kept her concerns out of her voice and ploughed on.

"Your nephew was found in my parish," she said. "I heard that you were alone. I wanted to come and offer my condolences and see if there was anything I could do for you in this terrible time."

On her last words, Adam's muscles contracted, pulling his head forward. He strained to contain another spasm of misery. She put her warm hand over his knotted one. "I am so very sorry."

He nodded jerkily and drew a ragged breath. "You knew Luke?" he asked.

"We never met, but Jim Postlethwaite, who runs the choir Lucas sang in, speaks highly of him."

Adam stared across at the photographs on the whatnot.

"You could see her in him sometimes. Trish was real proud of…" He squeezed his eyes shut, his face working.

"Where did you serve?" Faith asked in a calm voice, hoping to distract him onto firmer ground.

"Dubai. Hong Kong."

"That must have been interesting." She was running out of inspiration. "What did you do when you left the army?"

"Retrained. IT – did quite a bit of it in the corps."

So she'd been right after all. "There's plenty of call for IT wizards these days."

He lifted his forearms and slammed his hands down on the table, slopping the water out of the glasses and making Faith jump. "I let her down," he said, through gritted teeth. Faith rubbed the forearm nearest to her, feeling the locked muscles, making soothing noises. Everything in him was balled up tight. She felt the muscles relax a fraction.

"So you and Lucas have been living here alone since your sister died?" Adam nodded. "It must have been tough." He tucked in his chin and pushed out his lips like a little boy trying not to cry. She indicated the photograph of the small giggling Lucas, with the teenage Adam grinning down at him.

"You were close – you and Lucas? Looks like you had good times."

Adam's mouth twisted into a bashful smile. "Used to take him fishing." Looking closer, she noticed the fishing creel hanging from a military green strap over that younger Adam's shoulder. She hadn't seen any fishing gear in the house. Could that have brought Lucas down to the river?

"Did Lucas like to fish often?"

"Not for years." Adam Bagshaw's mood was slipping back; she sensed him approaching tears.

"What else did you do together, more recently, then?" she asked.

His answer was mumbled, almost as if he resented her lack of sympathy. "Have a pint on a weekend."

"Did you have a favourite pub?"

He shrugged, impatiently. "Lion's Heart." He rubbed his hands rapidly over his face, pressing down as if he wanted to rub his skin off. "Listen, what is this? You're asking a lot of questions for a vicar."

"I'm sorry," said Faith. "I suppose I just want to know what happened. I should think you do, too."

His eyes narrowed. "I guess so."

Faith let the silence linger. "Was Lucas in trouble?"

He blinked and looked at her sideways.

"Trouble?"

"Did Lucas seemed to be worried about anything? Was he getting on with his friends?" Adam looked away. He shook himself as if shaking her off. "He never said anything." His fork stabbed aimlessly at the remains of the Chinese. She wondered about the evasion.

"When did you last see Lucas?"

Adam hunched, and laid down the fork. "End of last week."

"Did something happen, Adam?"

He jerked his face toward her with tearful eyes. That wet, puppy-dog look again. "I drink – sometimes it gets the better of me."

Faith bristled, at least on the inside. She looked at the shell of the man opposite her. What was he saying? She hadn't even suspected for a moment that he might have done something violent, and she found herself unprepared for it. If he admitted anything now, she had a duty to call Ben.

"Go on," she said. She registered that she was marginally closer to the front door. A simple latch, unless he'd locked the deadbolt. She didn't think he had.

His eyes were fixed on her dog collar, as if she could offer him absolution.

"Blacked out. Must have got home, though. The police found me here."

"And you don't remember anything?" He shook his head, clinging to her with his eyes. She sat back a little in her chair, anyway, widening the distance between them.

"They found Lucas in the river," she said in a matter-of-fact voice, "but it wasn't where he went in. Do you know where he might have been that day?" Adam shook his head again. "Where would he go?" she pressed him.

"I don't know what Lucas did!" He pushed back his chair and stood up quickly. Faith flinched. "I need a drink." His gaze skittered over the floor to where she'd found the vodka. A slight frown creased his forehead; then he went over to the fridge and got out a can, popped it and stood gulping it down in the crook of the open door. He wiped his mouth. "I'd like you to leave now."

Her visit to Adam Bagshaw had raised more questions than it answered. She left him with both her own phone number and the details of the Citizens' Advice Bureau, and he took both with mild distrust in his face.

The convivial atmosphere of the hospital carol service helped lift her spirits. A pie-and-peas supper followed. Faith, glad of the normal, cheerful company of her parishioners, stayed until they all disbanded. She didn't get home until after 10 p.m., by which time her answer machine flashed accusingly – five messages, two of them from Ruth. Her sister's voice grated against her guilt. "*You said you'd call; I can't wait any longer. I am going out now.*" She texted an apology, setting a reminder to ring Ruth first thing next morning, and fell into bed to dream of donkeys.

A noise woke her in the dark. For a moment the space of the high-ceilinged room seemed unfamiliar. Living as a single woman in an inner-city parish had toughened her up some, and Faith had never felt unsafe in Little Worthy; but in that moment she was conscious of being alone, vulnerable in her pyjamas in this large, isolated house. She sat up, listening hard. She recalled her conversation with Peter about the spate of break-ins around Winchester, and cursed herself for not speaking to the dean about her alarm. She'd had to disable it because of the cat. A big old house like this might look like rich pickings, and the contents would be all too easy to see, as she never drew the curtains. She peeled off the covers and crept to the window. Beyond the glass, the night was charcoal grey and matt. The heating had gone off and she could see her breath, a fleeting presence before her. The window faced over the garden, the piece of lawn circled by the mature trees standing within the rectory boundary wall.

An unearthly scream resonated through the night, and her vision snagged on a movement below against the subdued luminescence of the snow. A fox slipped into the trees. Faith waited a moment for the adrenalin rush to stop buffeting her heart, and went back to bed feeling disorientated and uncharitable about Mother Nature.

CHAPTER

7

She had overslept. There'd be heavy lifting later, so she dressed casually: jeans, her waisted white shirt and old woolly jumper the colour of dried sage. Faith sat drying her hair at the kitchen table, gazing at the scrap of manuscript paper Jim Postlethwaite had given her. His writing was spiky and slanted. She liked that he used a fountain pen with real ink. A proper musician's hand. She clicked off the hairdryer and picked up the phone. Last chance on the donkey front.

Her call was picked up on the third ring.

"Joy Whittle." Ms Whittle's voice was gruff, her tone no-nonsense. Faith drew breath, gathering her confidence to take the leap – she *had* to secure this donkey!

"Hello, Ms Whittle? I am sorry to trouble you so early…"

"Not early. Been up for hours. Just on my way out to feed the ducks." The voice at the other end was clipped, and what Mother would call "County"; the kind of woman once known as a "gel" in certain circles.

"My name's Faith Morgan. I am vicar at…"

"St James's," Ms Whittle cut in. "Told you might call. Looking for a donkey."

"Yes, for our Christmas pageant." Faith hung on the edge of the silence, waiting. She deduced that Ms Whittle didn't appreciate small talk.

"My Banjo is a precious old boy," Ms Whittle stated, eventually.

Faith responded to the deep affection in her tone. "Of course he is!" she carolled down the phone, willing the woman to understand her respect for all living creatures, and most particularly donkeys called Banjo. "I should so like to meet him. I love donkeys." The pause went on so long, she wondered if it was a lost cause. Perhaps Ms Whittle didn't approve of the church or of animals performing in Christmas pageants. *Perhaps*, thought Faith, *she's waiting for an offer of remuneration.*

"I'm busy this week," the response came at last. "You can come over on Monday. Mid-afternoon's best. We'll discuss it." Faith scrabbled for a pencil to write down the directions to Ms Whittle's smallholding on the back of Jim's scrap of music paper. It wasn't far from the Markhams' place, by the sound of it. Ms Whittle rang off before she had finished her thank-yous.

Hardly a done deal, but she'd laid the groundwork. She had a prospect at last. Donkey doom loomed over her no longer! Then she saw the clock. No time to finish drying her hair. No time for breakfast. Her phone kept flashing at her. She couldn't take being harassed by electronic beeps today. She turned off the reminders, experiencing a spike of mixed liberation and guilt. She would have to ring Ruth later.

She squared her shoulders to face the day to come. The community carol service was one of her new initiatives, so she longed for it to go well. In a shady corner of her mind she glimpsed Ben, his wry expression questioning her motives – she with her comfortable congregation with their tidy little lives in their picture-perfect village. She shook off the thought. Ben Shorter's opinions were immaterial. She – personally – Faith Morgan, parish priest, thought it important for a Christian congregation to reach out and engage with the wider community around them.

Faith tugged on her wellington boots by the back door. Carol services were ideal for welcoming outsiders into the church. Everyone liked carol-singing at Christmas. Tonight's guests had been carefully chosen – in addition to the MP and local councillors, staff and residents from the local old people's home were coming, along with the co-ordinator at the women's refuge, and Mandy and Gerry from the Salvation Army with some of their regular clients. Faith had choreographed the service to give each of them a place to speak. She hoped, amid the carols and pre-Christmas cheer, to prompt her congregation to think beyond their natural acquaintance to their neighbours at large.

Locking the kitchen door behind her, she set off down the trail that cut through the back of the garden to the vestry door. This sort of service hadn't been done at Little Worthy before. Both her churchwardens had resisted the idea at first: Pat Montesque was plain outraged; even dear Fred Partridge had been wary.

When she had first floated the idea for this service, Faith had been very new to the parish – hardly two months confirmed in the post. She'd quickly discovered just how territorial churchwarden Pat could be about St James's. Sometimes, when she was feeling particularly tired, Faith fancied that the small Scotswoman mentally sat behind a desk vetting whoever dared to step across the threshold, as if "her" beloved church were some country club. It was a minor miracle this carol service was taking place tonight. At the time, Faith had been puzzled by Pat's capitulation. But since the revelations on Monday night, she realized that the turning point must have been when the ladies of the regional WI, headed up by their current president, Mrs Mavis Granger, had declared their intention to parade to demonstrate their civic commitment.

Her toe hit an obstacle and she nearly went flying. Faith caught her balance awkwardly, wrenching her knee. The large aluminium watering can lay turned on its side across the path. It was a chunky thing; surely too big for an animal to knock over? She righted it, placing it back against the fence feeling off-balance and jittery. There were footprints – not made by a fox but by a substantial boot with a heavy tread. Someone *had* been here in the night. She shivered at the thought, and cast a glance around her.

Her detective brain took over, detaching her from the implications of a stranger sneaking about her home. She followed the trail, across the lawn, and looping back to the kitchen window. A frisson of fear battered its wings in her pulse as she imagined someone peering in.

Pull yourself together, woman!

It looked as if her visitor had returned the way they had come. She made a quick inspection. She couldn't see any scratched wood or misshapen window frames; any sign that someone had tried to break in. There was nothing.

She must get on. Gerry, the Salvation Army co-ordinator, had been cheery but firm. If the gifts were to be sorted and distributed in the Christmas boxes, the Toy Service collection needed to be delivered to the centre in town by lunchtime today. Anyway, she had to get them out of the vestry before tonight. The trip would give her a chance to check details for next week when she and her volunteers were due to help at the Christmas lunch for the homeless.

She walked rapidly toward the squat presence of St James's, gripping the heavy Victorian key tighter than before. She fumbled it into the great iron lock. The Gothic vestry door felt reassuringly solid as she closed it behind her. She picked her way between the two stacks of gifts in their brightly coloured wrapping, and entered the chancel.

The walls of the Saxon church were three feet thick, and the storage heaters meant the temperature hovered a few degrees above that of the air outside. The light filtering through the stained-glass windows touched the polished oak pews and made the brass fittings of the lectern glow. The calm soothed her jangled nerves in an instant. She pottered about, feeling at home.

She tried to ignore the twinge of guilt. This was God's house and he welcomed everyone – but still, surely he didn't begrudge her some breathing space before Pat and the others arrived. Faith bent down to pick up a kneeler left on the floor, and hung it back on its hook.

Fragments of the past few days slid about in her mind. Though it was hardly conclusive, the physical evidence reported by Peter suggested that Lucas had been killed by someone he knew. Facing one's attacker and no defensive wounds tended to rule out stranger crime. Someone he hadn't thought to guard himself against.

She knelt down at the altar rail and tried to clear her mind to pray.

You don't know enough to get involved, she scolded herself. Leave it to the police – leave it to Ben and Peter – and Harriet Sims. Faith paused on the thought of the red-haired pathologist. Where had she come from, and what was she to Ben?

None of your business! Concentrate.

Adam Bagshaw in that hollowed-out home. His distress had seemed real to her. Ben had been right about the drinking, of course, and the combination of alcohol and shock was always unpredictable, but something about Adam Bagshaw told her he wasn't responsible. Bagshaw felt guilty about something, she could see. Perhaps something more than just letting his dead sister down. But not murder. Even if he had lashed out under the influence and following an argument, he couldn't have left his nephew to drown – could he?

She closed her eyes fast against the memory of Adam at his table. Marjorie Davis thought well of Adam Bagshaw, she repeated to herself; and Marjorie is a shrewd woman.

But then there was his admission of a blackout. She really ought to tell Ben about that. She saw herself standing in the kitchen at The Hollies with the vodka bottle in her hands. Bagshaw's drink problem was just the kind of weakness that brought out the self-righteous avenger in Ben. In the scene in her mind, the photographs on the whatnot were over her shoulder. Pictures of a loving family and Trisha holding them all together. The woman in those photographs had a good face. She wished she could have met Trisha. If she had lived, they might well have been friends. Regret blossomed in Faith's chest, filling her throat and stinging her eyes.

What could you have done?

The question came out of the ether quite kindly. It wasn't an accusation.

I should have liked to have been there to care when it mattered, she whispered back, knowing full well she was speaking of hypotheticals.

She got up off her knees. No. She couldn't unleash Ben on Trisha's mourning little brother. Adam had confided in her because she wore a dog collar, and she wouldn't betray that trust. She looked at her watch. If she loaded up the car now, with luck she could get away and be back before noon when she was due to meet with Pat and Fred.

Fetching Fred's wheelbarrow from the shed by the yew tree, Faith piled the multicoloured gifts into it, thinking about the children in the battered women's refuge. She hoped her congregation had chosen well. From what she could feel, they had majored in cuddly toys. At least there was no evidence of anything like the half-crushed tin of baked beans she had once found in a similar collection in a previous parish.

She wheeled the barrow to her car and piled the gifts into the back seat. She patted her coat pocket. Check. She *had* remembered the list of volunteers attending the Salvation Army Christmas lunch. She slipped into the driver's seat feeling more cheerful. She was catching up with life. She turned the ignition, and her faithful Yaris purred into life.

She sensed rather than heard her name being called. In her mirror, across the Green, she saw Pat coming out of her house in a bright puce coat. The puce arm lifted in a wave and Pat mouthed, "Vicar!" Guilt rushing in her ears, Faith floored the accelerator and drove off.

But when she returned to Little Worthy just after midday, Pat was there just inside the doorway. Faith had the strange notion that she had been waiting for several hours, but told herself that couldn't possibly be the case, could it?

"Pat!" she said, with as much bonhomie as she could manage.

"A word, vicar," Pat hissed.

The churchwarden's court shoes matched almost precisely the main heather shade of her plaid skirt. Pat would never wear outdoor shoes in the house of God. She always brought her indoor shoes in her bag when she came to the church, leaving her boots with their easy grip soles aligned dead centre against the wall beneath her coat, hanging on the vestry coat rack. Faith's eyes wandered over the purple cardigan buttoned up on top of the freshly laundered blouse with its Peter Pan collar. The well-concealed bosom heaved beneath the cashmere as Pat advanced toward her. Clearly she was not happy. Hovering beyond her in the chancel stood a substantial-looking young woman with a ponytail and a firm smile, making a meal of checking through paperwork on a clipboard.

"*If* you could spare a moment…" The churchwarden was standing so close, Faith had to incline her head down to make eye contact.

"The…" Pat cast a disparaging look over her shoulder, "*young woman* they've sent from the council offices says you've agreed to decorate the church."

"She does?" Faith frowned, trying to recall her intermittent email correspondence with the council.

"She says that the little ones and their parents will be expecting it. The Green Lane Primary have been making Santa Claus lanterns." Pat's disgust was almost palpable. She drew herself up. "*I* have informed the young person that she must have misunderstood." Pat pinned Faith with her steeliest of gazes. "In the Christian church we do not decorate in Advent."

Ah! She should have seen this coming. A manifestation of the crunch point between the Christian calendar and public expectations at this time of year. Pat was quite right. Advent was about death and judgment, heaven and hell, and moving from darkness toward light. Santa Claus lanterns and glittery baubles were inappropriate, liturgically speaking. (Though

– come to think of it – on occasion, being trapped in an overcrowded, over-decorated mall in the last shopping days before Christmas could seem like a vision of hell.) She pulled her attention back to Pat. The churchwarden was almost rigid with her intensity of feeling.

"We *might* have discussed this yesterday, had you been able to come," she began, ominously. "I *understood* – although perhaps I was mistaken – I *had thought* you said you were coming by to help with the Christingle oranges?"

Faith winced internally. *Had* she promised that? In the past few days, she had been so preoccupied with donkeys and incarcerated Josephs, she might have said something on autopilot.

"I thought Lucy Taylor and Alice Peabody were going to help you?" she said feebly.

"Mrs Taylor pushed a note through my door – I can't tell you when," Pat snapped. "It must have been the middle of the night; I found her note on my mat in the morning. She was *very* sorry, of course, but something had come up – and, as for Alice Peabody… I've told you before, that girl never keeps her promises. I was left facing two crates of oranges all on my own!"

"Pat, I am so sorry, I was diverted… a pastoral visit – to Adam Bagshaw. The uncle of the murdered boy. It seemed important that someone visit him. I am sure you understand priorities?" Pat sniffed. Faith pressed her advantage. "The only two family members Adam Bagshaw had have been brutally taken from him within the space of a year. The man is devastated. He needs – he deserves – compassion and support; *our* compassion and support." Pat blinked. "The gospel of love is for all our neighbours," Faith said gently.

Pat pressed her lips together in a tight line, as if she regarded Faith's sophistry as a little suspect. "Well, as it happened, Fred came by." Her voice strengthened. "And as for Alice Peabody, she turned up eventually – *forty* minutes late. She had that young man of hers in tow; the one in the army. All excited because he's come home from leave. Of course, we all support our brave boys. A bit on the rough side, but very willing." Pat gave her the brave smile of a Woman Who Copes. "Anyhow, the Christingles are all done. We got through them."

The council co-ordinator put her head through the door.

"Hello, vicar! Mrs Montesque, just to say, I'm off for a bit of lunch. See you back here at one?" she said brightly. Pat gave her a frosty nod.

"Well – that gives us a breather anyway," she said, as the woman departed.

"Sue and Clarisse will be here soon," Faith said. "We can discuss together what's to be done. Don't you want to pop back home and have some lunch?" she asked, hoping for a brief reprieve herself.

"I had a late breakfast," Pat answered, firmly. "I've brought a Thermos of coffee and some of my strawberry shortbread. Would you care to join me?"

They sat in a rear pew. Pat spread a large handkerchief between them and fetched a Thermos and a tin printed with transfers of Princess Diana and Prince Charles from her tartan shopping bag.

"Did you hear that it was Oliver Markham who found the Bagshaw boy on his land?"

Faith hadn't been expecting that. Had Pat finally realized that the pageant was missing its Joseph? And what had Mavis told her about seeing Faith at the scene? She quickly stuffed a piece of strawberry shortbread in her mouth and chewed to buy herself time. She widened her eyes enquiringly, but Pat wasn't looking at her as she poured out the coffee.

"The family's been away, of course – for the weekend. Mrs Markham took the girls shopping in London." Pat's tone was faintly envious. "They spoil those girls. Mind you, couples often do, when they have problems." Faith looked at her, startled. Pat tilted her head knowingly. "Money problems. Oliver's business is not doing well and *she's* keeping them going with that high-powered job of hers. If you ask me, that marriage is in trouble…" Holding her plastic cup delicately, she took a sip of coffee.

Faith wondered where this was going. She didn't approve of gossip – although she remained grateful Pat wasn't homing in on the pageant.

"Pat, we don't know anything about the Markhams as a family," she said, selecting another piece of shortbread. It was really rather good.

"Well, of course, they are new to the parish," said Pat, "but how often have you seen the pair of them together with their girls? She's always working away – Julie? Is that her name? A mother should be at home. Children need guidance, particularly girls, and the Markham girls are *that age*."

"That age?" queried Faith, feigning ignorance.

"*Boys*," said Pat, simply.

Without warning, the nursery rhyme sang in Faith's head – "*Snakes and snails and puppy-dog tails; that's what little boys are made of.*" She realized Pat was frowning at her. Faith swallowed.

"Well, it seems they were all in London together having fun as a family this weekend," she commented. "It's different nowadays, Pat. Often both parents have to work just to make ends meet."

"Well, they're back home now."

That was news. Trust Pat to know the latest. If Oliver Markham had been released, perhaps his alibi had checked out. Perhaps he had been cleared? Pat watched her with a speculative look. The Joseph question! Faith stood up abruptly.

"Pat – I must make a call, if you'll excuse me a moment. This shortbread is delicious."

She hurried off to the church porch, phone in hand. She found the Markham home number and pressed call. The phone rang and rang. Then the anonymous phone lady clicked in: "*The person you have called is not available at this time…*"

That could mean all sorts of things. Faith wished she knew how the checks on Markham's alibi were going. She left her name and a message that she'd try again later.

If only she could get hold of Peter Gray. What time was it? Lunchtime. She imagined Peter eating his lunch in the greasy spoon cafe by the police station where CID liked to hang out. Maybe he would tell her what was going on. Peter was a member of her congregation, after all, and the pageant was less than two weeks off. She needed to know if she should be looking for a replacement to play Joseph.

"Break out the tea! Reinforcements have arrived." A familiar voice hailed her from the wicket gate. Moments later, Faith was swept into Sue's warm embrace. Clarisse hugged Faith with more restraint, as befitted her elegance. They all beamed at one another. Faith felt her spirits lift.

"What do you need us to do?" Clarisse asked, her tawny eyes twinkling.

"We have a diplomatic situation," Faith declared with deliberate exaggeration. "The civic centre co-ordinator – the one who has been liaising with the schools? – she's expecting the church to be decorated. And as Pat has pointed out…"

"Ah!" They both appreciated the problem immediately. They followed Faith into the church. She could feel them close at her back. What a wonderful thing it was to have good friends. "The children from Green Lane Primary have made Santa Claus lanterns," Faith added, plaintively.

"Oh dear!" Sue responded. The three of them paused, gazing at one another a moment.

"I know. The Spicer wedding!" Clarisse exclaimed.

Sue nodded approvingly.

"Good thought! The Spicer wedding."

"The Spicer wedding?" echoed Faith, lost. They linked arms with her, one on each side, and marched her off toward the organ.

"Last year. Very posh. Loads of money," Sue said, rolling her eyes.

"They didn't want the decorations – they left them behind and we put them in the loft," Clarisse explained. "The theme was purple."

"Dark purple and cream. Very fitting," Sue pulled a face of clownish approbation. Faith laughed out loud. They stopped at the ladder leading up to the roof space behind the organ. "Clari can show you. I don't like ladders." Sue looked up at the nineteenth-century turned rungs with distaste. They look sound enough, Faith told herself, a mite dubiously.

Clarisse shimmied up the ladder with surprising ease. Faith followed her with less grace. Her knee was protesting. She paused at the top of the ladder, looking about. She'd never been up here before. Fred had always fetched anything needed from the loft.

The loft space was a shelf of floor above the rear of the church, inconspicuous from the ground. Faith looked out, admiring the bird's-eye view of her church. Clarisse pulled a cord and the yellowish light of a bare bulb revealed a space continuing much further back than she would have guessed. There wasn't enough head room to stand up straight. Clarisse crawled ahead of her down the narrow space left between stacks of boxes.

"I am pretty sure the Spicer box isn't very far back." Her voice came back to Faith deadened by the overfilled space. "I remember helping Fred put it up here. By the way…" Her slim brown hand pointed to a tobacco-yellow canvas trunk under the eaves of a tilted board at the left-hand margin. "The principals' pageant costumes are in there. We should get them out in the next day or so. Make sure they are OK."

"So *what* exactly are we looking for?" Faith asked.

"There were thirty or more pairs of dark plum satin bows for the pew ends, tied off with cream-coloured sprig arrangements. As I remember, it was quite effective. If we light lots of candles, it'll look fine, you'll see – and, best of all, we can put them up and take them down in half an hour."

The front half of Clarisse was absorbed in shadows. Faith thought that even at this angle she looked as if she could be posing for a magazine cover.

"How's Pat doing?" Clari's question came to her out of the dark.

"Well, I suppose, as a vicar you learn to cope with the business of having to work ahead of where you are spiritually at this time of year," Faith answered, thoughtfully. "But it is more difficult for laity, especially careful, faithful ones like Pat." Clari craned her head around to stare at her.

"What? I meant about her nephew. Wasn't he supposed to be coming to see her this morning?"

"What nephew? I didn't know Pat had a nephew." Faith was startled and then appalled. Not something else she had missed! Perhaps she hadn't been spending enough time on her parish. *That's what happens when you go nosing into police investigations that don't concern you any more...*

"Her estranged sister's boy," Clari was saying. "There is some family split. Fred's the one who knows the details. Pat's sister did something unmentionable and they stopped talking to each other years ago. The boy grew up without knowing anything about Pat. Then, just recently, he sent her a letter. I think he was tracing his family tree or some-such. Said he wanted to meet her. Pat was excited about it."

How shaming. For all her occasional quirks and annoying habits, Pat was a stalwart of the parish. As her vicar and pastor, how could Faith have missed something so important?

"You didn't know?" Clari's voice was kind. "Don't worry. Pat isn't a particularly confiding person. I just happened to hear her and Fred talking when we were clearing up together after pageant rehearsals."

At least Clari was there at the pageant rehearsals to hear, Faith chastised herself.

"And this nephew, he was supposed to come today?"

Clari nodded. "It looks as if he has stood her up."

"Poor Pat!" Faith suddenly saw the connection. In her way, Pat was as alone as Adam Bagshaw.

"Mmm." Clari sounded distracted. "Sue and I need to catch up with you over the pageant. Do you think Oliver Markham is going to be able to play Joseph with this awful murder investigation?"

Faith deflated with relief. "I am so glad you've thought of that too," she said. "I have been worrying and worrying about it. What should we do? I've tried ringing Oliver at home, but there's no answer."

Clari leaned further into the darkness, stretching out one slim leg for balance. Her voice was muffled. "It must be a dreadful time for them. It will hardly be a surprise if Oliver needs to drop out. But who can we get?"

Faith reviewed the possibles one more time. "Well, we need all the Wise Men. And Fred will be too busy marshalling everybody…"

"Besides, he hates making a spectacle of himself – as he puts it…"

"I did wonder about asking Peter Gray, but – being on the investigating team… well… murder enquiries are pretty intense. He most likely will say he doesn't have the time, and if he does agree, he'll probably get called away at the crucial moment and we will be Joseph-less anyway. You don't suppose Alice Peabody's soldier boyfriend might consider it? She is Mary and he's back on leave, I hear."

"Got it!" declared Clarisse, triumphantly. She edged backwards toward Faith, dragging a cardboard box. With a grimace of effort, she heaved it over between them, pulling back a flap. Faith glimpsed satin in a rich plum colour.

The box was unwieldy and dusty. Faith backed down the ladder, holding on with one hand, using the other to balance the cardboard box on her head. It was heavier than she'd first thought and her knee hurt. She wobbled uncertainly.

"Be careful!" Clarisse called anxiously from above.

Concentrating on holding her balance, Faith only dimly heard Fred shouting from across the church telling her to wait and let him do it. At last her lower foot struck reassuring tile and she turned, she hoped gracefully, to greet him with a triumphant, "Ta-da!"

Jim Postlethwaite was standing in front of her looking quizzical. He didn't take his eyes from her face. She thought she must be covered in dust. Jim lifted the weight of the box from her head with ease.

"Impressive," he said.

CHAPTER

8

Sue, Clarisse and Fred spirited the box of decorations off to the other end of the church, corralling Pat as they went. Faith shifted her gaze from their studiously turned backs. Casual in denim jeans and black peacoat, Jim Postlethwaite looked more like a dock worker than a choirmaster – a rather attractive dock worker. She pushed the unprofessional thought aside.

"Had a spare couple of hours and thought I'd drop by to see the church – I did leave a message…" He looked over at the group shaking creases out of the Spicer wedding decorations. "You've got something on tonight?"

"A civic carol service. It doesn't start until 6:30 p.m. Glad you could come by. Let me give you the tour. I was hoping the choir might be able to sing from the gallery." She led him away from the others, round to the curved wooden steps leading up to the gallery above the main door. She started up ahead of him. The treads were narrow and steep. Faith suddenly became conscious that her jeans fitted her rather snugly. She tugged her jumper down at the back. "It's a bit cramped," she said hurriedly, "but the effect will be dramatic, especially for the Midnight Mass." She glanced back over her shoulder. Jim lifted his eyes up to hers and grinned. She reached the gallery and stood back against the wall feeling flustered.

"The idea is to start with a solo voice singing the first verse of 'Once in Royal David's City…'" he said.

The gallery ran along the front wall of the old church. It only had room for two rows of chairs. When it was built in the early 1800s, the church band had played from here. Jim stood at the rail and looked out at her church.

"I know just the girl." He turned back to her. "Nice," he said.

"Our organist is very good." She was speaking too fast. She took a breath and deliberately slowed herself down. "Paul is studying music at the Royal College – an organ scholar. He plays for us when he comes home for Christmas. We're very lucky." She turned back to descend the steps. "The vestry is going to be a bit compact, given fifteen in the choir, I think you said?" *Detail. Concentrate on detail.*

He wasn't following her. He had taken the second seat in on the front row.

"I'm sure the vestry will be fine. Can't we sit? The view from up here gives me a good idea of the layout. Besides, your people look busy down there."

She sat down in the end chair, keeping her legs swung away toward the exit. It really was rather cramped up here.

"Numbers will be a bit down, what with Lucas and all that…" he was saying.

"Of course." She examined his face, full of concern. "Can they manage this? I will quite understand if you need to withdraw."

"No. It'll be fine," he said. "It is better we carry on – better for the kids."

"If you're sure…" His eyes were locked on hers. She noticed something shift, as if he was pulling her in, keeping her in place, looking at him. "You and the investigating officer – it seems like you know each other pretty well?"

A rather direct question, she thought. How to answer? She fancied he was judging her thoughts with every nanosecond that passed. She put a smile on her face and pretended to watch Sue and Clari fixing the decorations on the pew ends below.

"We both grew up around here. I used to know Ben Shorter pretty well some time ago, but we lost touch. I met him again when I moved back here, earlier this year."

There was nothing precisely untrue in that – though it hardly qualified as the truth.

"So you're friends?"

"Mmm." She made the noise as non-committal as possible. This was getting much too personal. What should she say? *We used to work together in another life when I thought we would be together forever, but I was wrong. No. Evasive is better.*

Jim was no longer looking at her. He sank his chin on his folded arms, gazing out over the rail.

"Do you know how the investigation is going into Lucas's…?" He trailed off, leaving the question hanging: death or murder? She glanced at him surreptitiously. Was he pumping her for information? Or maybe he was offering some?

"Not really," she replied, cautiously. "As far as I know, the investigation has only just got started. You knew Lucas. What do you think about it all?"

"It's shocking," he said simply. "You don't expect to come up against a murder, not in ordinary life." She wished she could say the same; but her life hadn't turned out that way.

"How are the choir coping?" she asked.

"It's been a bit hairy. Lucas's death has caused ructions – especially for V."

"V?" queried Faith.

"Lucas and he hung out together. Unlikely mates, in a way – but they were tight, even with the Dot in the middle." Faith wrinkled her nose.

"The Dot…?" She couldn't help smiling. Jim's face reflected her amusement, wryly.

"I know. The names they give themselves. The Dot is V's girl – at least, I *think* she is. It's hard to tell; one of those teenage group relationships. I get the sense V only joined the choir for her – though his voice isn't bad. The oddball trio."

Faith thought of the girl with the curls and the boy in the woolly hat at the cathedral; the short girl with the golden hair the PC had called Ben over to talk to – was that the Dot, maybe?

"So what happened?"

"Some nastiness – one of the lads in the choir – made a bad joke about V killing Lucas, over the Dot; typical teenage insensitivity. V took it to heart and socked him. Had to separate them. The verger was in a tizzy – fisticuffs in the chancel. The youth choir isn't very popular. We'll be lucky to see the week out."

"Not really?"

Jim shrugged. For the first time, she noticed the drawn look about his eyes. "Maybe. I guess; so long as it doesn't happen again… It was probably more cathartic than anything. A release of tension. They don't really have the emotional equipment to deal with death at that age. Especially when it comes so close – to one of their own, you know."

Down below, the Spicer wedding decorations were already up on half the pew ends. Fred and Pat, Sue and Clari were moving in pairs down two blocks of pews at a time. They worked well together.

"Do you do all this by yourself?" His question surprised her.

"Well, there's just me at the vicarage – but the congregation are very involved. We have a marvellous PCC, as you can see." She waved a hand at the team down below. Sue caught sight of her and waved back. She really ought to be down there helping, but she found herself curious about the man beside her. Well, if he was going to be personal…

"What about you? Do you have family?"

"Was married, once. My wife came from Edinburgh. She's gone back home."

Gone back home. Ambiguous. Divorced, maybe? She tried to ignore the pang of disappointment. Of course he was going to have relationships. He was in his thirties.

"Any children?" she asked. He was looking right at her and she saw something freeze. Only for a split second. He looked away.

"One. She lives with her mother. She's nearly ten now." His body language said clearly that the subject was closed. Faith watched Sue and the others, trying to think of something to say to dispel the tension. They were clustered together as if preparing to go off for a tea break. Perhaps she should take Jim down to join them. She caught the tail end of a look as his eyes flicked back to the church. He shrugged.

"Sorry – it's not something I talk about."

"Forgive me. I didn't mean to pry."

"It's…" he hesitated, looking off into middle distance. Faith chimed in softly, their voices blending, "… complicated." His lips quirked up. "And lonely, sometimes," he said, eerily echoing her thoughts.

This was too intimate ground. She should suggest tea. He tilted his head on his arms, crinkling his eyes at her.

"You're easy to talk to, you know that?"

The compliment warmed her. "It comes with the territory," she said, absently gesturing to her neck before realizing the dog collar wasn't there.

They were alone in the church. The others had disappeared, leaving the purple ribbons with their frothy cream accoutrements dressing the pews. Her church looked good. This could work.

"There's something about the space in these old churches." He spoke quietly. "Don't know why, but somewhere deep down in your psyche – it moves you. Doesn't it?" She watched his profile. At that moment she sensed no defences between them, just honest communication. "Do you…" He hesitated. He watched her with narrowed eyes, glinting through his lashes. "Do you ever doubt? Do you always just trust this?"

She tilted her head, considering. It felt important that she give him an honest answer.

"Well, life is complex and challenging. There's no denying that. But I think, in the end, I put my trust in love – and God." He stared back at her, his eyes willing her to go on. She attempted to elaborate. "Look at all your work with these kids. They've no connection to you; no rational call on your time. Yet you go out and you find them and you get them to sing with real joy – isn't that a material form of love?"

He laughed abruptly as if she'd startled him. "Thank you for that," he said after a moment. "You seem to think the best of people."

"I'm not naive, you know," she protested. He looked down his nose at her, unconvinced, the way Ben would do.

"I like that about you. But…" He looked away, articulating

his words as if this was something he really wanted her to understand. "I am a sinner; I am no saint."

"So are we all," she answered.

"Hi – Faith!" Sue called up to her from the vestry door. "What do you think?" She waved her hand at the transformed church. "Fab or what?"

"Definitely fab!" Faith called back.

"We're off to have something to eat – see you at six?" Sue waved backwards over her shoulder and was gone.

"I should go too." Jim unfolded himself from the chair. Faith stood up to give him room. They moved to the stairs inches apart.

"You doing anything tomorrow night?" His voice came from behind her as he followed her through the dusk of the narrow stairs. "I've got the evening off."

They'd reached the brighter light of the ground floor. He responded to the doubt in her face. "You've seen the kitchen in those lodgings they've got me in. I have to eat out." He tilted his head, looking down at her with a tentative smile. "It would be good to have company for a change."

He is a newcomer here, in a strange place at Christmas, she argued with her better self. *You saw those barely furnished lodgings he's in. That mini microwave would hardly heat a cup-a-soup. He is a guest of the church; what's the harm?*

Her lips were parting to answer him when she remembered supper with Peter and Sandy; that was tomorrow night.

But then, Sandy had said she was welcome to bring a guest. Why not? Why shouldn't she bring a church colleague to a friendly supper at the home of members of her own congregation?

"As it happens," she heard herself saying, "I am supposed to be having supper with friends – but perhaps you can come with me? Peter Gray and his wife – they'll be here at Midnight Mass…"

"They won't mind?"

"They told me to bring someone – come and meet some more people." There. That was just friendly – meet more of the congregation. Not a date at all.

"Cool," he said.

Jim rode a motorbike. He drove off, looking as if he was meant to be on it. She suppressed the urge to grin like an idiot after him. They were two professional colleagues and she had work to do. St James's was ready for tonight's invasion; the orders of service were laid out on the pews. She had nearly an hour before she had to be back in the church – time to put her feet up a moment, to turn herself around, grab something to eat and think about what had just happened.

As she locked the vestry door behind her, her mobile rang. Ruth! Oh dear, she had forgotten her sister *again*. She pressed the button without looking at the caller display, her mouth preparing apologies.

"Heard you've been to see Adam Bagshaw…" It was Ben. Disorientated, she struggled to adjust to the thought.

"Have you?" she responded, blankly.

"You left him your card." Amusement coloured the words. Faith grimaced, remembering.

"A pastoral visit," she said, a tad defensively. What did Ben want? And why just now, the instant after Jim Postlethwaite's unexpected visit?

"Got time for a coffee? Maybe we could swap notes."

Why did he do this? Ben was the one person with the ability to spring things on her, catching her off guard time and again. She scrabbled for her wits.

"Well…" She checked her watch. Now she had fifty-four minutes before she had to be back in the vestry. "There's a carol service at the church tonight. I only have half an hour or so."

"You've got coffee, haven't you?"

Yes. She did. For some reason she still kept a stock of that strong filter coffee Ben drank, even though she didn't like it herself.

"It will take you twenty minutes to get here from Winchester, and like I said, I've only got half an hour," she objected.

"Good thing I'm parked in your drive, then," he said, and rang off.

Ben was parked in the vicarage drive? Did that mean he'd seen Jim's motorbike leave?

Her heart rate had gone up, Faith noticed crossly. If Ben had driven up on the vicarage side, there was no reason for him to be aware of Jim departing from the church gate. And, besides, so what if he knew? It was perfectly legitimate that the choirmaster should come and check the layout of the church where his choir was due to sing. This was ridiculous! It was her vicarage, her church, her life. She stomped toward home feeling militant.

Ben was waiting in his long black coat by the kitchen door, his hands buried in his pockets. He tilted his head at her in acknowledgment.

"It's still cold."

"Isn't it," she snapped back. She unlocked the kitchen door and he followed her, looking irritatingly entertained.

"Coffee?"

"Thanks."

Ben was in her home. She turned her back on him, grateful to have something to busy herself with. He had sprung this visit on her without a by-your-leave. He could start the conversation. She opened cupboards and assembled the coffee machine. She was making herself a mug of tea when he finally spoke.

"You left the interviews at the cathedral early."

"I wasn't needed." *I am* not *going to discuss Jim Postlethwaite*, she added silently. She could feel his gaze on her back. "I had other things to do," she added hurriedly.

"Like sniffing around Bagshaw's place?"

"I've told you, it was a pastoral visit." She meant it as a statement; instead, the words came out defensive. Ben grunted. She plonked the mug of dark coffee in front of him. She'd made it extra strong. "The man's a wreck. He needs support."

Ben tensed and she winced deep in her conscience. She hadn't meant to reference that old business; perhaps the reason for their slow and painful split, perhaps a symptom of her emerging faith. Richard Fisher was the past, and should be left there. She didn't mean Adam was on the edge of suicide. She caught sight of the clock. No time to go into all that now. She fetched her tea.

Ben took a sip of the coffee. It was so strong it would have choked her. He didn't even flinch.

"Did you get much from the interviews?" she asked. He rubbed a long-fingered hand across his face. His five o'clock shadow stood out against his pale skin. He looked overworked.

"Teenagers aren't known for cooperating with the police these days." His bright blue eyes touched hers, reminding her of how close they used to be. She took her mug of tea and sat down across the table from him. She wondered if he had spotted the footprints outside and considered briefly mentioning them. Only pride prevented her from doing so. She didn't need looking after, and she didn't need Ben thinking he was the one to do it.

"Did you come across any particular friends who knew Lucas?" she asked.

"There's a couple, a girl and a boy. They weren't offering much, but I would guess the three of them hung out together more than most."

"The short girl with the golden curls and the tall boy – brown hair and a woolly hat?"

"That's them." His mouth curved in fleeting respect.

"V and the Dot," she murmured.

"What's that?"

"V and the Dot, I think that's what they go by. He's V, she's the Dot."

"Not the names they gave the PC."

"Probably not."

Lucas in a triangle with V and the Dot… how very *Dawson's Creek*, the girl between two boyfriends. Could that have anything to do with how Lucas got to the river? She thought of Jim's report about the fist fight in the choir. Could Lucas's death be the result of a territorial dispute between teenage boys?

"Come across anything else of interest?" Ben asked.

Her guard went up. This time she must keep her distance. She wasn't part of the police investigation. Clari's revelations about Pat's problems still stung. Her parishioners deserved her full attention.

"Not really."

He leaned in toward her, his eyes playful. She could feel the electrical tug between them.

"But you're developing sources?" he coaxed. She tried to stop herself smiling.

"Maybe," she said crossly. "Have you found out much about Lucas's movements yet?" Ben sat back and sighed.

"Nothing's straightforward. Lucas dropped out of school – never came back after the Easter break; not that anyone thought to report it since he was about to turn seventeen. So nothing there. A couple of teachers had him on their lists, but they didn't really remember him. His uncle's sitting on something – don't know what yet. Lucas didn't have a job that we can find. He had a bike we haven't been able to locate yet…" He spoke wearily.

"So all in all, day three of the investigation isn't going that well," she said.

"Thanks for stating the obvious."

"Did Oliver Markham check out?" Ben met her enquiry with his sphinx-like look. She held her breath. Did her pageant still have a Joseph? He lifted his dark eyebrows. He was teasing her. "He told you that he drove his family down on Friday night," she prompted, "and stayed over with them in their hotel through the weekend?"

"Right." His lips were pressed together at the corners. Was he flirting with her? "We're still checking," he said.

The clock reminded her that time was running short. She needed to be front of house in half an hour. She got up, taking her mug to the sink. He still nursed his.

"I've got to change and have something to eat. I have to be back at the church in twenty minutes," she said, surprised to catch a wistful note in her voice.

"Then go change. I'll put something together for you." He got up and opened her fridge. She watched him, baffled. He seemed to think nothing of the intrusion. "Omelette OK? You don't have much in."

She was hungry. What with changing and everything, she'd be lucky if she had time to grab an oatcake and some cheese. Ben's omelettes were OK, as she remembered. The minute hand moved on the clock. She gave up with a mental shrug. This was just a weird day. She headed to the door.

"Thanks," she said. "There's cheese in the butter drawer."

CHAPTER

9

Ben hadn't stayed more than a couple of minutes after she reappeared in her clerical clothes. He hated to see her like that. As she left the vicarage she saw her phone flashing. Another text from Ruth. Well, not really a text – just a question mark sent from her sister's number. The reproach itched under her skin. She stopped for a moment in her ice-bound garden and sucked up a lungful of freezing air. It burned the inside of her nose and made her head ache. Priorities. Focus on priorities. The civic carol service. Get back to the rest later.

She needed another moment to compose herself. She passed the vestry door and walked round to the front of the church. The musicians were arriving with their instruments and Pat was hovering like an irritated goose. She homed in on Faith.

"They won't stop to wipe their boots!" Muddy trails of melting ice marked the stone floor of the porch.

"Pat – don't worry." Faith attempted her most soothing voice; the one she used for distressed persons and unsettled beasts. "This church has stood for over nine hundred years. It can weather a bit of ice and mud."

Pat tossed her head. She was on edge too. What was it about this day?

"And who do you suppose is going to have to clean it all up?" Pat muttered.

Faith squeezed her arm.

"We'll do it together." Pat shot her a look of irritated affection. That was unexpected. They *were* in this together.

"Fred." Pat nodded a greeting at her fellow churchwarden and hurried off into the church.

Fred Partridge beamed at Faith. Her other churchwarden was a substantial man, but he had an inner peacefulness about him that meant that you didn't always become aware of him until he stood right beside you.

"She's in a fuss over that WI business," he said. "Wants to give a good impression. Mrs President herself is coming tonight."

Mrs Mavis Granger. Faith felt a slight chill run over her. She hardly relished another encounter with the imperious local dame. Fred smiled benignly at her and swept out his arm in a courtly gesture.

"After you, vicar."

The church was lit up with candles and movement. It looked cherished. The pew decorations were just right. Faith felt Fred's hand detain her. He drew her aside in the shadow of the gallery, away from the others.

"Just a word." He cleared his throat. His round eyes fringed by their stubby lashes were on Pat. "I don't know whether you know, but Pat's having a bit of a time."

"Her nephew?"

Fred looked relieved. "So you do know. It's not been easy on her. She's a bit..." Fred floundered. Faith touched his chest, feeling the fabric of his wax jacket with the flat of her hand.

"I know. We'll keep an eye on her."

Mavis Granger had already arrived. She must have come in from the vestry side. She stood in the midst of a group of women wearing blue sashes. Pat faced them. To Faith's eye the Scotswoman looked outnumbered. A wave of protective instinct rose in her.

"It's a small church," Mavis addressed Pat directly. The others stood in a crescent around her – her pack. Their leader's tone was condescending. "Only *serving* WI officers, otherwise we'd be parading all night. *I* would love to have you join us, Pat, of course, but I know you understand. This isn't the cathedral; there just isn't the space to have all the local WI members parade."

How mean! thought Faith. She could see Pat holding her shoulders back against the rebuff. She really shouldn't get involved, but…

She stepped forward. "Pat – I am sorry, ladies. I need my fellow host. Pat, the VIPs will start arriving soon. Can you help me do a final check to make sure the place cards on the seats are still right? You know how they can get mysteriously moved once the public starts arriving. We need to be at the door with Fred to start the greetings in five minutes or so." She smiled benignly at Mavis and her colleagues and swept away with her churchwarden.

"Mavis Granger thinks too much of herself," Pat muttered at her side. "The cathedral indeed! As if anyone sees her there except on high days and holidays."

Faith suppressed a grin. "Some people just feel the need to be seen parading," she consoled. She knew it was uncharitable but no one had the right to make Pat feel small in her own church. "We all know your importance to the WI. This is a night for hospitality. If that's what she needs, we can give her this."

* * *

The MP texted to say she was caught in traffic. Everyone else had arrived. Faith looked back at the full seats from the door. The atmosphere was cheerful – people chatting and catching up with friends. *It's going to be all right*, she assured herself.

"Vicar!" Mavis Granger sailed toward her with her hand outstretched. "I just wanted to pass on apologies from Neil – my husband. He did mean to come tonight, but he's been delayed in Stockholm. Plane trouble."

"How annoying," Faith said, taking her hand and shaking it since she wasn't sure what else to do. Mavis blinked. "I look forward to meeting him another time," she added hurriedly. A tall youth dressed in a black suit reminiscent of the sixties had followed Mrs Granger up the aisle. Something Mavis had said seemed to have irritated him. He was standing stiffly, staring detachedly over their heads. At first Faith didn't see it, then he turned his head to respond to a friend who called out a greeting. His curly brown hair was slicked back with gel. When she had seen him at the cathedral interviews, it had been trapped under a woolly hat.

"This is my son, Vernon," Mavis introduced him. "He's coming to sing at your church at Midnight Mass. He's in that choir."

Vernon – V. Mavis Granger's son, who goes out with the girl she employs in her shop. V and the Dot.

Faith reached out her hand. Vernon Granger made no move to reciprocate, his expression hostile. She opened her hand toward him instead.

"Welcome to St James's. I understand you were a close of friend of Lucas Bagshaw's – I am very sorry for your loss."

"Who told you that?" he said belligerently – or maybe he was just startled. He glanced at his mother. Faith could feel the tension between them.

"Vernon!" His mother's voice wasn't loud, but the energy she gave the word, combined with her expression, recalled the way she'd controlled her dogs down by the river. Her son seemed to shrink an inch.

"Sorry," he mumbled.

"Make yourself useful." His mother nodded toward Sue, who was talking to a couple of young volunteers. "Go and ask if there is anything you can help with," she dismissed him.

The proud mother from Monday night didn't seem very loving, thought Faith. What's going on with them?

"He's a good-looking boy," she said out loud to Mavis, as V moved out of earshot.

"My pride and joy." The words were curiously dispassionate. Faith's curiosity grew.

Mavis Granger turned her eyes on Faith, her head tilted slightly back. What now?

"You are close to the police, aren't you?" The angle of Mavis's mouth and her tone implied something disreputable. For one foolish, guilty moment Faith imagined that Mrs Granger had spied on her talking to Ben in her kitchen. "I hear that the sergeant who spoke to me down at the river is a member of your congregation. I don't see him here tonight… I suppose they're still busy with the Bagshaw thing."

Faith pinned a diplomatic smile to her lips. "No. I don't think the Grays were able to join us tonight," she replied. "As for the police investigation – at this stage, I imagine, they will still be establishing a timeline, trying to pin down how the victim spent his last hours, looking for witnesses, that sort of thing." She paused. "Your son, Vernon, was in the choir with Lucas, wasn't he? The police must have spoken to him?"

"He's upset. We all are…" Mavis said quickly.

"Of course. He was Lucas's best friend, wasn't he?" Faith pressed.

"I wouldn't say that. Vernon's always been popular himself. The Bagshaw boy was underdeveloped. Not the sort to make friends easily. Vernon took pity on him."

"Your son couldn't help the police?"

"Vernon will have told them everything he knows." She fixed her eyes on Faith and spoke with some emphasis. "He was with me the day Lucas died."

"Of course," said Faith. "I'm sure no one was suggesting…"

"Well, you know how people gossip," said Mavis.

Faith offered a wry smile and glanced at her watch. If the MP didn't arrive soon they would just have to start without her. The children from Green Lane Primary were getting restive, clamouring to light their lanterns. Mavis was still standing there. What was she waiting for?

"Your son's girlfriend, she's in the choir that is coming to sing Midnight Mass with us too, isn't she?" Faith asked. "She and your son were both friends of Lucas Bagshaw's. She works for you, I think you said?"

"Anna works in my florist shop, yes."

"Anna…?"

"Hope. Anna Hope."

Mavis Granger's eyes searched out her son. Sue had found him a seat with her family. It was probably a trick of the light, but Faith thought she saw yearning in Mrs Granger's perfectly made-up face.

"Her mother moved away with a new man after she and Anna's father divorced." Mavis Granger's tone expressed what she thought of women who discarded their husbands. "Anna's father's in the army. Anna is just eighteen, but she is keeping herself, living in a rented room." It sounded as if Mavis Granger respected the girl for that. "This is where she grew up; she wanted to stay."

"So you've taken her under your wing," Faith said with warmth. She had misjudged Mavis Granger. Who would have thought such an unappealing manner could conceal generosity? *That'll teach you to make snap judgments*, her better self scolded. Mrs Granger looked embarrassed by her approval.

"Anna's a good worker," she said brusquely. Pat had come up behind them.

"The MP's car has just drawn up – vicar…?"

The Civic Service was a success, despite a minor incident when two of the Green Lane Primary's Santa Claus lanterns clashed. Only Clari's quick reflexes and a bucket of sand contained the potential conflagration. The MP sounded sincere in her congratulations to Faith and, more importantly, had agreed to bring the local press to the Salvation Army Christmas lunch. According to Fred, the collection had raised nearly £400 for the women's refuge. The last stragglers didn't leave until past 10:30 p.m., when Faith had the church to herself again.

She shuffled the box down the pews between her feet, unhooking the glossy purple decorations one by one, folding them back tidily into their cardboard resting place, on autopilot, her thoughts drifting. It was nearly midnight by the time she finished. She looked up at the loft in its shadows. She really ought to complete the task, but she just couldn't face heaving the box up the ladder. Do it tomorrow. She left the box in the vestry, in a corner of the space that had been occupied by her Toy Service collection that morning. One task done and the next already reproaching.

The darkest hour comes before the dawn, and this is Advent: Prepare the way for the Lord.

Faith unlocked her kitchen door feeling bone tired. Her eyes fell on the washing-up from Ben's cooking congealing in the sink. She double-locked the door and left the hall light burning. At last she crawled gratefully into her bed.

CHAPTER

10

Faith stood on the pavement, arms full of artwork, looking at Mavis Granger's florist shop. Thursday began gently after yesterday's stresses and strains. She started virtuously, ringing her sister first thing. Ruth didn't pick up, but at least Faith had returned her call at last and left an apologetic message. She spent a pleasant couple of hours with the old people's home residents singing carols and show-tunes and discussing the most cheerful colours for a Christmas cardigan. After that, a quick dip into Green Lane Primary to collect a batch of Christmas-themed artwork for display in St James's, and that brought her here: across the road from Mavis Granger's small, exclusive florist shop.

Copper-banded tubs flanked the door, each containing a miniature tree with dense foliage clipped into a perfect sphere, lollipops of leaf. In the plate-glass window fronting the shop, sheaves of pussy willow with their delicate silver fur-buds stood in buckets next to evergreen confections where gold-sprayed pinecones mingled with red berries and crystal beads. The effect was very chic. Impeccable and perfectly conceived, with no rough edges or unsightly variations – a fitting expression of Mavis Granger herself.

Faith watched the girl behind the counter serving a customer – the girl with golden curls. Anna Hope. The Dot. Perhaps one of the people who knew Lucas Bagshaw best. There was no sign of Mrs Granger.

The bell over the door hung from a loop of iron lending a Dickensian charm. It jingled tunefully but not too loudly over her head. Faith examined a stand of tree shapes fashioned from crystal beads and reindeer made out of strips of twisted bark as she waited for Anna to finish serving her customer.

Standing poised to assist behind the counter, the Dot seemed taller than Faith remembered. The marble surface in front of her was stacked with understated wreaths decorated with gold and silver touches, the perfect complement to Anna Hope's hazel eyes, rosy lips and tumble of blonde-caramel curls. Right now in the glow of youth, she looked as delectable as a foil-wrapped toffee. Faith could see how she must enchant boys of her own age.

Anna waited for the door to close behind her departing customer. She looked Faith up and down, taking in the dog collar and the artwork.

"I saw you at the cathedral, didn't I?" she said. "What are you? Someone the police send in to offer witnesses comforting words and snoop for them?"

The accent was local, and the tone shockingly unpleasant issuing from such a sweet face.

"I am not with the police," said Faith. "I am the vicar at St James's. Your choir is coming to sing for us at Midnight Mass."

"So you're introducing yourself to every choir member?" The question was derisive.

"Lucas Bagshaw's body was found in my parish," said Faith.

Anna's posture stilled, shifting from belligerent to watchful. "So?"

This wasn't going as smoothly as Faith had hoped. Kids were more guarded than grown-ups, and in some ways more savvy – less likely to disguise their distrust with diplomatic words. Faith decided to reply in kind.

"So I think Lucas deserves justice. I want to find out what happened to him."

Anna dropped her head. She measured out a length of red ribbon, cut it in an economical movement and began weaving it around a half-made wreath.

"I met your boyfriend last night – V?" Anna cocked her head slightly at the use of Vernon Granger's nickname, but she kept her head down, blocking Faith out. "I have been talking to Jim – your choirmaster? He told me that you and V were Lucas's best friends."

"We were friends." Anna's voice was tight. She brushed a tear away with an angry hand, and kept on twisting the ribbon through the wire and spiky evergreens.

Faith asked her gently, "What was Lucas like, Anna?"

Anna's busy hands stilled. For a moment, Faith thought she wasn't going to reply, then she answered in a softer voice.

"He didn't say much but he had a wicked sense of humour. Dry, you know? He'd come out with just a single line and he'd crease you up."

"Did he have many friends?"

"Didn't need them. He had us. Didn't have time, anyway. He had to take care of things…"

"Take care of things?"

"There was just him and his mum; she was always working."

Faith nodded. "How did Lucas feel about that?"

"He worshipped his mum."

"What about his uncle?"

Anna snorted. "Waste of space! He was more of a kid than Lucas. Always having to look out for him; drag him home when he had too much. Did that a lot."

"It sounds like Lucas had it tough."

Anna shrugged. "Tougher than some."

Faith thought of what Mavis Granger had told her. The girl in front of her was already living on her own. Just like Lucas, she had to take care of things; no one else was going to do it for her. "Were there any signs that Lucas was having more trouble than usual recently?"

Anna's guard flashed up again. "Meaning?"

"Was he worried about anything? Acting secretive? Any change from what you'd think of as normal? Making dates and not turning up; not discussing where he had been or why he was late… that sort of thing?"

Anna almost smiled. "Know many teenagers, do you?"

"Fair point." Faith cast around for another angle. "Lucas's body was found on land down by the river, the Markhams' place. Do you know it?"

Anna shook her head.

"You haven't come across the Markham girls? There are two of them – fourteen and sixteen, I think. Dark haired; both tall. They live with their parents in a big house down by the river. They go to the secondary Lucas was at."

She didn't want to hear that Lucas was seeing one of the Markham girls, but she had to ask. Her arms were getting cramped holding on to the sheaf of artwork. She leaned the pictures against the counter. Anna was standing on a crate. That's why she looked taller. Flower stalks and bits of evergreen covered the floor around her.

"Taller one called Amy or something?" Anna sounded genuinely uninterested. "I've seen her about, but we don't know her." We. Was that just her and V, or was Lucas also part of her property?

"Did Lucas have a girlfriend?"

"No!" Anna smiled shyly.

"Did Lucas have feelings for you, then?"

"What do you mean?" Anna responded defiantly, but perhaps a little too fast. "There's only ever been V that way with me. We all just got on, that's all."

It was probably the truth, Faith speculated. But then what red-blooded teenage girl wouldn't have a soft spot in her heart for a little adulation on the side? Anna didn't have to want it to go anywhere, but it might have been different for Lucas. And what would Vernon feel about that?

"How did the three of you get together? Were V and Lucas already friends when you met Vernon?"

Anna looked lost for a moment, as if she'd never asked herself the question.

"I'm not sure. I think V already knew him from somewhere. They are… they *were* both mad about bikes. V wants to compete," she finished proudly.

"That's an expensive hobby," Faith said idly, watching Anna's skilful fingers. "Where did Lucas get the money?"

She knew she'd gone too far before the words were out. She could see Anna stiffen with resentment just by watching her hands.

"Maybe he won the lottery," Anna snapped, "or there was an insurance policy or something. His mother did die, you know." Faith nodded slowly, admitting her fault. "You sound more like a copper than a vicar," Anna said.

Faith let the comment sink. "When were you last in

touch with Lucas?" she asked. Anna straightened, meeting her eyes dead on.

"Friday… well, Saturday; but I was at work."

"Saturday afternoon?"

"V said we were going to meet at the pub but Luke cancelled. He said something came up."

"Which pub?"

"Lion's Heart, down on the river. The cider's cheap."

"V said…" repeated Faith. "You didn't see Lucas yourself, then?" The girl's expression was unreadable.

"No," she said after a beat.

"Then how did you know he'd cancelled?"

"He texted."

Of course he did. Faith sighed internally. Sometimes she felt rather old.

"Did you tell the police this, when they interviewed you at the cathedral?"

Anna shrugged sulkily.

"Might have done."

"But did you? Did you tell them about the text?" Anna pouted and shrugged again.

Well, maybe it wouldn't be important. And if it turned out to be, Ben and his colleagues could check the phone records.

"So, do you have any idea what it was that made Luke cancel?"

Anna shrugged yet again. It was an annoying habit.

"You can't think of anything? Anything Lucas was doing that might have got him into trouble?" Faith pressed. "He didn't seem distracted or worried…?"

"Luke was OK. You know, he could handle himself."

Not well enough, thought Faith. She'd seen enough teenagers in both her lines of work to know their confidence was fragile and tragically unfounded. "Anna, is there any chance Lucas had started drinking or doing drugs?"

"He wouldn't do that. He didn't even have the odd pint."

But when, at the Bagshaw home the other day, she'd asked Adam how he spent time with his nephew, he'd said they'd drunk together at his favourite pub – hadn't he?

"He didn't even drink with his uncle, to keep him company?" Faith insisted.

"They used to go to the pub," said Anna, "but Luke hated booze – seeing what it did to that uncle, I guess. Like I said, Luke spent his life having to look out for him – his uncle got to be the kid and Luke had to be the grown-up."

Faith thought of the guilt she'd seen in Adam Bagshaw's wet eyes.

"Could his uncle have got Lucas into trouble?"

Anna looked back at her for a fraction of second before she answered. "I wouldn't know."

Did she know something? Was she holding back?

Tears pooled in Anna's eyes. Rummaging in a drawer, she picked up a paper handkerchief and blew her nose.

"Luke didn't deserve this." She gave Faith a hard look and jerked her chin at the dog collar she wore. "How do you explain what happened to him? Luke was just a kid, and his mum, she worked so hard to keep it together; and she loved him, and now they're both gone; not that waste of space uncle of his – but Luke and his mum. You can't explain that, can you?" She shook her head angrily. "I don't see how you can keep on pretending."

"Believing in a loving God?" Faith's voice was gentle. Anna dropped her head again, concentrating on the wreath beneath her hands.

"I know – it's hard. All I can tell you honestly is that I have seen enough love – and God is love in essence – to believe that even tragedy like this doesn't have the last word." She wasn't putting it very well, but Anna seemed to hear her sincerity. Her anger ebbed.

"Nice if you can believe it, I guess."

"Shall I see you at Midnight Mass? We're looking forward to hearing you sing."

"Maybe." They listened to the sound of a car pulling up in the alley that ran at the back of the shop. "That'll be Her coming back," Anna said. "I need to get on. I'm behind with this order."

Faith didn't feel up to facing Mavis Granger again so soon after last night's service. She picked up one of the stripped-bark reindeer; it would do as a house gift for Sandy and Peter tonight. She paid Anna too much for it, gathered up her artwork and left.

CHAPTER

11

An illuminated Santa with a ruby-red belly and a drinker's nose occupied next door's front lawn. One of his bulbs was flickering. Faith found it quite distracting. Now they were here, walking up Peter's front path, she had to admit she felt nervous. Should she have invited someone connected – however loosely – to a current murder investigation to join her at supper at the home of one of the investigating team? It really shouldn't matter. This was just going to be a family supper with her and the Grays and now Jim. Sandy had told her to bring a plus one. They could talk church. Peter didn't need to mention his job. She hugged the stripped-bark reindeer – wrapping it in red tissue paper had been a challenge. Too late now. They'd reached the doorstep. Jim Postlethwaite stood beside her, smelling of aftershave and clean linen and the damp wool of his peacoat. He looked down at her beneath his lashes.

"Cold?"

"Mmm," she smiled up at him, and rang the doorbell. She really should say something about Peter's job. Peter and he had met at the cathedral. Jim surely already knew who Peter Gray was, but she should have checked. "I should have mentioned, about our hosts…" she began, but Jim's attention was on next door's decorations.

"I've got to say, I don't get that," he said. "Who wants a luminous giant Santa looming in at the window?" Jim grimaced. "When I was a kid, a weirdo like that would have given me nightmares."

"At least it doesn't play 'Jingle Bells'," Faith murmured. Then in a moment of resolution she turned to face him, saying hastily, "Just before we go in, I should mention…"

But rapid footsteps approached inside the house, the front door opened and she was illuminated in a flood of yellow light. There was Sandy dressed to the nines in a bold floral rockabilly dress, her fair hair held back in a wide Alice band. She looked very pretty, if a bit overdressed for a quiet family supper.

"Faith!" Sandy enveloped her in a warm-hearted embrace. "I was looking out for you. Welcome." She smiled sunnily at Jim. "I am *so* glad you could bring your friend."

"This is Jim – Jim Postlethwaite," Faith remembered her manners. "He runs the youth choir that's coming to sing for us at Midnight Mass – you'll be there, I hope? He's new to the area. I thought it would be nice for him to meet some more of us St Jamesians. Jim – our hostess, Sandy Gray." Jim reached out his hand.

"It's a pleasure," he said. Sandy's eyelashes fluttered.

"Welcome to our home, Jim. Peter, darling, Faith and her friend are here!" She called out, as she ushered them in. "You must tell me *all* about him," she hissed conspiratorially in Faith's ear as she took her coat.

Peter appeared in the doorway to the living room holding a bottle of wine in one hand and a corkscrew in the other. He too was looking disconcertingly spruce. His eyes met Faith's, smiling and relaxed until they registered her companion. Faith's heart sank. She *had* made a mistake. Peter recouped himself.

"Jim – isn't it?" He greeted Faith's plus one with a smile. "We met at the choir interviews on Tuesday."

"You're a policeman," Jim stated.

"Sergeant Gray."

"Right."

Sandy gave her husband a puzzled looked.

"Sandy, this is for you." Faith thrust the red tissue parcel at her.

"Oh, Faith! You shouldn't have," exclaimed Peter's wife.

The reindeer was released from its packaging and admired. Faith hadn't noticed it had quite such a fatalistic expression when she bought it.

"Shall we go in?" Sandy led the way. Faith felt Jim's fingers dig into her arm.

"You might have warned me," he whispered in her ear.

"I am so sorry! I thought you knew. They're members of the congregation and it's just a family…" The sentence faded on her lips. The table was set for a dinner party for six. Peter was staring at her with round-eyed significance.

"How are the boys?" she asked Sandy, hurriedly.

"Happy, healthy and a handful, as usual." Sandy was endearingly proud of her boys. She was one of those women born to be a mother. "They're upstairs, ready for bed. Faith, Daniel wanted me to ask you – you don't know anything about *Peter and the Wolf*, do you? Dan went to see it with his school and now he's got to write a piece about it…" Faith tried to recall anything pertinent about *Peter and the Wolf* and failed. It was a piece of music introducing different instruments in the orchestra, wasn't it?

"I know a bit," Jim volunteered.

"Can you draw an oboe?"

"I can try."

"You are my salvation. Follow me." Sandy led Jim up the stairs, chatting easily about her boys. Faith looked longingly after them. Perhaps Dan and Charlie wouldn't mind if she camped in their room for the evening. She turned back to Peter reluctantly. The table looked lovely – very elegant with its candles, soft green china and real linen napkins. At least she had put on a dress.

"Who else is coming?" she asked, with a feeling of doom.

"The boss and a plus one."

"Oh, good grief. Peter!" she exclaimed. "I thought this was just a family supper with us three – well, four."

"It was supposed to be." Peter was pink-cheeked with apology. "But Sandy was so pleased you were bringing a plus one… She called in at the office on her way back from some shopping today and Ben was with me, and before I knew it, she'd invited him. Work was crazy. I didn't have time to warn you."

Poor Peter looked almost as distressed as she felt. Faith's heart melted. It wasn't his fault; it was hers.

"Does Sandy know the background – I mean, our history, Ben and me?"

"I haven't told her."

"Really? That's very discreet."

"It's your business, not mine. I don't really know anything anyway…" Peter shuffled, embarrassed.

"This is terrible. What am I going to do?"

"Have a glass of wine?"

"Be serious!"

"Your face! It is kind of funny." He giggled. Faith cuffed him on the shoulder.

"It is not! This is going to be a disaster. Ben is not going to take kindly to my bringing a civilian caught up in one of his murder investigations to a social engagement at your house."

"I'm not so sure about it myself, Faith," Peter said, suddenly serious. Faith looked at him helplessly. She really had messed up.

"I am so sorry to do this to you, Peter. I was thinking church life – not police life. You and Sandy have become such a part of our congregation. Jim is bringing his choir to sing for us for free. He is a newcomer to the area; I was thinking hospitality. And anyway," she added, her tone shifting to defensive, "Ben is always stressing how I am not in the police. I'm just a vicar – well, I was thinking like one." Peter wrinkled his nose at her. "Do you think we should leave?" she asked anxiously. If she texted Sue, she might agree to ring her with a made-up disaster that could give her an exit.

Peter went over to the window. He lifted the edge of the curtain to look out.

"They're here."

Faith joined him to peer out. Ben was opening the car door for his date. Whoever it was, she had long legs. And she had red hair…

"That's the pathologist… Harriet Sims." *Could this get any worse?*

"Maybe it's just work-related," Peter suggested soothingly. Faith gave him a dark look. He backed away from her. "I'll go and open the door," he said.

Ben had obviously come forewarned and didn't bat an eyelid when he saw Faith. "Faith – good to see you." He was in a good mood. "You've met Harriet." The two women shook hands. Ben slapped Peter on the back, passing over a bottle of red wine. He glanced at the dinner table, noting the setting.

"Very nice. Where's your date?" he threw at Faith.

She wouldn't rise to it. "Upstairs; he and Sandy are discussing *Peter and the Wolf* with the boys."

"O-K," Ben said slowly. His eyes narrowed fractionally.

"So, how's the investigation going?" Faith asked, before he could start interrogating her. She might as well take advantage of Jim's absence upstairs. They wouldn't be able to say anything once he came down.

"Some tests have just come back." Harriet seemed happy to talk. "Analysis on the water in the boy's lungs…"

"What?" Peter was eager to hear the latest news.

"Traces of decayed watercress," Harriet said.

"Wild?" queried Faith. That wouldn't help much. Wild watercress grew all along the river where Lucas Bagshaw's body was found. Why, then, were Ben and Harriet so energized? She could feel the excitement of discovery running between them.

"No. A cultivated strain. One used commercially." Harriet was a head taller than her; much more Ben's height, Faith thought; *but angular, and that skirt is at least an inch too short.* Faith straightened her shoulders, wondering fleetingly if her own burgundy wrap-around jersey dress qualified as dowdy.

"We know that the victim went into the river breathing – if not for long. So when he took the water in, it looks as if he must have been pretty close to a commercial watercress bed," Ben elaborated. "We knew we were looking for an attack site upriver, but this narrows it down."

"Doesn't the heavy rain over the weekend complicate things?" Faith asked Harriet.

"Yes and no." Harriet was all confidence talking about her work. "The concentration of particles suggests the water

131

he fell in was passing through a dense area of watercress cultivation."

"We've been looking at maps," Ben locked in on Harriet's eyes. The pathologist was mesmerized. Faith knew that look. It made you feel as if you were the only person of significance in the whole wide world. "There are a couple of big commercial watercress farms within a mile upriver from the Markham place."

"That's still quite a stretch to cover," Faith commented. She thought of what Anna had told her earlier in the shop about the plans to meet Lucas on the afternoon of his death, and how Lucas had texted to cancel. "Did you manage to get anything off the smashed phone in the boy's pocket?"

Harriet turned from her contemplation of Ben reluctantly. She blinked.

"Sorry?"

"It was too damaged," intervened Peter, as he leaned between them to pass a glass of wine to Harriet and Ben.

Harriet thanked him, but Ben held up a hand. "Just water for me," he said. "Driving."

Peter withdrew the second glass. "We've got the account details," he continued. "We're still waiting on the records from the provider."

"Christmas!" Ben said. "Gets in the way of everything; all the keyboard tappers off getting drunk and disorderly at the office party – we could be waiting for weeks."

"Faith, what can I get you?" Peter asked. 'We've got cranberry or orange juice, or water – or a mug of tea?" She felt as if her smile was made of cardboard.

"Cranberry juice sounds great, thanks," she said.

"So is this new squeeze of yours coming down?" Ben was teasing her. Out of the corner of her eye, Faith caught the puzzled look on Harriet's face; presumably Ben hadn't filled her in on their past relationship.

"About that…" Faith's back was to the stairs. She saw Ben stiffen as he looked beyond her.

"Mr Postlethwaite," he said, with a stare that could cut glass. Faith didn't dare move. It was like watching a car crash in slow motion. She felt Jim arrive beside her. In that moment she was glad of his solid presence. He stood close, almost as if they were a couple.

"Jim is bringing his choir to sing at Midnight Mass at St James's." Her voice was a notch too high. "Being new to the area, he doesn't know many people. So I brought him to meet Sandy and Peter." She flashed a smile at Sandy. Peter's young wife wore the anxious frown of a hostess watching her carefully planned dinner derail. "Jim – this is Ben."

Jim Postlethwaite didn't flinch. He leaned forward with confidence. Faith watched, fascinated, as the pair of them gripped hands. She could see the tendons flexing under Ben's skin.

"Detective Inspector Ben Shorter, isn't it? We've met before. How's the investigation going?"

"I can't discuss that," Ben answered flatly.

"Of course," Jim acknowledged with a polite smile.

"I think we should all sit down." Sandy waved both hands at them as if she were trying to shepherd unruly children. "Peter, get everyone settled and I'll fetch the starters."

"Let me help." Faith darted after her into the safe haven of the kitchen, grateful to extract herself, however temporarily, from the field of tension.

Sandy had set out their plates in two neat rows on the countertop, a bowl of garnish beside them. She retrieved warm cheese tartlets from the oven, manoeuvring them expertly to the plates with a spatula before draping each one delicately with an artistic curl of garnish.

"Faith – what *is* going on?" she asked in a low voice, as she deposited the spatula and oven tray in the sink.

"Sandy, I am so sorry! I made a mistake. I didn't realize it was a dinner party with Ben Shorter or I never would have brought Jim. Because – you know the murder victim of the case Peter and Ben are on? Well, he was in Jim's choir." Sandy's guileless blue eyes widened with shock.

"He's not a… a suspect?" she asked.

"No! Of course not. I would never—"

"Of course you wouldn't," Sandy said. "Oh well, never mind – Ben Shorter'll just have to get over himself. He can be a bit too sticky at times." That was an understatement, but then, Sandy didn't realize how well Faith knew him. "Jim was quite charming upstairs with the boys; they've really taken to him," Sandy smiled reassuringly at Faith. "I think he's a nice man. Well, there's nothing to be done right now. We'll just have to get through it. You take those and I'll take these."

Balancing three plates, she pushed the kitchen door open with her hip and sailed through. Faith followed less confidently; she wasn't used to carrying three plates at once.

She made it to the table safely and distributed her starters. Peter had taken the head of the table. Ben and Harriet were sitting across from Jim and a spare chair with her name on it. The battle lines were drawn. She dropped into her seat, avoiding Ben's confrontational stare.

"So how are things, Faith?" Sandy asked her, as she picked up her fork. "I know how desperately busy it gets for you this time of year. Did you find a donkey?"

"Why would Faith want a donkey?" Peter asked gamely.

"For the Christmas pageant, darling – you know. Mary and Joseph have to have a proper donkey." Out of the corner of her eye, Faith saw Harriet put her hand on Ben's thigh as she whispered something to him. *How rude.*

"Well, actually, thanks to Jim – I think I've found one." Faith smiled gratefully at her companion. He grinned at her sideways. He didn't appear to hate her, despite her dropping him in this.

"Glad to help," he said. "So Ms Whittle's come through?"

"Not yet confirmed, but I am quietly confident. He's called Banjo," she said, and forked a piece of tartlet into her mouth. The pastry crust melted on the tongue.

"Banjo?" Ben asked, as if the name had snagged his waning interest.

"The donkey," said Sandy, as Faith was chewing. "For the Christmas pageant."

"Sandy, these tartlets are divine," Faith said. Sometimes she wished she could cook – but it took so much time and practice to get really good at it. Across the table, Harriet echoed her approval in a murmuring sound, her eyes on her hostess, though Faith noted that most of her tartlet remained in bits on her plate.

"So, Harriet, what do you do?" Jim asked.

"I am a forensic pathologist."

"Do you work with Peter and Ben here?"

"Sometimes. Yes." The burning look the redhead gave Ben was hardly colleague-like. "At the moment we are working together on a murder case."

"The death of Lucas Bagshaw?"

"Yes." Harriet flicked a startled look at Ben. He was concentrating on clearing his plate.

"He was in my choir," Jim said. Faith thought she

detected a hint of stubbornness in his voice, as if he wanted to show Ben he *would* talk about the investigation, whether the policeman wished to or not. He took a sip from his glass of water and replaced it precisely in the damp circle it had left on the tablecloth. He smiled a friendly smile at Faith. "We seem to be surrounded by law enforcement."

"Didn't you know? Faith used to be in the police force too," Ben's deep voice curled across the table. Faith could almost feel it vibrate the air. Jim swung to face her. He was keeping the social performance going, but she read the shock in his eyes and something else – the thought that she had deliberately deceived him.

"She didn't tell me." The warmth had gone from Jim's face.

"Nor me, neither!" Sandy exclaimed from her other side. Faith felt trapped. Dear, sweet Sandy was staring at her as if she had suddenly displayed horns. "Why on earth did you never tell me, Faith?"

Why did Ben have to do this? Faith knew she should have told Sandy before, but they had always met on church ground with the boys there. The opportunity had never arisen.

"It never came up," she said, inadequately. "It was a long time ago. But yes, that's where we met, Ben and I. I was a cadet at Hendon, the police college, and he had been sent back for a refresher course – sensitivity training, wasn't it, Ben?" He was leaning back in his chair, his eyes bright. His lips twitched up reflexively at one corner, then he became impassive once more.

"I knew you and Ben had met before, but…" Oh dear! Sandy sounded hurt. Faith wished they could talk this through in private. This just wasn't the time. "I thought it was just because you both grew up locally. I didn't realize you had *worked* together." The emphasis she put on the word implied something else – Sandy was catching up fast.

"No, we didn't know each other here. We met in London." Faith's words were measured. Harriet was watching her with a cat-like look on her face. How much worse could this night get?

"So what happened to make you change careers?" Jim made the question sound as if he was genuinely interested.

"She found God," Ben cut in derisively. Harriet snapped her head toward him. He drained half his wine glass, not looking at her.

"Is that a problem for you?" Jim asked him directly. Bless him! The question was right on, but Faith wished she could warn him – it really wasn't a good idea to poke the bear like that.

Ben picked up the wine bottle. He stretched easily across the table to fill Jim's glass. Jim put his hand over it to stop him.

"I am on water, thank you. Driving."

"Of course." Ben smiled, but not with his eyes. Faith wasn't sure if Jim recognized the test or not. Ben never touched a drop when he drove, and he expected the same of others. He sat back and refilled Harriet's glass. Faith imagined a meter in his brain ticking up suspicions. If his hands hadn't been in plain sight, she would suspect him of running checks on his BlackBerry under the cover of the tablecloth.

"So – Jim. What brought you to your career choice? Choirmaster for disadvantaged youth," Ben smiled, with a hint of derision.

Faith glared at him, wishing her legs were long enough to kick him under the table. Ben ignored her.

"I was a music scholar at Cambridge," said Jim. "Trained as a teacher. I've always enjoyed music and teaching."

"And how long have you been doing it?"

"A couple of years. You've always been a police officer?"

Ben nodded slowly, then took another sip of water. "Oh, yes," he said. "Always."

They survived. Faith hardly knew how. Sandy's food helped. She was a great cook. Between them, Faith, Jim, Peter and Sandy bravely kept the conversation going with occasional loaded interjection from Ben.

She watched for her moment. The red-haired pathologist went upstairs to use the bathroom, and Faith cornered Ben by the coats.

"You are horrible sometimes, Ben Shorter," she hissed. "What are you playing at?"

"Me? What the devil do you think *you* were doing bringing *him* here?"

"I *was* intending to have a nice supper with friends."

"He is not a friend."

"Not yours, maybe – but my social life is none of your business."

"Do me a favour! This is not about your social life. This is about an active –" Faith could see Ben's anger in the stiffness of his jaw; he forced his words out between his teeth, "I repeat *active* – murder investigation."

The justice of his point disarmed her.

"I didn't realize you'd be here," she said. "I thought it was just a supper with the pair of us and Sandy and Peter, members of my congregation…" He still towered over her, but his shoulders relaxed a fraction. Staring him down at this angle gave her a crick in the neck. "Anyway, we haven't discussed anything pertinent in his hearing," she carried on in her most brisk and professional tone, "and he isn't one of your suspects…" She sensed his stillness. Her throat went dry. "He isn't, is he?"

"Not at the moment," Ben said. "But it's early days." He took a step back and ran his fingers through his hair, as he used to do when he felt baffled by their relationship. "But really, Fay, you know better than this. You've put Peter right in it."

He was quite right; she had.

"I am sorry!" she said. "It was an accident – a case of cross-communication. What can I do about it now?"

He touched her shoulder lightly, and his face softened. "Just keep your distance, will you? At least until this is done? With luck this won't have consequences."

"That was fun," Faith said. Jim made no response and put the car into gear, focusing on backing out of Sandy and Peter's drive. She tried again. "Well, now at least you know all my deep dark secrets." Jim snorted – and not in an entirely convinced way.

Five minutes later, defeated by a series of monosyllabic answers, Faith gave up her attempts at conversation. She watched the street lights chasing over Jim's profile. He had moved far away from her. She hunkered down in her coat. The roads were glassy with ice and Jim drove cautiously, leaning forwards toward the windscreen. At last he drew up at her vicarage door. He kept the engine running, his hands on the wheel.

"So goodnight, then," she said. He dropped his head before he turned his face toward her. His expression was closed.

"Goodnight."

"Do you want to come in and talk about it?"

"I need to get the car back. Borrowed it from a friend."

She sat there feeling sad. She didn't want to leave it like this. All at once he dropped the hand nearest to her from its grip on the wheel, leaned over and kissed her lightly on the lips. It was sweet. He sighed.

"It's certainly complicated," he said.

"I know."

They stayed like that, inches apart for a moment, then she got out of the car and went in, closing her front door behind her.

CHAPTER

12

The light on the old-fashioned answer-phone was blinking, and the digital display read "22".

"You're not answering the phone, then?" she said. Faith stood in the doorway to the barn Oliver Markham had converted into his joinery workshop. It felt cold by the door. She suspected her nose was red. Oliver Markham sat on a stool by his workbench, a tubby yellow Labrador lying at his feet. His thick, unruly hair looked uncombed, and underneath his wax jacket, his shirt hung out untidily below his jumper.

"Is this about the church Christmas tree?" he asked in a flat voice.

"What about the Christmas tree? Are you having a problem with your supplier?" Faith felt a pulse of panic. If Oliver couldn't produce the tree, where was she going to find another 15-footer this close to Christmas? He looked at her under his heavy eyebrows.

"You still want me to fulfil the order?"

"Of course I do." Faith was puzzled. Oliver frowned at her as if she was being obtuse. He gestured toward the battered answer-phone with its blinking light.

"Word's got around," he said. She looked about at the machines, the piles of wood and the floor covered with fresh blond shavings; then she noticed that there was very little work out on the benches.

"People have been cancelling their orders?"

Oliver snorted. "And some."

"Oliver, I am so sorry!" He looked so forlorn sitting there. His bitch got up and put her head on his knee, staring up at him with anxious brown eyes. He tugged her silky ear between his fingers. Faith pulled the door shut behind her and walked over; she crouched down to pet the dog.

"Who's this?"

"Name's Podge. She's my daughter's dog. Started out as Hodge, but then she grew up big-boned, didn't you, girl?" He shook her muzzle gently. Podge licked his hand and then, to be polite, Faith's cheek.

"She's a friendly girl."

"So you still want the tree?"

"Absolutely." Faith nodded vigorously. This close to Oliver, she felt perfectly at ease. She sensed no tension or violence in him. Oliver Markham was a big, strong man. If Lucas had faced him in his last moments, he would surely have had defensive wounds. Every nerve in the boy's body would have been signalling to him to protect himself.

She thought of Ben's attitude in her kitchen on Wednesday when he'd told her that they were still checking Oliver's alibi. He had left her with no impression that Markham still featured in his suspect list. They now knew that the Markham farm was only where Lucas's body had ended up; he had not been attacked there. In other words, the suspicions concerning Oliver had arisen from insubstantial evidence resting on no more than the cruel accident of circumstance. There was the gunshot incident, but Ben had been a detective long enough not to let himself get carried away with coincidences.

"Are Julie and the girls back?" Faith asked in concern, horrified at the isolation and damage Oliver's arrest had caused.

"They were – but they're not now."

"What happened?"

"Brought them back on Wednesday but then the girls' so-called friends were saying all this stuff and it upset them… Julie's taken them over to her mother's."

"So you're on your own here?"

"I thought I'd have work to do…" He looked around at the still workshop. She remembered Pat's gossip about Oliver Markham's business having money troubles. This wasn't going to help.

"Haven't the police finished checking your alibi?"

"Not that I've heard."

"I am sure it won't be long."

"You think that'll end it?" he said fiercely. "People suspect me of being a murderer, don't they? I didn't even know this kid."

"I think he went to your daughters' school."

"Did he?" he shrugged. "They never said." He stared down blindly. "I can't get my head around it." He stood up abruptly. "Walk? Podge needs to go out."

The sun had come out, melting the ice from the paths and sparkling on the snow-covered fields. They walked out down to the river, Podge trotting along beside them, her nose to the ground. They found themselves back where it had all started. The ground was trampled, but the crime scene paraphernalia had been cleared away. Oliver picked a stray piece of police tape from some scrub and mechanically tucked it in his pocket.

"I can't believe I didn't see him," he said staring down the bank. "Do you know anything about the boy?"

"His name was Lucas Bagshaw, he was sixteen – almost seventeen – years old. He grew up around here. His mother worked as a carer for Marjorie Davis, among others. Maybe you've met her at church?"

"That shrewd old bird who used to work in the civil service?"

"That's Marjorie."

"How's his mother doing?"

"She died in February this year."

Oliver screwed his eyes tight shut a moment. "That poor kid! What about his father?"

"No one knows. He was never a part of Lucas's life."

There were the holes for the tent pegs where the forensic tent had stood. Markham took a couple of steps. He stared down at the spot where Lucas's body had been examined.

"I was on the tractor," Oliver recited as if he was trying to get it straight in his own mind. "It's a noisy old beast. I wanted to clear the debris brought down by flood, and I needed to think."

"What about?"

"Family stuff." He glanced at her. She was dressed in the dog collar today. She tried to recede behind it.

"What's going on, Oliver?" He bent down and picked up a straight piece of stick and threw it. It sped through the sky in an arc. Podge, showing an unexpected turn of speed, raced after it, ears flapping. "Are you and Julie having problems?" she prompted. His dark eyes looked at her, suspicious beneath the shelter of his thick eyebrows. She shrugged to placate him. "It's just that I know Julie has to work away a lot. That can't be easy."

"That's part of it." He paused. "She's pregnant." That was a surprise.

"Well, congratulations! That's good news, isn't it?"

"I think so," he said softly, his lips curving in the bashful smile of a man who loved his daughters.

"And Julie's not sure?" He nodded, his jaw clenched. Faith realized he was on the edge of tears. He straightened his shoulders like a good soldier.

"I presume this wasn't planned?"

He shook his head. "I know Jules worked really hard to get where she is, professionally. She loves her job…"

"And she thought she'd done the mothering bit? How old is she, forty?"

"Nearly forty-one." He tossed his head back, looking blindly at the sky. "She said it was a mistake!" She could sense the pain radiating out of him.

"I am so sorry, Oliver."

"She knew *two weeks* before she told me. Two weeks! I knew something was up. She didn't want to talk; the silent treatment. I even started thinking she might be having an affair." He turned his back on Faith, hiding his face from her. He went on, his voice fractured with emotion. "Just before she took the girls to London we had a row and she told me. She said she was going to make her mind up what to do about it while they were away." He swung back to face her, his voice raised, his face contorted. "Make up *her* mind. Like it was nothing to do with me!"

Oliver's fists were clenched and his eyes full of tears. Faith stayed where she was.

"That must have been so hard for you."

Oliver drew a shaky breath. "So I was sitting on that wretched tractor," he continued more calmly, "wondering if Jules… if she was going to decide to get rid of our baby, and how could we – us – how could we survive that? And just asking myself how could twenty years – the twenty years we spent together, making a family – how could all that just fall apart out of nowhere? And this postman appears…" The words tumbled out, gathering speed. "He's asking for a tow and there's this boy, dead in the reeds, and the police are here and I have no control over anything any more. I am just caught up in this utter mess…" He shoved his hands in his pockets, rocking back on his heels, bracing every muscle. "That poor kid. I didn't even see him."

Faith felt the urge to slip her gloved hand under his arm, but fought it. She didn't want to be misconstrued. They stood like that, looking out across the river, for some time.

"So where are you now?" she asked at last. "Have you and Julie been able to talk by yourselves, without the girls?" He shook his head.

"They're at her mother's." He laughed bitterly to himself. "And Jeanie's never been too fond of me. She wanted a higher earner for her daughter."

So money was in there too. Wasn't it always? Faith thought about how the Markhams came to the parish earlier that summer, and how she had wondered about the tensions between the couple, apart so much of the time.

"What made you move here, Oliver?"

"We always wanted to move out of the city; bring the girls up in a proper home."

"And what made it possible?"

"Julie got a promotion – a partnership in her law firm. She's really great at her job."

Faith waited a moment to let that sink in. "So now she's carrying a baby unexpectedly, and your life here depends on…" She left the sentence unfinished.

He hung his head. "I know," he said. "I just need to build up the business. We can make it work. We have some savings."

"But you can see how hard it must have been when Julie found out. Did she go to a doctor here?"

"No. She works in London in the week."

"Just because she took two weeks to tell you doesn't mean she doesn't love you or that she doesn't want to make this work. It's no good sitting here brooding. You've got to talk to her – properly, calmly. Do you love her?"

"Of course I do!"

"So go and find Julie – her mother can look after the girls; you two need to go somewhere private where you can have the space to talk it out. If you can talk to me, you can surely talk to the woman you love, the mother of your children."

His face broke into a weak smile. "You're bossy, you know that?"

"I've been told."

"Thanks."

"Of course, what I really came here for was to check that you're still on for being Joseph in the pageant." He frowned at her. "I really need you, Oliver. The Little Worthy pageant is the highlight of the village's Christmas weekend – just ask Pat. I am already on my last chance for a real donkey; I have one slim prospect. I *can't* lose my Joseph. Oliver, you will do it, won't you?"

"And what if I'm taken up for murder?"

She waved her hand dismissively. "You're not going to be. So, will you still be in the pageant?"

His smile broadened. "OK."

"Hallelujah! Thank you." she beamed at him. "Who could be more perfect than our very own carpenter?"

"Cabinet-maker, please," he corrected her with a mock frown. "Come to that – if the real-life donkey can't make it,

I could always cut you out something in MDF. I could pull it along beside me on wheels." The joke and smile were thin, but it was a good attempt.

The river had fallen back to its normal winter levels. The water pushed on idly by. Faith thought of the evidence of watercress in Lucas Bagshaw's lungs.

"How well do you know the river upstream from here?" she asked. "Do you know where the nearest commercial watercress beds are?"

"There's a farm not much further up. You see it on the left, just down from that big pub, just under a mile on – by the road at least."

"Which pub?"

"You know, the big one that has all the tables out in the summer. The Lion's Heart."

The Lion's Heart pub on the river where the cider was cheap; the pub where V and the Dot had planned to meet Lucas the day he died, before he cancelled. She paused the car at the top of Markham's drive. She really ought to go back and get on with Sunday's sermon and a whole desk-worth of admin. But… the dashboard clock said 11:55. Almost lunchtime… She put the car in gear, swung the wheel left and took the road upriver.

The Lion's Heart pub was a big whitewashed building. Some parts of it looked at least seventeenth century. The large beer garden must have been quite an attraction in summer, but now, in December, the tables were all empty and several of the pub's windows were shuttered up. Even the B&B side was closed. Only the main bar remained open for the locals. In the car park the snow had been cleared into dirty mounds of ice and grit, leaving a central block of frozen spaces. A solitary red estate with patched panels was parked in the end bay. Faith reversed into a middle spot. She turned off the engine and wrapped her colourful winter scarf around her neck.

The bar was almost empty. She put her bag on the counter and climbed up on to one of the round-seated wooden bar stools. A middle-aged man with a beer drinker's belly and a seventies rocker's haircut came out of the kitchen behind the bar.

"What can I get you?"

"Orange juice, please."

He fetched a tiny bottle out of a glass-fronted fridge.

"Want ice and lemon with that?"

"Thank you." She looked about the ill-lit space. It was a large room. In this light it seemed to be entirely upholstered in tobacco colours. "Not many in today," she commented.

"Regulars don't usually come in until half past." He went into the kitchen and came back with a tray of clean glasses, and started to place them on the shelf above the bar.

"I've never been in before," she said.

"That right?"

She leaned over the bar and stretched out her hand.

"Faith Morgan. Pleased to meet you." He wiped his hands on a tea towel and clasped her hand. His was clammy and cold.

"Rick Williams. The landlord." He narrowed his eyes at her. "You on the job?"

"I'm sorry?"

He grinned. "You're not the first copper we've had in here."

Faith half-smiled down at her orange juice. Was it that obvious? She tugged her scarf aside to show what was beneath. "I'm not with the police. I am the vicar at St James's, Little Worthy."

"Really?" For a moment Rick's cultivated impassivity cracked. "I could have sworn…" He put another couple of glasses away. "Hang on – you're not the one who found the lad down by the river?" That surprised her. She hadn't realized that gossip had spread.

"I didn't find him. I happened by soon after he was found. Lucas Bagshaw – did you know him?"

"He came in a few times with his mates. Not that I serve underage drinkers or anything," Rick added. "I run things strictly legit here. They only get alcohol if they've got the ID."

"Of course. So Lucas came in with his mates – you mean Vernon Granger and Anna Hope?"

Rick looked at her curiously. "Yeah. Those three were always together. The Goth and the Good Boy – odd couple; and then him tall and her short. They kinda stood out." Like Jim had said, Lucas and Vernon were unlikely mates.

"Were they always tight?"

Rick brought a tray to the bar, with a small knife and a handful of lemons. "Well, the two lads, they got into it once. Had to transfer them to the car park. But then lads can be like that, can't they? All pals one minute, pounding on each other the next. They made it up. Only happened once."

"Any idea what they were quarrelling about?"

Rick shrugged his meaty shoulders. "Not interested."

Could it have been over the Dot? Faith wondered.

"When was this?"

"Earlier this year – summer, I suppose."

"You can't be more precise?"

Rick looked into mid-air, knife poised. "You ask a lot of questions for a vicar."

"I'm naturally curious," said Faith blithely. "I suppose a death, at this time of year… it makes you wonder if you could have done something."

Rick began chopping again, and nodded. "They knocked over one of the flower tubs by the door; got the last of the tulips. I had to replant the whole thing…" He focused on the memory. "It must have been late May – no; it was a mix of Flaming Parrot and Queen of the Night and they were late this year. Early June."

Rick didn't look like a gardener, Faith thought. Just goes to show, you never know with people. She could feel the landlord's interest fading. Her eye fell on a computer printout of a picture stuck to one of the pillars holding up the bar shelves. It was of a fit young man grinning in bright sunshine beside a baby elephant taking a shower. Beside him was an Asian man with a wooden switch, presumably a local. Someone had scribbled in the margin: "Latest from Stewie!"

"Nice elephant."

Rick followed her gaze. "One of the bar staff. Gone travelling for a couple of months. Only left a few days ago and now look at him." Rick jerked his head to the frosted windows and the winter light beyond. "All right for some!" A couple of days ago, Faith thought. Today was Friday. Lucas's body had been found on Monday.

"Stewie – he wasn't working here last Saturday, was he?"

Rick's eyes narrowed, focusing on her. "Yeah, his last night," he said slowly. "I'd forgotten that. Karen was off sick and Stewie came in to help clear up after the lunchtime crowd. Gave him some extra travelling money for the favour. He flew out on Sunday night gone."

Faith wondered if Ben's team knew about the absent Stewie. They would have found out at the cathedral interviews about the plans of Lucas and his mates to meet at the Lion's Heart that Saturday afternoon. Ben was bound to have sent someone in to look for witnesses, but the picture might not have been up if the interviews had been done earlier in the week. She wondered what they had found out. Had Adam Bagshaw been drinking here that day?

"So was it just Lucas and the other boy and the girl who hung out together?"

"Normally, yeah. Well, not all the time. There was an older guy they talked to; seemed to know him."

"One of your regulars? Lucas's uncle, maybe?" The bar manager looked blank. "About forty, ex-soldier, drinks a lot."

"Oh no, not him. Another guy."

"And who's this?" It was a man's voice and not a pleasant one. Faith turned to face a lean man about her height with leathery skin and sandy hair. He looked dirty.

"Who's asking?" she quipped, trying to go for light. The newcomer had dead eyes.

"This lady knew Lucas Bagshaw," said the landlord. "The kid that died." His manner had shifted to distant, drawing the line between his side of the bar and theirs. "What are you having?"

"Pint of the House."

If Rick's intention had been to distract the newcomer, he failed. The man didn't move his eyes from Faith's face. He was standing too close. He stank of stale cigarettes and some sweeter, more chemical smell. She steeled herself.

"So what are you? Po-lice?"

"No," she replied calmly. "Clergy." That puzzled him for a moment. The vicious expression returned. He reached out a sinewy hand for the pint Rick had poured him, and dropped coins on the bar with the other.

"No good comes of sticking your nose where it don't belong," he said, "and you don't belong here." With that he slouched off.

Faith watched him go to the far end of the room and slip into a booth, out of sight. She reached out for her glass, propping her elbow on the bar to steady herself.

"How unpleasant."

"That was Keepie. Best stay away from him."

"Drug dealer?"

Rick held her gaze. She heard the distant sound of a truck drawing up outside. He looked over his shoulder toward the back. "Like I said, best stay away," he repeated.

"Did Lucas?"

Rick ignored her question. "Delivery's just come. I need to deal with it." He went out the back.

She was down to the last inch of orange juice. She twisted the glass between her fingers. This place meant something in the Lucas story, she was certain of it. They all drank here – Lucas, V, the Dot, Adam Bagshaw. And now this fellow, Keepie. Faith recognized the type. Not one of the more careful drug dealers; he had all the marks of someone who used his own product. A short fuse, probably, reliant on aggression rather than brains. She wondered what the local police had on him.

Anna – the Dot – had been so sure that Lucas didn't use or drink. *He wouldn't do that.* That's what she'd said. Maybe the connection wasn't that Lucas took drugs, but that he didn't. But Lucas had money. He had dropped out of school; he didn't have a job Ben and the police could find. Where was he getting it from?

Had one of the oddball trio stuck their nose in, as the fragrant Keepie put it, and Lucas had been the one to pay?

She ran through the possibilities in her head. Lucas wasn't using, but dealing for Keepie, and Vernon found out and they fought… But then they reconciled. And if they'd fought over that, and Lucas's death had somehow been a consequence of changing his mind, why the delay? They had fought in June. He was killed in December. She knew she was grasping at straws, looking for neat cause and effect in a world that rarely followed those rules.

Maybe Vernon had got involved with drugs and that was what the fight was about? But that didn't explain the money. Could Lucas have been blackmailing Keepie? Taking money to keep quiet about what he knew? Unlikely. Keepie struck her as too unstable, not the sort who responded rationally to being threatened. His kind didn't have the patience for strategy. Men like Keepie were more likely to turn to violence or flight as the first option.

Vernon Granger was the blank piece in this puzzle. She wished she had a better sense of him. From her glimpse of him at the service on Wednesday night, Vernon had struck her as a wary, possibly angry boy. That on its own was nothing, but she also knew that Anna Hope was fiercely loyal to him. She liked what she had seen of Anna. The Dot was a strong young woman – the kind of young woman Trisha, Lucas's mother, might have been once. If only she could gain Anna's trust somehow. Between them, V and the Dot held the key to what had happened to Lucas – she was almost certain of it. Faith finished the last of her orange juice and picked up her bag.

She took a detour home along the river. The country lane ran between hedges. Occasionally, through a gap, she could see the river flowing toward Winchester, wild watercress beds floating at its margins. Her phone buzzed from the bag on the passenger seat. She found a convenient lay-by and drew up. She'd missed a call. The churchwarden's Scottish accent was more pronounced than usual in the voicemail, the tone softly conspiratorial.

"Vicar – I thought you should know as soon as possible. I've just run in to young Alice Peabody on the Green. She tells me she's off to Wales for Christmas. Her young man's proposed and he's taking her to meet his parents…" Pat had the grace to stop short of "I told you so," but it was implied. Faith put the phone back in her bag. Well, that was lovely for Alice, of course. She wished the engaged pair mental congratulations but, as far as pageant was concerned, flighty Alice from the Hare and Hounds had proved Pat right – again. Faith put the car in gear. Just as she secured her Joseph, she was down a Mary.

As she prepared to pull out, she saw a police van in her mirror. It sped past and she glimpsed uniformed officers. She followed in its wake with a sense of urgency. They rounded a couple of bends and then the van slowed. It drew up among a group of vehicles parked by an old wooden bridge spanning the river. The van door slid open and a pack of uniformed officers disembarked. A forensic team hovered around the bridge and there, tucked up against the hedge, was Ben's metallic green Astra.

CHAPTER

13

Whiteness sprang up from the bridge. Someone had turned on an arc light. Getting out of her car, Faith could hear the generator chugging. The river here was deeper, the water faster flowing than further down by the Markham place. Ben stood at the end of the bridge. Harriet Sims had just moved beyond him onto the walkway carrying a metal forensic case.

Ben's gaze fell on Faith. He didn't seem surprised to see her. He strode toward her, his eyes, his whole posture, crackling with energy.

"We're in business," he said.

"You've found the attack site."

Ben grinned. He did love it when investigations started moving.

"It was obvious, really. Even with the recent flooding, the currents in this stretch of the river aren't strong enough to carry a body more than a few yards, unless…"

Faith glanced down at the water running under the bridge. "It falls into mid-stream," she concluded for him.

"And since this isn't the time of year for boats…" He

flipped out a hand toward her, palm up, inviting her to supply the answer.

"Bridges," she answered, to indulge him.

"So I sent out a couple of teams to check bridges and points overlooking the faster currents upstream from Markham's place, and…"

"Routine police work and the hard graft of others found you your attack site," she teased.

"Only took them a day and a half," complained Ben.

The old bridge was made of roughly shaped pillars of weathered wood in rustic style. This must be private land. It looked as if it had been neglected for years. A technician was examining the downriver rail.

"I see the logic, but why this bridge? There's nothing obvious that I can see…"

"No," Ben leaned over the rail and pointed diagonally back toward the bank, "but that is easier to spot." Down below in the mud and reeds, a scene of crime officer was taking pictures of an expensive-looking bicycle.

Peter Gray struggled up the steep bank, his wellington boots slipping on the frosty mud. He made a final long-legged stride and came up to join them.

"We're lucky it wasn't nicked." His smooth cheeks were flushed from the cold. "It's a good machine. Custom-built. Italian hand-crafted carbon frame with FAR 240 tubular carbon wheels – nice. Very sleek. I asked Santa for one of those…" Faith couldn't help smiling at his enthusiasm.

"I had no idea you were a bike man, Peter. How much would something like that cost?"

"Two to three thousand."

"Pounds? Wow! Where would Lucas get that sort of money?"

"That's a good question," said Ben. He looked over at the uniformed search officers being briefed by one of his team, a soberly dressed young woman with hair scraped back in a severe bun. She finished her speech and the officers fanned out along the bank.

Ben and Peter walked across to consult with their team member. Faith's curiosity drew her onto the bridge.

Harriet crouched down near the further end, beyond the forensic technician concentrating on a warped join at a roughly midway point on the downriver handrail. It was six days on and there had been rain and frost and snow between. Faith wondered what they could hope to find.

Harriet glanced up at her sideways. Ben and Peter might be sufficiently distracted by the discoveries at hand to overlook the last time they'd met at that disastrous dinner but, given the way she'd been eyeing her on Thursday night, Harriet Sims seemed unlikely to. Faith was trespassing on her crime scene, and she had every right to ask her to leave. Crouching down there in her overalls, with her hair held back in a ponytail, the pathologist suddenly seemed vulnerable. It was a desperately awkward situation for her. Harriet Sims had fallen for Ben Shorter's charms without realizing what came with the package, whereas she, Faith, was a veteran. Faith found herself smiling reassuringly as she approached, and was met with a baffled look in return.

"Faith."

"Harriet."

Harriet straightened up. "Ben tells me your insights can be useful," she said, with her eyes lowered. "I understand the victim was connected to your church?"

"Loosely, yes," she said. Harriet nodded, and seemed uncertain what to say next, so Faith spoke instead. "This can't be an easy surface to work, especially six days on with all the rain and frost."

"I don't have high hopes of much in the way of viable traces – but if the victim went over here, we may get lucky."

"You're not sure he did?"

"The chances are this is the place. See…" Harriet bent her face to just above rail height, indicating along the surface down to where the technician was working. At that angle Faith could see a distinct split in the rail.

"There's a recent break there – it gives at least four or five inches if you push against it."

"How tall was Lucas?"

"Five feet eight, and a bit."

"Just a touch taller than me." Faith measured herself against the height of the wooden rail. It was relatively low. "Someone five feet eight and a bit falling against this rail – they'd be struck about here, would you think?" Faith marked the place on her body with her hand, allowing for an inch or so.

"That would explain the bruise on his hip," said Harriet.

"And the broken phone," Faith added. Harriet nodded slowly.

"Yes. So…" She moved to face Faith, who turned instinctively to keep her in sight. She felt the rail in her lower back. "Lucas had a contusion on the upper right temple. Say someone hits him with the proverbial…" Faith recoiled as Harriet's pantomime swipe passed uncomfortably close. The movement unbalanced her and she turned with it, catching herself on the rail. It was so low, for a second she thought she might go over. She froze, clutching the rail. The water swirled and eddied glassily beneath.

She turned back to Harriet and looked her in the eye. "You think this is the place?"

Harriet nodded, and gave the broken rail one more experimental push before crouching again to resume her search for any missed evidence.

Faith's winter coat and city boots weren't enough against this cold. She really should get in her car and leave them to it. The rest would be painstaking, boring graft. She had work of her own to do.

Just wait a *little* longer, whispered her old self. Ben's junior, the young woman with the scraped back hair and sensible shoes, was approaching him to report from the search team.

"Nothing of interest so far, sir. Just litter, looks like – but it's being bagged anyway."

"Keep at it," Ben instructed.

"Want a look?" the junior asked.

"Pete," Ben detailed Sergeant Gray off with a jerk of his head. He turned to Faith. "You look like you need to warm up. I owe you a coffee. I've a Thermos in the car – join me?"

"That would be welcome," she admitted. "Just for a few minutes…"

As they turned toward the cars she noticed a right of way sign and a footpath running alongside the river back upstream.

"Where does this go?" Faith asked.

"It's a short cut," said one of the uniformed constables, looking up. "It ends up in the car park of a pub just up the road."

"The Lion's Heart?"

"That's right. Five minutes' walk or so."

They sat in Ben's Astra with the engine running and the heater on full blast. The coffee tasted of Thermos and was way too strong. Faith wrinkled her nose.

"Pete keeps some packs of sugar in there," Ben nodded toward the glove compartment. "He doesn't appreciate my coffee, either." His eyes scanned the operation of his team outside. "By the way, Oliver Markham's in the clear." Ben took a swig of coffee. "Hotel housekeeping confirms seeing him over the weekend. There's CCTV footage of the whole family in the lobby leaving for the theatre just before 18:30 on Saturday night."

Around the time Lucas was going into the river sixty miles away. So Oliver could get back to his life.

"And that's it?" she asked.

Ben looked at her, nonplussed. "Well, we have several lines of—"

"No, I mean, with Oliver. You put the man through hell and—"

"Just a moment," said Ben. "You're hardly the person I thought would misuse *that* word. We treated him fairly."

Faith's blood was boiling. "We must have different ideas of fair."

"Didn't we always?" said Ben, rolling his eyes. "You know we have to pursue the lead. The bloke waved a firearm at a bunch of nuisance kids a couple of months back."

Faith simmered. She knew there was truth in his words, but did he have to be so… so… complacent about it?

They sat in silence for at least a minute. Faith swirled her cup in an effort to dissolve the sugar. There was no spoon, and the coffee was too hot to stir with her finger. Her black mood passed.

"What did the Markhams go to see?" she asked irrelevantly.

"*Wicked*". According to his wife, he fell asleep." Ben looked at her sideways, his eyes twinkling. "That's one you never dragged me to."

"I knew you better than to try," she said. "As I recall you, too, had the tendency to sleep in theatre seats." Ben had never shared her love of musicals. But he had taken her to them once or twice when they were together. She focused on him in her peripheral vision, looking ostensibly into her coffee. Was he the same still? Those odd little chinks in his armour.

He chuckled to himself. "I've told you a hundred times, there's no street cred left to a DI caught humming show-tunes over a corpse." He shifted in his seat, leaning against the driver's door, adjusting his legs. Now he could watch her face as she drank his abominable coffee.

"So what's the Saturday timeline so far?" she asked.

"Lucas left his home in The Hollies around 12:30 or soon after – we have him on traffic cams on his bike at a couple of junctions. Looks like he was heading into town. After that, we lose him – too much CCTV footage to go through without some clue as to direction. According to Vernon Granger and Anna Hope, the victim was due at the Lion's Heart at 3 p.m. or thereabouts. But he never showed. Said Vernon has a text timed at 14:46 sent from Lucas's phone to the effect that something had come up and he'd catch up with him later, but no more than that."

"You've canvassed the Lion's Heart?" Ben gave her a patronizing look. "Of course you have," she amended quickly.

"According to staff, Lucas never showed, but Vernon and the girl were there for an hour and a bit. Landlord is certain they had gone by 4 p.m."

"The time of death?" Faith asked.

"After five and before 7 p.m. – as near as we can figure. The immersion in freezing water confuses things a bit."

"And the attack site is just a few minutes' walk from the Lion's Heart," she pondered. Ben grunted. "Was Adam

Bagshaw seen at the pub that afternoon? I understand the Lion's Heart was a favourite watering hole of his."

"Not that anyone has reported. Bagshaw had been in on Friday lunchtime. The landlord said he was doing some serious drinking, in for the long haul… He got into enough of a state to be asked to leave. According to bar staff, Bagshaw senior wasn't seen back after that."

"Isn't there any CCTV in a big pub like that?"

Ben grimaced. "Only in the car park. Inside the pub, the system is down for repairs – has been for *some* time."

Faith picked up on his emphasis.

"Deliberate, d'you think?" Her mind shifted to Keepie. No dealer wanted electronic eyes on his place of business. "Do you know a man they call Keepie?"

Ben flashed a look on her. "Sebastian Keep? Local drug dealer – low level, but known to carry knives. You're very up to speed, vicar."

Faith shrugged. "I just met him this lunchtime – when I went in for a drink. He saw me chatting to the landlord. He told me to keep my nose out of where it doesn't belong."

Ben sat up. "He threatened you?" His jaw set.

"No need to get all protective. I can look out for myself."

Ben's face was a picture of scepticism. "You know addicts. They're unpredictable and Keepie's a skunk. You're a woman and you haven't kept up your training – have you? You're bound to be at a disadvantage, and as a vicar you're easy to find. Try to stay out of his way, will you?"

"I have no plans to get acquainted," she reassured him. "But Keepie's stage warning did make me wonder. It could just have been routine territorial stuff, but could Lucas have run across him? According to Anna, he was quite anti booze and drugs, and they both were regulars at the Lion's Heart."

"A teenager, in this day and age?"

"You're too cynical. You can't assume things about real, live individuals – not even teenagers. Remember the context. Lucas had been a carer for an alcoholic uncle from an early age." Jim had told her Lucas was mature for his age, but then, Thursday night being such a tender subject, it probably wasn't diplomatic to mention the choirmaster by name. She edited her words. "Lucas was said to be mature for his years – it's possible, isn't it?"

Ben's attention had wandered. He checked his watch.

"It is strange that no one saw Lucas at the pub…" she mused, thinking of the elephant picture on the bar. "Did you know about Stewie?"

Ben swung his full attention back to her. If she hadn't been familiar with his intensity, she might have found it intimidating.

"Who's this?"

"A barman at the Lion's Heart who left to go round the world just this Sunday, but he was filling in for a sick colleague on Saturday afternoon."

Ben frowned.

"Says who?"

"The landlord – Rick Williams. There's a picture up on the bar – I saw it this lunchtime. Stewie must have posted it on Facebook or something – the picture is a computer printout. It looked to me like he was in Thailand, I think."

"Oh, great! Tracing a backpacker on the opposite side of the world; that's going to be fun. I suppose I'll have to get someone onto it."

"If Uncle Adam was drinking heavily…" Faith remembered Adam's tearful guilt and his admission of a blackout. "What if Adam went on a bender; you don't know if he came back home on the Friday night – do you? What if Lucas went out looking for him on Saturday?" Ben was wearing his "you and your imagination" expression. She pressed on. "Anna Hope – the Dot? She told me that…"

"When? When did she tell you?" Trust Ben to pounce on the irrelevant bit.

"Earlier this week. I saw her at Mavis Granger's florist shop on Thursday…" She was about to add, *I was buying a house gift for Sandy* and cut herself short just in time.

"You've been busy, haven't you?" She couldn't tell if he was cross with her for butting in or just for not updating him sooner.

"Stop interrupting," she scolded. "As I was saying, Anna told me that Lucas spent much of his life looking out for his uncle; fetching him home when he drank too much. That could be an explanation for his movements that afternoon."

Ben thought about it. "Possibly. But then he would surely have checked the Lion's Heart first – it being Uncle Adam's favourite watering hole."

"Maybe he did – and the now nomadic Stewie was the only one to see him." Ben obviously didn't like the idea, but she could see him turning it over. His bright blue eyes fixed on her, pinning her back against the car seat.

"And do you think Lucas might have found him?" He was asking the question she didn't want to ask herself. In the confined space of the car she couldn't get away from it, or him.

Did she think Adam Bagshaw might be guilty of murdering his nephew? She focused her memories of the shell of the man she had encountered in that empty home.

"I think Adam Bagshaw is self-destructive," she said slowly.

"OK – but he might lash out in a drunken fit."

"Yes – he might. But here?" She gestured out at the isolated, frozen bridge before them. "What reason would the pair have to meet here? It's not on the way to their house. And if they did, and by some terrible accident, Lucas was hurt and fell in the water, I can't believe Adam wouldn't try to pull him out. They were family. Lucas was all he had left."

"Maybe he passed out."

"If he had, I think you would have found him here too. I don't see Adam Bagshaw as a man with the wherewithal to cover up murder." She waited. Ben was contemplating the bridge; thinking it through. At last he nodded, briefly.

"I agree with you. Adam Bagshaw is a messy drunk, and whoever did this is organized enough to cover their tracks."

"So who's left? Suspect unknown? I presume V and the Dot have alibis for the time of the murder?"

"Sort of. Anna was with friends; two girls back her up – but teenage girls lie for one another as a matter of course, don't they? Mrs Granger gives Vernon his. Ma Granger says she was doing the Christmas baking while her son was playing some video game in the lounge."

"Not what you'd call unbreakable alibis."

Ben raised his eyebrows in agreement.

Faith's mind slipped back to the tension between Vernon and his mother at the Civic Service on Wednesday. Did Mrs Granger know, or suspect, something about her son? She saw again Mavis Granger's painted and wistful face and heard the dead weight of her words as she gazed after him: "*My pride and joy.*"

"What?" Ben used his low, seductive voice; the one he used to tease things out of her. She should have averted her face. He was too good at reading her, and at this distance, cramped together in a car, he became a living, breathing lie detector.

"It's not evidence – just hearsay." She had to give him some of it. "Something the landlord told me at lunchtime," she said.

Ben rolled his forefinger at her to say *go on…*

"The landlord said that Lucas and Vernon were tight; good mates – all except one time they had this fight in the pub."

"A fist fight?"

Faith nodded. "They were thrown out of the bar and continued it in the car park."

"When was this?"

"June – early June, I think." Faith paused. June. There was something connected with this case, another reference to June – what was it? She almost caught the tail end of something and then it slipped away.

"Anything else?" Ben prompted.

"Well, I suppose there was the fight in the chancel this week – Vernon and another member of the choir got into it because the other lad accused V of knocking Lucas off over rivalry for Anna's affections. I think that really is nothing – just a sign of tension…"

"Tension can arise from guilt," Ben began, then his expression shifted and he leaned a fraction toward her, examining her face. "So when did your choirmaster tell you this?"

She overlooked the contempt in his voice. "On Wednesday afternoon, when he came to check the layout of the church," she answered. They could be grown-ups about this.

"Wednesday afternoon *and* Thursday evening… You two are being very social." Apparently only one of them in the car was a grown-up. "Don't be silly!" she snapped.

"You planning to see him again?" *He's interrogating me like a suspect*, she thought.

"Jim Postlethwaite is bringing his choir to sing at Midnight Mass at my church. Of course I am going to see him again!" She closed her eyes briefly and tried for reason. "The engagement was fixed long before Lucas Bagshaw's body turned up and you got this case."

"Is there something between you?" He remained tight-lipped.

In the confines of the car, she remembered the brief kiss the day before. "That's none of your business."

He swung his head away from her. She imagined his expression as he glared out of the fogged side window.

"So you're not going to stay clear…"

She gazed at him nonplussed. How had they flipped from discussing the case in the old familiar way, to this? It was ridiculous.

Ben leaned over her and opened the passenger door. He picked her half-finished plastic cup of coffee from where she'd balanced it on the dashboard and handed it to her. "You can take that with you," he dismissed her. "I've got to get back to work."

CHAPTER

14

She spent Saturday morning at her desk. By eleven o'clock, Sunday's sermon was done. She went into the kitchen and made herself some tea, thinking that she really ought to get a head start on another of her Christmas sermons, but her mind was in turmoil. She pressed the tea bag against the inside of the mug with a teaspoon. This was all Ben's fault. Why did he have to keep trampling through her life? She'd run out of milk, and crossed the hall and opened the front door. At least the milkman had been. It was one thing she and Pat had in common – supporting the local dairy farm, even though it was nearly twice as expensive as buying from the supermarket.

She'd had another delivery too. A small square cardboard box stood beside her pint of skimmed milk, with a note attached written in Fred's round hand. Faith remembered her churchwarden had promised to drop off the orders of service – good old Fred; as good as his word. She hugged the box to her chest with one arm, clutching the milk in the other hand and shutting the door with her rear.

She ought to be writing about the power of God's love and instead her curiosity was leading her to poke holes in strangers' lives, trying to satisfy her need to know what had happened to Lucas Bagshaw. She should be focusing on her vocation; on teaching the faith and caring for people who were sick or struggling. She still hadn't had a moment to talk quietly to Pat, to find out how the churchwarden was coping with the issues of her estranged family and newly discovered nephew.

Talking of estranged families, she still needed to get in touch with her sister. She picked up the phone and dialled Ruth's number. Her nephew, Sean, took the call.

"Aunt Faith! How's the God business?"

"I am very well, thank you, my philistine nephew. So you're back for Christmas already?"

"I can do my reading here as easily as at uni. Besides, Mum's food is better."

"Is your mother in?"

"No. She went into town early, Christmas shopping. I'll tell her you called."

"How's she doing?" Faith cradled the receiver between her ear and neck, freeing her hands to open the box.

"We-ell… Has she told you about Dad?" The box was sealed with resilient brown packing tape. She picked at an edge with her fingernail.

"What about dad?" Sean's dad, Brian, had left Ruth when he decided to upgrade from the suburbs to a younger wife and a townhouse. Ruth had never really regained her balance and Faith found it hard to forgive Brian for it, although he remained in touch with Sean. He loved his son. The end of the tape loosened and she pulled it free with a satisfying ripping sound.

"Susie left him." Susie was the stepmother.

"Really?" She stopped pulling the tape, focusing on Sean's voice.

"Dad's a bit of a mess. I think he's been crying on Mum's shoulder."

Well, that was another disaster in the making. "How do you feel about that?" she asked cautiously.

"I'm good, but I feel a bit worried about Mum. I know you have loads of stuff to do, but it'd be really cool if you could check her out at some point – just, like, when you can. She doesn't really talk to me."

She ended the call feeling ashamed at her neglect. She resolved to make it a priority to get Ruth on the phone in person. She could do with more hours in the day. She took a deep breath.

She left the box half-opened on the kitchen table while she washed her mug up and wiped down the surfaces. If she could just put a solid hour in on her next sermon then she could go into town and do some Christmas shopping. She was beginning to think she should be planning to entertain her family at the vicarage on Christmas Day.

She sat down at the kitchen table and spread her papers out before her. Isaiah 52, verse 9:

> *Break forth together into singing,*
> *you ruins of Jerusalem;*
> *for the Lord has comforted his people,*
> *he has redeemed Jerusalem.*

The ruins of Jerusalem – when expectations crumble, you have the opportunity to rebuild on sounder foundations… Guiltily her thoughts slipped sideways to the distance between her and Jim after the revelations of the Thursday night dinner. She wondered about the sweet kiss. She wanted to see Jim again, to talk to him, to clear the air before he brought the choir to sing at St James's. She hated the idea that he could think she had deliberately deceived him. Idly, she opened the top flap of the box revealing sheaves of orders of service for the Midnight Mass on the 24th. She took out the top copy and checked through. No immediate typos jumped out. That was a relief.

She turned the pamphlet over in her hands. The choirmaster should see the order of service. It would only be a small detour if she was shopping in town. And if Jim didn't happen to be in, she could always drop it off with a note.

She wouldn't be making the trip for personal reasons. She had legitimate parish business.

And besides, a little unwelcome voice said, perhaps Jim could shed more light on the dynamic between Vernon and Lucas.

She took the short cut through the cathedral Close. As she turned out of the King's Gate, she spotted Jim standing outside his lodgings a bit further down the street. He had been running. He wore sweat pants and a dark grey hoody, his door keys in his hand. He wasn't alone. A shorter man, a lean man with a pointed nose and sunken cheeks, confronted him. Faith's heart skipped a beat.

It was Keepie.

She took a step toward them but something stopped her. Where could Jim Postlethwaite have run across Sebastian Keep?

You met him at the Lion's Heart.

When Rick Williams told her Lucas and his friends sometimes drank with an older man, she had assumed it was Adam Bagshaw, but what had the landlord actually said?

"Oh no, not him. Another guy."

She dropped back into the shadow of the King's Gate, staring at the two men arguing in the street. She couldn't hear their words, but Keepie's posture was angry and Jim's defensive. Keepie backed away, stretching out an arm pointing back at Jim. His words carried across to her hiding place, but indistinctly.

"Don't forget, I know all about you."

Jim was turned three-quarters toward her, his face clearly visible. Her phone was in her hand. Hardly aware of what she was doing, she took a picture of the pair of them and then framed Jim's head in close-up and clicked.

Blood buzzed in her ears. She felt cold and isolated from the street around her. What had she just done? Guiltily she dropped the phone into the depths of her bag.

"*I know all about you*" – what could a man like Sebastian Keep know about Jim Postlethwaite? Jim was a stranger to Winchester; he had only arrived in the summer – hadn't he? Then again, had he ever told her that?

Jim had unlocked the door. He walked back into his lodgings. The door closed behind him. She didn't know what to do.

She had acted like a police investigator; capturing evidence of a potentially incriminating nature. She didn't want to face the implications of that. She told herself she had acted on autopilot. She could delete the pictures from her phone.

But her phone stayed in her bag.

This was so silly! She should just go in and ask Jim what his connection was with Sebastian Keep. She took a couple of firm strides into the street. Except – if she asked him, she didn't know where his answer might lead. This wasn't just about her and her world. She was trespassing into an active murder investigation. Both Sebastian Keep and Jim Postlethwaite intersected with the life of a murder victim. The caution of her police training asserted itself. Lucas Bagshaw, who would now never make his seventeenth birthday, was the priority here – not her petty curiosity or her emotional "need to know".

Jim appeared in the tall window of his lodgings on the second floor, looking away from her, down the street. She hesitated. She was out in plain view. Jim turned his head and saw her. He waved and she waved back.

"This is a surprise," he said, as opened the door.

"Bad timing?"

"Well…" He looked down at his sweats with rueful charm. "I've just been for a run; I should have a shower."

"I don't want to disturb you."

"No – come on in."

The tiny apartment was a mess. Was it only Monday when they had sat here before? It seemed an age ago. The room was not as she remembered it. Now there were clothes and a used towel draped over the anonymous, ugly geometric furniture with the Scotchgarded covers. A half-filled duffel bag protruded from behind the sofa. She looked at Jim, with the sweat on his skin, framed against the vast window. What did she really know about him? She prided herself on her estimation of character. He had seemed so controlled, with a gift for apparent honesty. Now, in that room, she felt as if she was intruding on something that was unravelling. *You're projecting*, she scolded herself. She had merely called unexpectedly on a rare day off and had caught an undomesticated bachelor coming back from his run before he had time to pick up.

"I was in town – tackling the dreaded Christmas shopping," she heard herself chattering. "I thought I'd leave you this." She held out two copies of the order of service. "You might like to see it before you bring the choir on the 24th."

"Thanks." He took them from her. "That's useful."

Her nerves were jangling. Her phone was radiating guilt like a red-hot coal from her bag.

"How are the rehearsals going?" she asked, just to be saying something.

"Not too bad. We've had a couple drop out, but the rest are in good voice." He paused. "Have you heard how the investigation is going?"

She felt a thump in her chest. Suddenly a kaleidoscope of fragments resolved into a pattern. In each of their encounters, the subtle pressure of interest about what she knew of the investigation... No! She pushed the suspicion away. Jim had every reason to be curious about that. Someone he knew had been killed. He had said it himself – murder was an extraordinary intrusion in "ordinary" life. It would be odd if he *hadn't* shown interest. She analysed his expression. He was distracted. His eyes seemed to meet hers through glass.

"I think they've got a few more pieces of the puzzle... maybe."

Rick Williams had implied the "older guy" had been seen drinking with the trio more than once.

When they had first met in this room and when they had talked in the choir loft at St James's, Jim had spoken as if he barely knew Lucas and his friends; as if they were just three faces among many; the relationship you'd expect between a choirmaster and the young members of his occasional choir. Suspicion pumped out its toxic fumes once more.

"What do you know of Vernon Granger's family?" she asked.

Jim pushed up the sleeves of his sweatshirt impatiently. His forearms were well-muscled with prominent veins.

"His mother, Mavis, came to a rehearsal once. V wasn't keen to have her there. I don't know her, but she struck me as a pushy mother and not a particularly understanding one. His father's still around, but absent a lot – at least that's my impression."

He lifted his arm and ran his fingers through his sweaty hair. The inner skin of his arm just below the crook of his elbow was flecked with little white scars, like random dashes. Faith tried to keep her composure.

He pulled down his sleeves. "I should go have a shower…"

"And I need to tackle my shopping. I only wanted to drop off the service sheets."

"Thanks."

"So I'll see you at Midnight Mass."

He bid her goodbye with little emotion.

She was outside on the street again. She should report what she had seen to Ben, but… She needed to be honest with herself. She couldn't trust her judgment right now. Her feelings were all mixed up. She had started this day with such different thoughts. Now she felt betrayed by that short, sweet kiss.

She took out the phone, and looked at the photos, then pressed "Delete".

Are you sure you want to delete this item?

Faith couldn't. This was a potential part of a murder investigation. And even without the photographic evidence, she couldn't forget what she'd seen and heard.

She slipped the phone away.

She did her shopping on autopilot. She put too many figs and boxes of mince pies in her trolley at the supermarket and was startled by the bill. She thought of Detective Inspector Shorter's antagonism toward the choirmaster over the dinner table Thursday night. Ben certainly wouldn't be inclined to give Jim the benefit of the doubt. She felt responsible for that.

If there was an innocent explanation, she should find it and use the evidence to convince Ben.

The road out of Winchester was clogged with Christmas shoppers, harried by the clock counting down to the Big Day. As soon as she could, she turned off on to the back roads. She found herself approaching the Lion's Heart pub.

The piles of dirty snow in the car park had resolved into mounds of hard ice. The bar door was closed but there were lights on. She pressed her face to the glass. Rick Williams stood alone behind the bar. He saw her. He wore an irritated expression as he came to open the door.

"We're not open until six."

"I know. I won't keep you long." Standing there, looking at him, her purpose almost failed. But she had come this far. She had to know. She got out her phone. "I was just wondering… When we talked, you said that Lucas – the boy they found down at the river – that he and his friends used to meet up here sometimes with an older man?" She flicked up the headshot of Jim. "Do you recognize this man?"

Rick leaned over the phone in her hand, peering short-sightedly at the screen. He wore Brut aftershave – a flashback to her childhood.

"That's him," he nodded. "Started coming in this summer. Now I think of it, he came in with the three of them. He's been in a few times since then. I think he works in town."

"Did they ever drink with Sebastian Keep?"

Rick stared blankly at her as if he was trying to calculate her purpose and its implications. She kept still, holding his gaze, willing him to answer her. He backed away from her, retreating into the shelter of his pub.

"Might have." Her face must have fallen or he saw something that made him reconsider. "The older guy knew what Keepie was. He didn't encourage him," he said roughly, and closed the door on her.

She got back into the car and sat there in the frozen car park. What did all this mean?

Jim Postlethwaite had lied to her – or at least he had been economical with the truth. All he had said – at his rooms, when they first met, in her own church and afterwards – only suggested the normal interaction of a choirmaster with his choir. He had even emphasized his distance – "*They talk to me about non-choir stuff only if and when they want to*"... But he had got involved to the extent of socializing with choir members; and not just any members, but the crucial three. Jim had been seen drinking with Lucas and V and the Dot, and not in some pub across from the cathedral but at the Lion's Heart, way out of town.

Jim Postlethwaite and a drug dealer?

"*Don't forget, I know all about you.*"

What could Keepie know about Jim? Something that had happened at the Lion's Heart pub?

She could imagine where Ben's line of reasoning would lead him. Jim was acquainted with Sebastian Keep, a known local drug dealer and he, Jim, was running a youth choir with vulnerable kids. Talk about being in a prime position to distribute. Put that together with the white flecks on Jim's arms. She knew needle scars when she saw them. Jim had been a heroin user. At the very least, he must have lied on his application form.

A group of memories coalesced. Jim's sudden coldness at the cathedral interviews when he had observed her familiarity with Ben and Peter. His distance after she had led him into that Thursday night dinner: "*We seem to be surrounded by law enforcement.*"

A mixture of denial and anger blossomed in her chest at her own stupidity. Ben had tried to warn her. She had refused to listen because Ben was some sort of electrical disturbance to her; his proximity breached her composure and scrambled her wits. She had been feeling vulnerable and she had allowed herself to be deluded, to fall for illusory charm and a gift for apparent honesty. In her self-indulgence she had blamed Ben for interfering with her personal life, when his concerns had been professional and valid. Now Jim's secrets had exposed her.

Jim had been a user.

Had been. Those scars were old and well-healed. He'd got off the stuff.

Do you believe in redemption? The voice rose unbidden, as it always did.

Of course she did. But she wasn't a fool.

Sometimes love demands you risk being a fool.

From what Rick, the landlord, had just told her, Jim could just as well have been protecting the teenagers, warning Keepie off.

The choir had been working together through the summer. Perhaps it wasn't so strange that the trio might have invited their choirmaster to a pub by the river on a hot summer's day.

But then, why hadn't Jim been open about his relationship with them? She recalled the cynical look on his face the day of the cathedral interviews when he had thought she had deliberately concealed her relationship with the police from him: "*I appreciate the value of discretion.*"

That night she found it hard to sleep. She kept seeing Jim in vignette, his head on his arms, in the choir loft. She felt again his stillness.

"*I am a sinner; I am no saint.*"

CHAPTER

15

She shifted about in her big bed, pummelling the pillows in futile efforts to find a comfortable position. The clock passed midnight, and then one o'clock. She awoke from a fitful doze. There had been a sharp sound. It was near – almost in the room. She sat up, her heart beating rapidly.

A scatter of hard substance hit the windowpane. A human voice hallooed from down below. She got out of bed and pulled on her thick cord dressing gown, slipping moccasins on her feet. The outer coverings made her feel a little more defended. In an afterthought, she picked up her phone from the nightstand and put it in the pocket of the dressing down. She opened the window and peered out.

There was a figure down below. A man – a drunken man. He lifted his head toward her then staggered, as if the movement had made his head swim. A vagrant. She called down to him to go and sleep it off.

"Vicar?" She recognized the voice. She leaned out to get a better look. Adam Bagshaw was leaning against her wall looking up at her, his head tilted to one side.

"What time do you call this?" she asked irritably. He

wrinkled his forehead and looked about him as if there might be a clock in the bushes.

"Dunno."

"I'll come down. Go round to the kitchen door – that way…" she instructed, making an exaggerated gesture around the house toward the back garden. She didn't want him traipsing mud and slush over the carpets. If Ben could see her now, he'd be screaming, she thought. She touched the phone. If anything happened, she didn't think she'd have much trouble locking a door and dialling 999.

On second thoughts, she brought up Ben's number on-screen, her finger poised over the call button. On Saturday night, she'd probably get a quicker response from him.

She found Bagshaw sitting half on her flower bed, humming. The tune was familiar – "Away in a Manger".

Any tension went out of her and she let the phone drop into her pocket. "Come on," she said, inserting an arm under his and heaving. "Ups-a-daisy, I think you need some coffee."

"'Away in a manger, no place for his head,'" he sang out, then stopped. "Used to like carols," he confided. "Cheery." He looked at her owlishly. At this proximity his breath was toxic. "I've come for a visit."

"So I see." She tried to sound like a disapproving schoolmistress.

"You visited me," he said anxiously. His cartoon-like expression made her smile.

"That I did," she admitted.

She got him into the kitchen and sat him safely at the table. His skin was freezing cold. Adam heaved a gusty sigh.

"He died a week ago. You know?" She could only look back at him, witnessing his sorrow. She nodded slowly.

"Many a time he's dragged me home. Luke never gave up

on you. Just like his mother." He looked into middle distance as if he saw something there. "So I got drunk." He smiled humourlessly at himself.

"When did you last eat?" she asked.

"Huh?"

"I'll make you something. How about some toast?" Adam Bagshaw began a nod, then thought better of it. He held his head in his hands.

"I don't know what to do! Trish, she always knew what to do – what I am going to do? I can't be without her or him. What's the point?" His eyes were full of tears.

She put some of Ben's strong coffee in a mug, sweetened it liberally and placed it in front of him. "Drink this – it'll warm you up."

She set about toasting some bread. She heard rustling, and turned around to see Adam fumbling in his coat. It took her a moment to realize that he was looking for something. After a couple of tries he pulled out a piece of paper. It slipped from his grasp and floated to the floor between them. She bent down and picked it up.

"Read it," he said. "I'm homeless. *No place for his head*," he sang mournfully. "I miss her. I miss him. I hate Christmas."

The header read Whittier, Panner and Trusk Solicitors. The letter was short but to the point. It invited Mr Bagshaw to an appointment to discuss the winding up of the trust fund set up for the benefit of Trisha and Lucas Bagshaw and alternative arrangements for paying the mortgage at 5, Benson's Close, The Hollies. She looked up and met Adam's eyes.

"Can't pay the mortgage. Don't have a job," he explained. "Trish, she did all that. She said I would lose my own head if it wasn't tied on. She did," he waved a clumsy arm and hit the tabletop, "all that."

Faith brought him a piece of buttered toast, sitting down to watch him eat.

"There was a trust fund paying the bills?"

"And some," Adam replied, with his mouth full.

So that was where the money came from; not drugs or crime…

Adam had stopped eating. He stared at the slice of toast, his hands resting on the table.

"I loved the boy. I loved them both. I should be homeless. I was never worth anything – they just thought I was. And now they're gone." He wasn't crying any more. He just looked at her with such empty despair it brought tears to her own eyes. She leaned toward him.

"You are made in God's image," she said passionately. "You are not worthless! You loved them, and Trisha and Lucas loved you; and God loves them and you too. There is hope and I will help you find it." She blinked away the tears and sat back. "But first, you need to eat."

He did what she told him, messily.

As she washed his plate in the sink, Adam rambled on about how he loved his lost family. Despite her wish to be a kind ear, sleeplessness kicked in; she began to tune in and out.

"I knew it upset him," Adam was saying. "Perhaps I could have done something more – but I couldn't, you know?" She put down the tea towel, focusing her wits.

"Why couldn't you, if Lucas was upset?" What were they talking about, precisely?

"I promised her," he said solemnly.

"Trisha?"

He stared at her, his eyes wide and sincere. "She made me promise I would never tell."

About what? The trust fund had been set up by someone

with money who cared about Trisha and her son but was keen to remain anonymous. The biggest missing component in this scenario was Lucas's father. Faith made a guess.

"About Lucas's father, the source of the trust fund?"

Adam looked surprised that she had to say it out loud, as if she should know that already. "I kept my promise to Trish," he said.

Her sleep-starved brain tried to review what Adam had said in the last hour. It sounded as if Lucas had discovered something that led him toward the identity of his father.

"Did Lucas know who his father was?"

Adam frowned as if the thought hadn't occurred to him. "No."

"But he found something out before he died?" Adam nodded slowly. "When?"

"Sometime during the summer, I think. He started asking more questions."

"And you know who Lucas's father is?" Adam blinked. He yawned a tremendous yawn. His eyes were unfocused. "Do you?" she insisted, but she was no longer sure he heard her. With a soft grunt, Adam's head dropped onto his folded arms on the table. He started to snore.

He was too big for her to move. She fetched a duvet and wrapped it round him. She left a glass of water and a bucket beside him in case of emergencies, and left him sleeping against her kitchen table. She needed to get some sleep herself. She had to be ready for the Sunday services in less than three hours.

When she woke again it was barely light. Outside promised a day of fog and ice. She had made it to the third Sunday in Advent – sermons on love and readings on John the Baptist. She came down to the kitchen. Adam had gone, leaving the duvet neatly piled on the chair he had occupied. The Beast, her visiting cat, had ensconced himself in its soft centre. Adam must have assumed he was hers and let the creature wander in.

"I am not running a B&B here," she scolded him severely. "This is a vicarage and I have to conduct services." The Beast didn't take her seriously. He watched her fetch food and his bowl from the cupboard. She rubbed his head as she passed. It was nice to have his company. Lack of sleep had sapped her energy and powers of speculation. She found her sermon notes, donned her cassock and set out down the path to her church.

It felt as if daylight never turned on properly that day. The fog refused to move. After lunch, her services done, she felt too restless to stay still; but if she walked about the village, people would talk to her, and she wanted time to think. She got in the car and drove.

Lucas's absent father had been contributing to his upkeep all these years. Her mind roamed around the dramatis personae of this case. Was he local? It seemed likely, in so far as Trisha Bagshaw had been a local woman who had lived here all her life. The insistence on anonymity suggested a married man; Trisha's swearing Adam to secrecy suggested she cared for Lucas's father; and the trust fund suggested he was a man of means – sufficient means to support two families and disguise the fact. But speculation could take her no further.

The fog got denser down by the river. Fortunately, not many people ventured out on these country lanes on a cold, dark Sunday afternoon. She drove slowly. The fog wrapped itself around, cosseting her in the private world of her car. It felt peaceful. She drew up at the old wooden bridge where Lucas had met his end.

Something just off the side of the road caught her attention – a dead animal, she thought at first; for an irrational second she thought it might even be the Beast.

She got out of the car. She heard only matt silence, and water dripping off leaves, flowing in the river below. The fog had closed in with the failing light. She felt uneasy. It was isolated here.

She approached slowly. Misty trails drifted over the walkway, resolving into a dense bank of fog sealing off the sight of the river and the world beyond it. The tarred surface flexed and cracked under her boots as she walked out to the middle of the bridge. Not roadkill, she saw as she moved closer. A bunch of flowers. A bouquet wrapped in plain white paper. Twisted willow radiated in a frame around paper-white narcissus, pussy willow and sprigs of purple heather and, at the centre, like a bleeding heart, an open flower of red amaryllis a handspan wide. A card rested amid the stalks. She leaned over, being careful not to touch or disturb anything. The message was short and written in block capitals.

SORRY I WAS NEVER THERE FOR YOU.

She flipped on the lights. Her church welcomed her with its peaceful familiarity and a lingering smell of the coffee on offer after morning service. Fred had kindly returned the box of Spicer decorations to the loft. She was going to take advantage of the Sunday afternoon lull to check out the pageant costumes.

Sorry I was never there for you.

The words were such that almost anyone could utter them at some point in their lives. But in the context of Lucas Bagshaw's death, what did they mean? Faith's first thought had been Anna Hope, the unrequited crush who, perhaps, in keeping her distance, hadn't been the shoulder to cry on that Lucas needed. But *never* was such a strong word; so weighty. She could imagine Anna writing "Sorry I *wasn't* there for you", but "never" didn't quite make sense. And hadn't Anna insisted that there were no romantic feelings on either side?

She climbed the ladder into the loft and turned on the light. The afternoon was so dark, the bulb seemed to burn brighter than before. She crawled toward the tobacco-yellow trunk. A large board rested against the lid, wedging it shut. She tugged at it, cramped in the confined space. It was heavy and she could feel her cheeks flushing with the effort. All at once, it came free, jamming a sharp edge into the flesh of her thigh. *Ouch!* She subdued the childish temptation to fling the board over the edge and resign it to the dump. She tilted the surface to the light, ruefully rubbing her bruised leg.

She opened the trunk. Her fingers touched the heavy weave of robes and cloaks. It was too cramped up there and hardly any light penetrated the gloom. She found the trunk too heavy for her to move by herself, so she threw the costumes down to the foot of the ladder – robes for the three Wise Men, followed by two turbans and a Persian fez, then Mary's blue gown and headdress, a couple of cloaks... But there didn't seem to be anything for Joseph. She heard footsteps below.

"Hi!" She leaned over the ledge. Ben stood looking up at her, his arms full of costumes. "Having a clear-out?"

"What are you doing here?" she asked. She turned off the light and climbed down. He waited rather close to the foot of the ladder. She wondered if he intended to step back and give her space. He grinned at her over his armful of fabric.

"Only passing. I've just been to the attack site."

"You have?" She was startled into openness. "Me too.

Did you see the flowers?" He quickly disguised his surprise, and his eyes crinkled in acknowledgment of her enthusiasm.

"They're bagged up in the car."

His voice contained a hint of challenge, but in this case, she knew he really had no other option.

"I didn't know the site was common knowledge."

"If the local vicar knows, I guess everyone does," said Ben.

She felt a flush of outrage. "I certainly didn't tell anyone!"

"Relax," said Ben, grinning. "A local pap showed up on Friday evening. We shooed him away, but it was on the local radio an hour later."

Faith's cheeks cooled, and she cursed herself for falling prey to his teasing. Ben seemed to sense her shame and offered a neutral question. "Don't suppose you saw who left them?"

She took the costumes from him, laying them out one by one over the back of a nearby pew, so she could sort through them. "No, but I have my theories."

"The father?"

"Possibly. Or Adam."

Though it hardly rang true for Adam, either. She couldn't imagine him holding it together long enough to carry out such a gesture.

Maybe she had miscounted. Joseph had to have a robe somewhere.

Ben's mouth turned down in a sceptical frown. "What are these things?" He picked up a purple turban shaped like a giant onion with blue inserts and silver trim.

"Pageant costumes. Adam paid me a visit last night. He was very drunk – I thought he was a vagrant. He woke me up."

"What?" Ben's bark made her start. "Do you get many vagrants calling in the middle of the night?" he asked.

"Vicarages attract them," she said soothingly. "Especially around Christmas. It's the reputation for charity."

"You must have an alarm?" His frown had deepened.

"Yes, but I don't use it. You see, I sort of have a cat…"

Ben rested his palm against his forehead. "Fay, come on," he said. "You know better than that."

She shrugged, deliberately casual. "They're just hungry for food and human company."

Ben's jaw set stubbornly. He would come back to the alarm system, she was sure, but right now he decided to return to the case in hand.

"What did Bagshaw want?"

"He was grieving – the first week anniversary of Lucas's death. And he had some bad news." She took a breath. This was important news. It could alter the course of the case. "Apparently Trish and Lucas benefited from a trust fund that paid the mortgage and more on that house in The Hollies. Now they are dead, the trust is to be wound up and Adam is likely to be homeless."

She had to admit to a flicker of disappointment. Ben didn't seem surprised. He was just watching her with his usual acuity, as if aware of every breath and eyelash. "You knew about the trust fund," she said.

"I only found out a few hours ago," he gave her the consolation prize.

"Do you know who's behind it? I am presuming it's from the absent father?"

"Best guess – but he's keen not to be identified. Legal are negotiating their way through various roadblocks. We haven't identified who it is yet, but we will. Meanwhile, we know the money was purely for the benefit of Trish and Lucas and ends with their deaths."

"So it was clearly not in Adam's interests to do away with Lucas," she pointed out, glad for the opportunity to emphasize Adam Bagshaw's status as a victim, not a suspect.

"If he knew about the trust." Ben never gave in without a fight. She held his gaze.

"He knew about the trust."

"Then I'll give you that," Ben conceded.

The costumes were in a neat pile on the pew. She sat down on the other side of them, so they formed a fabric boundary between her and Ben.

"So what did *you* think of the flowers?" she asked. Ben got his phone out of his pocket and flicked up a series of pictures of the bouquet on the bridge. He held it out, leaning over the costume barrier so that she had to join him there to see the screen.

"Those aren't cheap flowers from a petrol station," Faith said.

"No?" His bright eyes behind their long black lashes were amused.

"Well, look at it – twisted willow? And that red amaryllis, that won't be cheap. Not what I would expect your average man to choose. That's a sophisticated selection put together by a professional."

"OK. So he went to a florist."

"So he must have bought them yesterday, which indicates pre-planning. Any clues in the card?" Ben flicked up fresh photographs with his thumb, views of the card front and back. Faith leaned closer.

"He used capitals – but it's not like he can't write. He doesn't want his handwriting to be recognized – that suggests he's local."

"And cautious," she commented. "Fingerprints?"

"We'll check, of course. But gloves in this weather wouldn't be uncommon."

Their faces were only a few inches apart. She could feel the energy emanating from his skin. She realized that she was biting her lower lip. She sat back and flicked her hand over the fabric between them, erasing the dent made by the pressure of her arm.

"Do you think Adam Bagshaw knows who the dad is?" Ben asked. His face was turned away as he put his phone in his pocket.

"I think so. He told me he was keeping a secret Trisha had asked him to keep. I am not sure he will tell you, though. He is desperate not to let his sister down again. Keeping the secret she left him with is the last piece of loyalty he can show her."

Ben snorted derisively. "He's a drunk. If I get him in my interview room, I can make him talk."

"Surely you'll know via the lawyers soon enough," she said gently. "You don't need to take that last thing from him."

Ben rolled his eyes at her. "I'll see."

She felt the shift in mood. He propped himself up against the pew end.

"Thursday night was fun," he said. She gave him a hard look sideways – he was really going to go there? He smirked at her.

"I have one word for you," she said. "Immature."

"Immature?" he teased. "I wasn't the one bringing a potential suspect to a social occasion at an investigator's house in the middle of a murder enquiry."

"Oh, come on, there's no 'potential' about it," said Faith. "Anyway, how about the lead in an active murder investigation playing footsie with the pathologist off duty?" she retorted.

"I didn't know you cared."

An unworthy thought slipped up from her subconscious. Had Ben been trying to make her jealous? She pulled herself back, crossly. No. That was absurd and dangerous self-regard. Ben was a master at this game; a reflexive flirt. It didn't have to mean anything. Time to return to safer ground.

"So this trust fund – do you think Lucas's death could tie to that?" asked Faith.

"In what way?"

"Well, both beneficiaries die within a few months of each other." She hesitated as an awful thought struck her. "Trisha Bagshaw's death was so sudden. She was only in her early forties…"

The corners of Ben's mouth twitched up. "Checked the autopsy report. A brain aneurysm, probably there all her adult life. It blew and she was gone."

"Just like that?"

"Pretty much. According to the dates she was in a coma for twenty-four hours or so at the hospital before they turned the life support off."

"That poor boy, Lucas, and her poor, poor brother," she said.

Ben shifted in his seat. Sentiment made him uncomfortable. "Let's stick to what we know. This is about drugs, I'm sure."

Faith looked past him for a moment, thinking automatically of Jim. "Sebastian Keep?" she said.

Ben shook his head. "Not Keepie himself. He alibied out."

Faith felt something inside her slump with the disappointment. It would have been so much simpler if Keepie, a career criminal, had been to blame; then Jim would be in the clear and she would never have to tell what she saw. "Keepie was picked up on suspicion of supplying banned substances in town that Saturday lunchtime," Ben explained. "He was held at the central station and questioned. Released just after 10 p.m. that night – so he's out."

She checked her watch and stood up, contemplating the pile of costumes with her eyes, but Jim Postlethwaite with her mind. She wasn't ready to bring him up. Not here, and not now. "Well, it's official. I am short a costume for Joseph. This pageant is not what you would call going smoothly."

"What does Joseph wear?"

"One of those sort of stripy, Eastern-looking robes with undershirt and sandals, I imagine." Ben rolled his eyes. He didn't have to say anything. She got the message. *So this is how you spend your days...?*

He was lolling at his ease on the pew. She hadn't seen him this relaxed in a church before. The sight of him was so familiar. He had always liked smart suits in dark colours – never brown or green or anything wild like that. You wouldn't catch Ben Shorter in a peacoat – unless he was undercover.

"What are you doing for Christmas?" she asked.

A shadow passed over his face. He straightened up. "Working." He had always been impatient of the empty fuss around the Christmas holiday. "You know it's not my thing. Those who can, huddling together, pretending they like one another, just to show that *they* aren't alone, like the rest of the human race."

"There's that, but there's also the real meaning of the festival," she suggested quietly.

"What? You're telling me there's something real under all the tinsel and carolling? Come on, Fay. You can't pretend you're some naive suburbanite. You've glimpsed the real world. Christmas is no more real than the painted nativity scenes wheeled out every year. You know what Bethlehem looks like these days, don't you? There's not a lot of gold, frankincense or myrrh to be found."

"That's rather an impoverished view," said Faith quietly.

Ben shrugged. "It's what I see. Boxing Day morning, real life's still waiting. You just get to face it with a hangover, indigestion and a pile more debt."

CHAPTER

16

From behind the doors with their square safety glass windows, came the murmur of classes in progress. Faith had finished her Monday morning assembly. She waved goodbye to the school secretary in her office and crossed the car park. She had failed to get Ruth on the phone all weekend. This was getting ridiculous. Her sister would be at work at the council offices only five minutes' walk away. Why not go and call in? She paused on the kerb opposite Mavis Granger's florist shop. Ruth liked flowers.

Mavis herself stood behind the counter today. "Did you enjoy the reindeer?" she greeted Faith as she stepped into her shop. So Mrs Granger was letting her know that she knew all about last Thursday's visit and her chat with Anna. *She'd have made a good interrogator*, Faith thought.

"It's charming," she answered lightly. "I chose it for a friend as a house gift. It was very much admired." She looked about the shop. The wreaths that had covered the counter before were gone. "How's business? I would imagine things are pretty hectic just now in the run-up to Christmas."

"Our busiest time – although it is a little easier now that the wreaths have gone out, but there is still plenty to do." As they talked, Mavis was shaping what looked like one of a set of table decorations with poinsettias and frosted silver-white stars on pins with quick, assured fingers. "There are a lot of dinners this time of year."

Faith pondered the selection of flowers on offer. Ruth liked tulips, but it was hardly the time of year for them.

"The policemen investigating the Bagshaw boy's death came to talk to me the other day," Mrs Granger offered conversationally.

"They did?"

"They were checking my Vernon's alibi." The statement had a flicker of accusation behind it. Faith met her eyes coolly. "He was with me," Mavis stated, "that Saturday afternoon when the boy disappeared." She dropped her eyes. She simpered like the silly woman she most certainly wasn't. "The truth is Vernon's been rather naughty. I blame his friends for leading him astray." She punctuated the words with a little laugh to take the sting out of them. "The police tell me they've been seen drinking at a local pub. Not alcohol, of course. Vernon knows better than that – a shandy at most. I spoke with young Anna about it. She may be eighteen, but I don't want her leading Vernon into bad ways – though I don't think she meant any harm. It was most likely that Bagshaw boy."

Faith thought about mentioning Lucas's teetotal habits, but she'd rather the conversation didn't become antagonistic. "Did they give you any idea of what happened to Lucas?"

She caught the tail end of a speculative side-glance but it was so quick, she wondered if she had imagined it. Mavis had finished one arrangement. She started on the next.

"A motherless and fatherless boy," she was saying. "He left school as soon as his mother died, you know. Well, it's hardly surprising he slipped into bad ways."

"Not in Vernon's company, surely!" Faith interjected unkindly. She couldn't help it. Mavis Granger seemed so ready to blame Lucas for his fate.

"Of course I didn't mean that!" Mavis flashed back. "It's just…" she hesitated. *She's making a performance of it*, Faith thought. *She knows what she is going to say.* "It's just that Lucas Bagshaw – well, he had money when he shouldn't." Mavis's limpid eyes met Faith's with just the right measure of regret and sorrow for the poor, misguided boy. "I had my suspicions." She tilted her well-groomed head. "Perhaps you'll remember – Pat Montesque mentioned it at that meeting we had in your church hall; we had a break-in at home earlier this year."

"Ah yes – I remember; in the first week of June, wasn't it?"

Faith caught the flicker of a double take at her guess. Mavis pursed her lips.

"The police called it a crime of opportunity," she went on. "An amateur, they thought – but some valuable items were taken."

"What sort of things?"

"Portable; easily sold – gold jewellery, small silver, that sort of thing."

"How distressing for you. And you suspected Lucas?"

Mavis gazed at her significantly across the counter. "It was soon after Vernon began bringing Lucas Bagshaw into our home – my son and Anna were kind to Lucas after his mother died."

"Did you tell this to the police at the time?"

Mavis wouldn't meet her eyes. "It didn't seem right," she said. "The boy had only just lost his mother. But I did warn Vernon."

In other words, you didn't like the boy, he was poor and so you thought it would be neater if it were Lucas who had stolen

197

from you, thought Faith sourly. The fight at the pub! Her attention was caught. But the boys had made up…

"So you told your son you thought his friend might be responsible for your break-in?"

Mavis nodded, her lips pressed together in a thin, reddish-orange line. Her hands were still on the decorations. "Lucas convinced my son that he hadn't been anywhere near us on that day. Vernon believed him. I never did entirely. Lucas was never short of money, you see; an orphaned boy; his mother was a cleaner…"

Faith felt a pulse of revulsion at this contemptuous dismissal of the loving Trisha.

"I am keeping you too long," she said. "You are so busy. I just wanted to buy something cheerful for my sister."

Her eyes roamed over the riot of colour and texture in the window. Pussy willow, and in a blue enamelled bucket on the counter, heather sprigs. At the back, a stand of twisted willow shafts, and near the front a pail of white, six-petalled stars with their delicate yellow centres – paper-white narcissus. She looked again.

"You don't happen to have any red amaryllis?"

Mavis's eyes inventoried her stock. "We did have some in," she answered, "but Anna must have sold the last of them on Saturday. We'll be getting another delivery this Wednesday."

Faith picked out a poinsettia in a ceramic pot wrapped round with a crushed taffeta ribbon in an edible caramel colour and tied off with a bow.

"This will be perfect," she said.

She set off for the council offices clutching her peace offering for Ruth. She hadn't thought of it before, because Winchester had plenty of florists, but Mavis's shop was well situated on the way out of town toward the Lion's Heart pub and the bridge. Her blood quickened with the delight of the chase. If the chain of her speculation was sound, and if Anna Hope had sold the last of the amaryllis on Saturday, she might very well have met Lucas's father. It was frustrating that Anna hadn't been in the shop. Faith glanced back over her shoulder at Mavis, standing in her window. She didn't have any other means of finding the Dot. She would have to wait until tomorrow to talk to her.

The Winchester City Council offices resided in an ugly eighties' building faced with contrasting dirty pink and reddish brick with window strips of dull glass. Her sister worked as a valued administrator in an open-plan office on the second floor. Her desk was near to the boss's office.

Ruth spotted Faith at once. She pushed back her chair and stood up.

"What are you doing here? Is everything all right?"

Seeing her sister's anxious face, Faith realized that the unexpected visit was ill-conceived. Her sister must be thinking something awful had happened to one of the family.

"Oh, nothing to worry about," she said. "We keep missing each other, that's all. I should have called ahead. This is for you." Faith put the poinsettia on Ruth's desk, and bent to give her sister's cheek a kiss.

"You shouldn't have." Ruth shifted the pot a few inches and fluffed the flower's petals. Knowing her, she was figuring out whether she still had any plant food in her drawers.

"They're Christmassy – don't you think?" Faith said. "Remember how Mum always had one on the hall table?"

Ruth's mouth tilted in a small, fond smile of shared memory. "On that blue and white dish to stop it marking.

She still has it. It's on the front room windowsill."

Ruth was petite and neat. All their adult lives Faith had envied her that. She always picked up such bargains in the clothes department, but today she looked extra well-groomed. Her thick dark hair in its smooth bob shone. Her eyebrows had been recently plucked.

"You're looking well."

"I've got news." Ruth cast a glance around the office. She seemed satisfied that the coast was clear. "Brian and I, we've been spending time together." She looked so vulnerable and pleased. Faith's heart sank. "Susie's walked out on him. Apparently the relationship hasn't been good for years." She squared her shoulders defiantly. "He's been having a tough time of it, poor thing."

"Ruthie…"

Her sister's face set in its stubborn look. "I know what you're going to say, but I have my eyes open. I am just being a friend."

"Right."

Ruth put out her hand and touched Faith's arm. "I've been wanting to talk to you for ages, but you've been so busy."

Guilt and love overwhelmed Faith in a rush of feeling. She wrapped her arms around her sister and hugged her. Ruth wasn't a demonstrative person, especially in public, but she gripped her back. Why had she left it so long? They released one another.

"Once this week is done, I am all yours," she said. "We'll have a good, long catch-up, OK?"

Ruth surreptitiously wiped moisture from her eyes. She pulled a paper handkerchief from the box on her desk and blew her nose. "We really need to talk about Mother," she began.

Faith frowned. "Oh yes?"

"You know Cindy – from accounting?" her sister asked.

"Cindy?" Faith's puzzlement deepened.

"You know! We do quiz night together on Wednesdays. Cindy's been through it already with her gran."

"Her gran…?"

Ruth's pause was pregnant with meaning. "Forgetting things," she prompted. "It's the first sign. Cindy's given me some leaflets. I can lend them to you."

An involuntary giggle, like a hard bubble, ascended from Faith's gut. She choked it off. "You think our mother…?" she heard the outrage in her tone and caught herself. She tried a lighter note. "Oh, come on!" she teased. "Mum's only in her early seventies. She's as bright as a button."

"I know Mum's not stupid," said Ruth. "She's very clever at covering up. It's not her mind, it's her memory. You only see her on visits. I talk to her every day. There are signs…" There was a quiet conviction in Ruth's voice that got under Faith's skin. Annoyance prickled at the back of her neck.

"Like what?"

"Losing things – glasses, her keys… The other day, for instance; I called at 10 a.m. and she was still in her dressing gown. Mum never gets up late. She was notorious for popping wide awake at 6 a.m. 'I'm an early bird, not a night owl,' she always said."

"Maybe she just wanted a lie-in," said Faith. Did her sister really speak to her mother every day? "She's retired, after all. And everyone mislays things – I do it all the time." Faith caught her breath.

Her sister inhaled deeply. *Here it comes.* "If you made more time for your own family instead of trying to save the world, you might have an idea of what is actually going on with our mother."

Faith felt the kick deep inside of her. Ruth had never understood her vocation. She unclenched her jaw. I am not going to be drawn into these old childish routines, she repeated to herself. I am *not*!

"Come on, Ruthie, you know you can be over-solicitous sometimes." There! That sounded perfectly rational and kind. "Has Mum asked for help?"

"You don't see because you are never here to see; I am. I know what is going on," her sister argued stubbornly. "I think we need to take her to the GP to be tested."

"Surely you're overreacting? Let's just hold fire before taking drastic action. Look – we'll be together at Christmas. We can discuss it then. OK?"

A young woman with bleached hair approached them, carrying a pile of manila folders.

"Hey, Ruth. These are for you. Peter says he needs them processed as soon as you can."

The woman eyed Faith's dog collar with open curiosity. Ruth dismissed her with a firm: "Thank you, Kim."

In the space of the distraction, Faith made up her mind. While part of her wilted at the thought of the extra pressure, it was beyond time she paid attention to her family. There seemed to be a lot of catching up to do.

"Before I let you get on," she began, "I've been thinking of what you said about Christmas. How about you bring Sean and Mum to me for Christmas Day this time? I'll be tied up with the service until one-ish, but then, it's traditional for Christmas lunch to be late, isn't it? We can eat at three or so. That front room at the vicarage is made for Christmas. We can give the Aga a run…"

She knew Ruth had been yearning after the Aga that came with her vicarage ever since Faith had given her the tour and she'd laid eyes on the glossy, four-door beast. It was one of life's little ironies that Faith, who considered food just something you needed to consume to live, had ended up with a country kitchen and an Aga, while Ruth, the great hostess, was stuck with her doll's house kitchen in her modern semi. Ruth's expression reflected the conflict between irritation and the possibilities of the vicarage kitchen. The Aga won the day.

"Sean and Mum and I can have everything ready for you for when you're free," she agreed thoughtfully. The decision was made. "You don't have to worry about the food," she added. "You can email me what you want and I can bring all that. We can settle up later. Just give me a set of keys."

Faith winced internally at the thought of her space being invaded. She could see the plans bubbling up in Ruth's brain. Would she ever get her keys back? But Ruth looked happy.

Her job was done. After swearing that, however busy she got, she would not forget to have another set of house keys cut and would drop them off with Ruth just as soon as possible, she left her sister making lists at her desk.

She had almost all her Christmas presents. Just one more purchase to make – an overpriced and nicely presented box of soap for Aunt Hilda. She headed down Great Minster Street toward a shop that stocked Crabtree & Evelyn, when she spotted George Casey hurrying toward her on the opposite pavement. She tried to turn her face away, but he'd already seen her.

"Ms Morgan! I *thought* it was you." The diocesan press officer fussed toward her, his pink mouth full of news. "Something's come up – that fellow who ran the youth choir, Postlethwaite? He was coming to you with the choir in a few days, I believe?"

"Was?" She felt a shot of adrenalin peak through her heart.

"He's gone. Resigned this morning." Casey's eyes goggled with anticipation and excitement. "I've just been with the dean. Such a crisis! We've been composing the press release. It's embargoed until noon, but I thought you should know, what with your church being on the tour. Need to know and all that."

"What's happened?"

"Well, I'll tell you, it was a shock. Not that, as I told you from the first, I didn't have my doubts about the diocese hosting a choir of urban youth – especially at this time of year – but I didn't dream of anything like this."

"Like what?" Faith prompted irritably. Why wouldn't he just spit it out?

"Drugs!" Casey announced dramatically, then lowered his voice. "The fellow had a criminal record. And him running a choir with vulnerable young people! It could hardly be worse." His voice lifted suddenly, eyes sparkling. "But I think we've got it under control. Swift action just as soon as the deception was revealed; culprit dismissed within hours, et cetera."

"Deception? What sort of deception? That Mr Postlethwaite had once used drugs himself?" Jim Postlethwaite had been a heroin user, she knew that already; but he had recovered and straightened his life out. It was foolish and wrong of Jim to have lied on his application form, but his reasons were perhaps understandable. Many people were loath to give a reformed addict a second chance.

"Oh, it's much worse than that." George Casey's little mouth pursed up, savouring the revelation. "Prison sentence," he confided.

"I don't believe you!" Faith was horrified. A custodial sentence. Jim had been in prison for a drugs offence? *I am a sinner; I am no saint.*

"So the dean called Postlethwaite in first thing this morning and he didn't deny it," Casey exclaimed. "Just tendered his resignation. An hour later he had cleared out of his lodgings. I checked with the cleaning staff." He seemed pleased with his own diligence. "I knew that choir would bring the cathedral grief, but the dean *would* have his social engagement…"

"His lodgings are cleared out?" Faith repeated, stunned. "Already? Where has Jim gone?"

Casey responded with an indifferent shrug. "No idea. Good riddance, I say. The dean's secretary and I are contacting the members of the choir to notify them of the disbandment. The tour will have to be cancelled." Belatedly, he registered her expression. "The dean was as shocked as you," he sympathized. "He thought it all a mistake at first – but then the dean is a very holy man." Casey seemed to think the quality akin to adorable foolishness.

"When did all this happen?"

"This morning," Casey answered, as if she were stupid.

"No. I meant, when was this offence supposed to have taken place?"

"I have no idea." The press officer didn't seem to think it mattered. But Jim might have been in his teens at the time – just a foolish, misguided boy.

"How come the dean found out about this just now? Mr Postlethwaite has been working in the diocese since the summer."

And then she knew the answer before he gave it.

"The dean got a call from the inspector heading up the enquiry into the murder of Lucas Bagshaw. It must have come to light while they were investigating his association with the youth choir." George Casey adjusted his long woollen scarf.

"Must dash. Too much to do – but I thought you should know as soon as possible about the choir tour being cancelled. Very difficult at this short notice, I am afraid. But you can see – *force majeure!*" The press officer took his leave with a flourish and hurried off on his busy path of destruction.

Faith stared after him.

"Ben," she muttered. "What have you done?"

CHAPTER

17

Faith abandoned her list. She would have to pick up the gift soap another time. She fought her way through the crowds of Christmas shoppers, her overstuffed bags catching and bumping all the way to the car park. She stowed the bags in the boot of her car, her head full of what had happened to Jim Postlethwaite. Now she was ashamed of her own suspicions. She, personally, knew nothing but good of him. Those scars on his arms had healed long ago. His choir seemed to trust him. And what about his kindness to her – going to the trouble of finding that donkey contact when she was a complete stranger? Even the landlord at the Lion's Heart had said that Jim hadn't encouraged Sebastian Keep. And as for the confrontation she witnessed outside his lodgings, Keepie was just the kind to blackmail Jim if he had discovered his secret. Maybe one day Keepie had seen the scars on Jim's arms and drawn his conclusions, as she had. Perhaps he'd found out about the time Jim served behind bars.

Her anger focused on Ben. The bottom line was that Ben Shorter had hounded a man out of his job and lodgings, not because he had discovered a lie in his job application but because of his ridiculous bulldog attitude toward *her*. Ben just couldn't let go of a woman he had once thought of as his. Fuming, she got into the car and turned the ignition. She had a couple of hours before her appointment with Ms Whittle and Banjo the donkey. She was going to have it out with him.

She found a parking spot not too far from the public entrance to the central police station. After several tries she squeezed in between a Range Rover and a Volvo. Her first flush of anger cooled in the concentration of parking. Was she being self-indulgent? It would relieve her feelings if she could just give Ben a piece of her mind, but was this about her guilt, not his?

No. There was no sound reason for Ben to make that call to the dean. Not right now. An active murder investigation gave the DI in charge many more important things to do with his time.

She got out of her car and was surprised to see Vernon Granger. He stood between her and the police station. In contrast to her last sight of him, with his mother at the Civic Service, he had dressed today in his teenage persona, wearing a baggy jumper over jeans and engineer boots, his curly hair untamed. He was arguing with a man a little shorter than himself; a middle-aged man dressed in a fashion-conscious, double-breasted pale fawn wool jacket embellished with exaggerated lapels studded with overlarge buttons. The man's hands, gloved in smooth brown leather, were on Vernon's chest. At first glance, Faith couldn't judge whether he was assaulting the youth or pleading with him.

"Your mother wants you home," she heard the man say.

"I am not coming with you! Anna's here."

"They won't let you stay with her. She's being interviewed."

"Then I'll wait until they're done."

"Come on, son, think of your mother – she's worried about you."

Son? Mavis's husband – Neil, wasn't it?

"I'm *thinking* of Anna."

"She's not your family; we are."

"Oh yeah? How do you figure that?" The boy gave a bitter laugh. "Anna and Luke, they're the nearest thing I ever had to family."

"You're upset. Don't say that. We're your parents; we love you."

"Is that what you call it? Just leave me alone." Vernon wrenched open the glass door and disappeared into the police station.

Neil Granger turned. Faith saw him face to face. He had that well-groomed sheen of a prosperous CEO. *He doesn't know how to deal with this situation*, Faith thought, *and he's used to being in charge.* She tried nodding politely to him and walking on past, but he stopped her.

"You're the new vicar at St James's, aren't you? My wife says you've been mixed up in this from the start."

His aggressive tone took her by surprise. "I don't know that I would put it like that. I happened to be visiting the Markhams' farm on the day the body of Lucas Bagshaw was found. Your wife came by with her dogs and that's how we met." Maybe he would find the detail calming.

Neil Granger stared at her for a moment, grinding his back teeth, as if he wanted to draw something out of her by sheer attention. Abruptly he turned on his heel and marched away. *Interesting family dynamic*, Faith thought. She watched Neil Granger get into the Range Rover across the street. He swept out into the road, missing her Yaris by inches.

* * *

Faith couldn't see Vernon inside.

"The DI's interviewing, ma'am," the sergeant on the desk confirmed as he put the phone down, "but Sergeant Gray says you can go up. Room 315 on the third floor."

Room 315 proved to be the case HQ. Peter was the only one in. The rest of the team must be out on assignment. Whiteboards stood against the wall covered with timelines and notes in different coloured markers and, on a large table, pieces of evidence were spread out in plastic bags. Peter was typing on a laptop. He looked up.

"Hi, Faith. Come to see the boss?"

"I was hoping to. I hear he's interviewing Anna Hope. What's brought that on?"

"We finally got Lucas's phone records in. There's a text unaccounted for."

"From Anna to Lucas?"

Peter nodded and shifted his weight. Faith recognized the signs. Ben must have warned him against telling her too much. She had caused Peter enough trouble over the Thursday night dinner. She stifled her curiosity.

"OK if I wait?"

"Of course." Peter glanced down at the laptop. "You don't mind if I get on?"

"Not at all! Don't let me disturb you."

The room was peaceful with just the soft, plastic sound of Peter tapping away at his laptop. Faith examined the murder boards for clues as to why Anna had been called in. A piece of paper Blu-Tacked to one side carried a forensic sketch of the wounds on Lucas's head and the likely shape of the weapon that made them – a shaft about an inch in diameter. Alongside, a forensic report was circled in yellow highlighter pen at a paragraph that drew attention to traces of cellulose embedded in the second, deeper wound on the crown of Lucas's head.

She moved on to the large table, where a collection of debris gathered from the fingertip search of the attack site was laid out in evidence bags. It looked like a lot of old rubbish – cigarette butts, an old mealworm pot, a tangle of fishing line and the rubber heel of a shoe, each with meticulous details attached, including a sketch map marking where the item had been found. It was the litter of a dozen lives that had happened to pass over that spot for half a day, an hour, or just a moment; walkers and fishermen and tourists and lovers – and a murderer, perhaps. It seemed such an impossible task to sift through all that debris and strike lucky, identifying the one elusive piece that fitted into the puzzle they were trying to solve.

There was a piece of twisted and curled plate metal, maybe an inch and a half wide and four long, with two holes from what must have been screws. The label said it had been found under the hedgerow along the road leading away from the bridge.

"Have you seen this?" she asked Peter.

He came over to join her. "Yes, we're not completely sure what it is, to be honest. No prints."

He opened the bag and tipped it into Faith's hand. The metal was light, one side completely smooth, the other marked with letters and numbers, but it was badly scratched at one side and hard to make out the full inscription. The tagger had labelled it "metal plaque, partial engraving: 'WRS, 987'".

"We resorted to Google," said Peter. "No matches that make any sense."

As Faith put it back and zipped the bag, her eye snagged on another group of bags, set out at the far side of the table. Not litter, but Lucas's personal effects. The glint of silver from a key ring caught her attention. The bunch of keys was labelled "Lucas Bagshaw/house & misc". There was a silver shape attached to them, like a fob. She admired the platinum disc appliquéd with a sinuous shape in contrasting silver.

"This is Jensen," she said.

"Meaning?" Ben was standing in the doorway, and his voice made her start.

"Georg Jensen, the Danish designer. Very sought-after."

"And expensive?"

"Yes." Faith shifted the keys around within the bag to have a better look. "This isn't a key fob. It's a pendant – a woman's pendant."

"Maybe it belonged to his mother."

"Could be – it's an expensive piece of jewellery for a cleaner."

"Another gift from the absent father?" Ben suggested.

"How did it go?" asked Peter.

Ben shrugged. "Inconclusive. The transcripts are being typed up now. You can read them later."

The windows of the investigation room overlooked the public entrance. Down below, Faith saw little Anna Hope leaving under the shelter of Vernon Granger's lanky frame. Ben was contemplating her cynically from afar. Suddenly she remembered the reason she had come here.

"I need to talk to you – in private," she said.

"So?" Ben waved her out with an arm. "We'll be in Exam 2," he said to Peter.

He opened the door for her to pass into the bare little interview room with the hose-down floor and utilitarian chairs, and table with the recording machines. He drew out one of the chairs for her and sat down beside her. She noticed that at least he had the decency not to put her on the opposite side of the table like some suspect.

"Shoot," he said.

"I have just been told that Jim Postlethwaite resigned his job and left his lodgings this morning." She was pleased with her self-composure. Her voice came out measured and controlled. "Why did you phone the dean to tell him about his drug use? There's no evidence he's been using recently."

Ben's eyes narrowed. It had been some time since she had seen him look so hawkish. "How long have you known?"

"That Jim once used heroin?" She felt embarrassed, as if she had deliberately concealed something pertinent from an investigating officer; well, she had. But she hadn't judged it pertinent… "Only a couple of days."

"He told you?"

"No. I saw the scars on his arms.'

"And what were you two doing?"

"Don't be childish! It was nothing like that."

Ben shifted. He reached out an arm. She felt the pressure on the back of her chair. He leaned toward her, crowding her space.

"It wasn't just drug use. Did your pet choirmaster tell you he did time with Sebastian Keep at Her Majesty's pleasure?"

She tensed. She knew something was coming; something she wouldn't like. "Of course he didn't."

The control in Ben's voice hinted at the force of held-back emotion. "Do you know what he was in for?" His expression held no triumph at all, only sympathy. "Eight years ago, James Richard Postlethwaite, Cambridge graduate and middle-class waster, was shooting heroin, but he was married with a kid. A little girl. And like many an addict, Jim was too busy getting high to look after her. His two-year-old got into his stash. She nearly died. His wife left him and took the kid, and he served eighteen months for possession and child endangerment."

She pressed herself back in her chair to get away from him. She wanted to close her eyes, shut him and what he was saying out. But she kept her eyes open. Jim had risked the life of his child for his addiction. The worst crime in Ben Shorter's book. Of course, neither Ben nor she had ever experienced the grip of an addiction. They didn't really know what it might be like, but in Ben's world that wasn't the point. A proper man protected his family. She swallowed.

"That's terrible. But it was eight years ago. Jim Postlethwaite served his time. He's worked hard to get his life back together. He was doing a good job with those kids in the choir."

Ben stood up. The energy of his movement and the chair legs scraping against the floor made her start. He strode away from her and leaned against the wall, his arms folded around his chest as if to contain his irritation.

"You know the statistics. Once a user…"

"And you don't believe in redemption," she commented sadly, more to herself than him. He answered her anyway.

"No. I live in the real world." And there they were, on opposite sides of the room again.

"You didn't have to make that call," she said.

He stared at her, unflinching. "You were the one who brought in Sebastian Keep. That's how it came up. Mr Postlethwaite and he were cellmates. So you could say it was your fault. Consequences, Fay. You can't control them."

Faith blinked. He wasn't just talking about this situation, right now.

"Unlike you, I don't buy the redeemed sinner act," Ben went on. "Your Jim endangered his family and betrayed them for his drug of choice. Being an addict is part of a person's character; you don't change that. You say eight years is enough to change a man? He owes a lot more than that."

She stood up to face him on more equal terms.

"Your job is to be an investigator, not an avenger, Ben. Tell me this. Are you seriously considering Jim Postlethwaite as Lucas Bagshaw's murderer?"

"He says he was running a music workshop at the cathedral from 11 a.m. to 5 p.m. that Saturday, followed by a rehearsal in the chapter house," Ben said glibly.

"So there will be witnesses to that."

"A number of God-fearing types say they saw him there, but then they broke up into groups for some sessions. We haven't finished tracking him through those."

"In other words, you know he didn't do it, but you're still going to hound him?"

"I'm an investigator. I investigate."

They glared at one another across that hideous, lightless little room.

"Shame on you, Ben Shorter," she said.

Banjo had silky soft ears covered with the most delightful silver-grey fur, blending to charcoal tips.

"He likes his ears rubbed. He's a lovely boy." Ms Whittle, Banjo's fond owner, was maybe in her early seventies, all sinew and leathery skin contrasting with clear, innocent eyes. Her hair was cut in a wispy grey bob, held back from her face with grips like a child from the 1930s. Somehow, from their first phone call and introduction, Faith had imagined the animal sanctuary as a place of ramshackle charm barely held together by an eccentric enthusiast. The reality was much more shipshape. Ms Whittle's various charges were housed in a large nineteenth-century barn that had been fitted with pens and stables. Ms Whittle must have a substantial private income. She evidently expended a good deal of it on the care of her animals.

Ms Whittle's reddened hands with their prominent knuckles ran over the donkey's flank. Banjo sighed and gave Faith a look of pure lordly contentment.

"So can Banjo take part in our pageant?" she asked.

"He won't want to do it alone," Joy Whittle said anxiously. "He'll want a friendly face beside him. I'll need to be there too."

"But of course!"

Ms Whittle gave Banjo's neck a couple of slaps. "He'll enjoy it, won't you? He's a very smart boy. Banjo likes an outing."

"That's wonderful."

They discussed fees (surprisingly moderate) and transport and timings. In half an hour, Faith's donkey doom had been vanquished. She had the final principal of the pageant in place – or at least, she would have had, if Mary hadn't decided to drop out in favour of a trip to Wales to celebrate her engagement. Faith pushed that problem aside for the time being, permitting herself to enjoy her brief moment of triumph. Ms Whittle offered a mug of tea to celebrate and went off to the tack room to brew it.

There remained the disaster with the choir to be dealt with. Small mercy that Pat hadn't answered her phone when Faith rang to deliver the bad news about Jim Postlethwaite. She avoided details of course, only mentioning unforeseen circumstances. With Fred she'd been a little more candid. He had said he would discuss with Pat the possibility of recorded music. Faith could just imagine the sour turn of her face at *that* suggestion.

Faith heard a female voice murmuring from a pen down the far end of the barn. She couldn't make out the words. She wandered over to investigate. She leaned on the chest-high wooden partition. Looking down, she saw familiar golden curls. There, crouched in the straw, was Anna Hope, crooning as she scratched the back of a pygmy pot-bellied pig.

"Anna! What on earth are you doing here?" You had to give credit to the facial control of the average teenager. Anna's expression didn't flicker at the sight of Faith.

"I'm always here Monday afternoons."

"I thought you worked at the florist shop?"

"Monday's my day off. Ms Whittle lets me volunteer here. I love the animals. This is Brandy. Sherry's asleep over there." She indicated a small dark mound curled up in a corner of straw. "So, have you got Banjo sorted out?"

"It was you who gave Jim the contact?" Anna tossed her curls in acknowledgment. "Thank you so much. Banjo is going to be perfect for our pageant."

"He's a smart boy," Anna echoed her mentor. "He'll enjoy it."

"I was at the police station earlier. Are you OK?"

Anna shrugged. Brandy jerked up her head and trotted off on tiny trotters to the water trough. She dipped her pink snout and began to guzzle up water noisily. Anna stood and leaned on the partition a little further down, facing away from Faith.

"The police say I sent a text to Lucas that Saturday, asking him to meet me at that bridge."

"The one down the path from the Lion's Heart car park?"

Anna nodded. "But I didn't. I told them, I was shopping with a couple of friends; we were in town until seven. They back me up – and anyway, I didn't have my phone."

"What happened to it?"

"I lost it – I couldn't find it when I finished work Saturday lunchtime."

"So you've had to replace your phone, then?"

Anna shook her head. "I got it back. The cleaner, she found it in the cuttings on the floor that Monday. It's really busy at the shop at weekends. I must have knocked it off the counter – it's only small."

A lost phone – that sounded a bit convenient.

"So you got it back when you went to work on Monday, the day they found Lucas?" Faith was distracted by a passing wisp of thought, the hint of a broken connection. She couldn't pin it down, but a more serious thought overwhelmed it.

"No. Like I said. I don't work at the shop on Mondays – that's why I'm here," Anna insisted. "V's mum gave it to him, and he brought it back and gave it to me at choir that evening."

Who had the most obvious opportunity to lift Anna's phone and return it without raising suspicion? The very person who gave it back to her: Vernon, the solicitous boyfriend. And Vernon's alibi rested solely on the testimony of his mother. Faith could readily believe that Mavis would lie for her son.

Was she back to her old speculation, that Lucas's death was a consequence of a territorial dispute over Anna? She thought of Vernon's emotion when she overheard him and his father outside the police station: *"Anna and Luke, they're the nearest thing I ever had to family."*

Unless Vernon had the lying skills of a psychopath, it just didn't fit. Could there have been something else at stake between Vernon and Lucas?

"Did Lucas ever talk to you about his father?" she asked. Anna dipped her head, her curls falling forward in a curtain over her face.

"He didn't know who he was."

"Are you sure about that?" Anna shrugged. She spun around and leaned on the partition facing out of the barn.

"He had a secret – well, sort of. More like a project. He didn't talk about it much. He was very loyal, Lucas." Faith heard Adam's voice, talking to her in her kitchen, in her head: *"Sometime during the summer... He started asking more questions."*

"Do you think Vernon knew what it was?" Anna shrugged again.

"Could be. They were close, almost like brothers." She slipped Faith an odd side-glance. Faith couldn't quite interpret it. But there it was – that family thing again.

"I meant to ask you – just this last Saturday, did you sell a bouquet at the florist shop – a combination of narcissus, pussy willow, heather sprigs, twisted willow..."

"Maybe, yeah. It was a busy day, like I said."

"Do you remember who you sold it to?"

"Nope, why would I?"

Anna's posture changed. Her head lifted. Faith thought she detected an anticipatory stillness. Anna wasn't looking at her.

"Hi," she greeted someone. A soft voice spoke from behind Faith.

"Vicar – what are you doing here?" Faith swung round. Vernon Granger was standing in the barn. Anna skipped around the partition and went over to him. He put his arm around her protectively. She smiled up at him.

"I came to arrange for Banjo the donkey to take part in our church pageant," Faith answered Vernon. "I hadn't realized that Anna worked here."

"Yeah. Loves it; don't you?" His wrapping arm squeezed the Dot gently, his expression loving. If a human could purr, Anna did then.

Faith was nonplussed. Neither of them remotely looked as if they might capable of murder.

CHAPTER

18

Sometimes she wondered how she would ever make it through that week. There seemed to be fewer and fewer hours of blessed sleep in her bed at night as she struggled on from task to task: from writing service sheets to sermons, to rehearsal, to clearing up, to service, to meeting, to carol singing, to cleaning up and back again. The keys she cut for Ruth turned out to be a blessing. She and her sister hadn't actually set eyes on one another since Faith's Monday morning visit to the council offices, but a tree appeared in her front room at the vicarage.

At five-thirty in the morning of Friday, 23 December, Faith stood in her dressing gown sipping her mug of tea, admiring it. The Christmas presents she finished wrapping at one o'clock that morning adorned the foot. The tree had lights and baubles and smelled like Christmas. The Beast, who had been taking an early breakfast in the kitchen, padded through to investigate. He reared up on his back paws, bracing himself on paper-wrapped parcels that crinkled beneath his feet, and sniffed the canopy.

"Yes. I like the smell of pine needles too," she said.

The Beast took a quick bat at a low-hanging bauble. She went over and re-hung it out of his reach. Christmas was nearly here.

The supermarket opened early to accommodate the rush of frantic shoppers. Faith was at the doors at 7:30 a.m, realizing that she had forgotten several items in the list she'd sent to her sister, including both chipolatas and turkey foil. She hurried up and down the aisles, claiming the last rather sad-looking packet of Christmas crackers as well.

Her mind followed another path entirely – the pageant tomorrow. Everything was in place except for Mary, and Joseph's robe. She hoped Sue might have the solution to the missing robe dilemma, and as for Mary – worse come to worst, one of them would have to fill in. They would be meeting up at the Salvation Army centre in town later to help with the Christmas lunch – they could figure it out then.

Faith almost crashed into an oncoming cart.

"Hi, Faith, you're out early." Oliver Markham beamed down at her. His wife, Julie, was beside him. They looked domesticated and relaxed. She felt her face light up in a responding smile.

"It's the only way to survive this time of year."

"I hear you," Julie returned with feeling. "I love the actual celebrations, but isn't it hard work until you get there?"

"So, how are you both?"

Julie threaded her arm through her husband's. "We're expecting again," she announced. She looked happy.

"How wonderful! Many congratulations," Faith exclaimed. As she spoke, the obvious smacked her between the eyes. Why hadn't she thought of this before? "Julie, I don't suppose, by any chance… You know Oliver is playing Joseph in our pageant tomorrow? You couldn't bear to dress up as

Mary, could you? You don't have any dialogue, and we have a charming donkey. He's called Banjo…"

"But why are we setting off so early?" Pat complained, as she settled herself into the passenger seat, her tartan shopping bag containing her apron and rubber gloves on her knees. "Surely we are not expected at the Salvation Army until eleven?"

"I have a stop to make on the way," Faith replied.

Fifteen minutes later she drew up in the drive at 5, Benson's Close, The Hollies. Pat peered out at the anonymous semi, a frown on her face.

"What are we doing here?"

"Calling on a friend. Won't you come in? I'll introduce you. It may take a moment, and it is going to be cold sitting in the car out here." Grumbling under her breath, Pat hauled herself out of the car and inched her way carefully up the icy drive.

Faith mentally crossed her fingers as she rang the doorbell. To her relief, Adam answered the door both dressed and quite sober. They had only ever met when he was drunk or suffering from a hangover. She wondered briefly if he would remember who she was. She needn't have worried.

"Faith!" He actually seemed pleased to see her.

"I've come for a visit," she said with a smile. "This is my friend, Pat Montesque. We were passing and I thought we'd drop by to see how you are doing." Out of the corner of her eye, she saw Pat stiffen with suspicion. "Pat, this is Adam Bagshaw. I don't think you have ever met?" For a moment she wondered if Pat was going to resist. So she didn't look back as Adam invited them in. Pat followed. Faith heard her mutter something about "Sorry for your loss."

The carpet had been vacuumed since Faith's last visit.

The cardboard box of debris had been cleared away. Pat was looking about the room. She spotted the whatnot in the corner with Trisha's treasures and photographs on it.

"I remember that Neapolitan cart," she said. She cast a glance at Faith. "That belonged to Marjorie Davis."

A pleased smile blossomed on Adam's face.

"I remember Marjorie – what a lovely lady! Is she well? Trish was so fond of her. She gave Trish that as a memento, a thank-you for nursing Mrs Davis after her accident. All these are gifts from Trisha's ladies." He waved a hand at the little silver clock, the fairyland bowl and the rest. Pat stared belligerently at him a moment.

"Marjorie is very well, thank you," she said at last. "She mentioned you the other day," she added. Her attention shifted to the ironing board set up by the kitchen counter.

"You iron your own shirts?" Pat demanded.

"Army training," he explained.

"You're an army man?"

"I was. Served in the Signal Corps." Pat gave a brisk little nod. She composed her limbs neatly and sat down in the leather chair, watching the pair of them attentively.

"So how are you doing? Are you eating all right?" Faith enquired. Adam nodded.

"I've been to the Citizens' Advice, like you suggested," he answered. "They've given me an adviser. He says he can help me apply for benefits; I might even be able to stay on here."

"That is good news."

"Aren't you looking for a job, young man?" interjected Pat severely.

"Yes, ma'am," Adam responded. Pat contemplated him with pursed lips for a moment.

"You can call me Pat."

Faith smiled privately to herself. Maybe this could work.

"We're on our way to help at the Salvation Army Christmas lunch," she explained.

"Why don't you come along with us?" Pat piped up unexpectedly. "Come and help someone more unfortunate than yourself. It'll do you a lot more good than sitting alone brooding."

What had she done? Faith thought, amused. Adam Bagshaw didn't stand a chance.

The Salvation Army centre was little more than a large shed with a catering kitchen, an office, and bathrooms attached. Sue had arrived before them. Together with the other volunteers, they set up folding tables covered with red paper tablecloths, laid cutlery and Christmas crackers, prepared food and decorations. The atmosphere was convivial. Adam proved a dab hand at peeling potatoes. Faith watched Pat in her apron, supervising as she chopped carrots beside him.

"Hello, Faith!" Sue stood nearby with her arms full of bunting. She jerked her head at a ladder alongside her. "Do you mind? You know I have no head for heights."

Sue held the ladder as they moved around the room, Faith clambering up to fix the decorations as they went.

"I meant to tell you, Faith, the Joseph costume isn't in the trunk with the others."

"You know where it is?" Faith asked eagerly, glancing down from the top of her ladder.

"My Em borrowed it for her school's production of *Jesus Christ Superstar*, earlier in the term. She's bringing it back this afternoon. We'll have it ready for tomorrow, don't worry."
Faith executed a victory wiggle on the top rung.

As they completed the decorations and returned the

ladder to the store room, Faith examined Sue's face. She didn't seem to be her usual bubbly self.

"What's up?" she asked. Sue glanced over to the main entrance where a straggle of early birds had just come through the door.

"Can we have a word later?"

After that, it got so busy, the lunch passed in a blur. Faith helped at the serving table with Adam and Pat. She saw the MP arrive with reporters and a group of local business people. The Right Honourable Philippa Fawcett had done well. She had brought some of Winchester's most successful and wealthiest entrepreneurs – Neil and Mavis Granger among them. Camera bulbs flashed as Mrs Fawcett made a short speech and took interviews. The VIPs spent fifteen minutes perched next to suitably deserving-looking lunchers having their photographs taken. The guests were remarkably gracious about it. Another flurry of photographs followed when the visitors handed over a cheque to Gerry, the centre manager.

As the group of VIPs prepared to leave, their good deed accomplished, Faith noticed that Adam, standing beside her in the line, had stopped serving. He stood quite still, staring across the room with an odd, distant intensity. She followed his eyeline to the dispersing group of entrepreneurs. The red of the paper tablecloths made her think of the red amaryllis at the heart of that bouquet on the bridge. Lucas's mystery father must be wealthy, and Ben and she had agreed he was probably local… She glanced back to Adam, piling roast potatoes on to plates again, his head down.

Faith finally caught up with Sue over the washing-up. The Salvation Army building had two sinks, and they were assigned to the one in the cramped janitor's closet. It was quite private there.

"So what's up?" Faith asked, plunging her rubber-gloved hands into the near-boiling water. Sue sighed. She looked really worried.

"Did you see the Grangers?" she asked.

"Yes. Good photo-op, huh?"

Sue took a deep breath. "It's about the murder. Well – I am hoping it isn't, but it might be." Sue's dear, kind face was sad. Faith had never seen her this troubled before.

"Come on. Spit it out."

"It's about Vernon Granger. His mother made a point of telling – she made it quite clear – that he was at home with her that awful Saturday when Lucas died?"

Faith recalled Mavis saying the same thing to her. "Yes?"

"It just didn't register with me; I didn't know the details but… Em reminded me – she's talked quite a lot about Lucas. He didn't often make it into school, but they got on well when he showed up. She liked him. Anyway, Em and I, we went into town shopping that Saturday afternoon and we saw him."

"Lucas?"

"No," said Sue softly, "Vernon Granger. On a bus, coming out of Winchester."

"What time?"

"Five o'clock – or maybe just before." So Vernon didn't have an alibi for the murder after all.

"You're sure?"

"Yes. We've known Vernon for years."

"Have you told the police?"

"I spoke to Peter before I came here. He's asked me to come in to the station to make a statement this afternoon. Will you come with me?" Sue pleaded.

"Of course I will."

* * *

So Faith found herself back in Room 315. Peter and Sue had gone off with a WPC to an exam room to take down Sue's statement. Ben was shuffling paper at a desk in his shirtsleeves. He barely looked up at Faith. She recognized the focus from when they were together. Little else mattered to him at the moment.

"What will this mean?" she asked him. He kept writing.

"We've found CCTV to support what your friend says – it wasn't hard after we knew where to look. I've sent a team to pick the kid up."

Faith recalled her last memory of Vernon with his arm around Anna, their affection for one another so plain on their faces. "Do you really think this is right?" Ben ran a hand through his thick dark hair. She caught a mere flash of his intense blue eyes.

"Gotta go where the evidence takes you."

"His parents have just been at the Salvation Army lunch. They only called in for a short time. They're probably back home by now."

He grunted. She tried again. "Did you ever track down the travelling barman?"

"We did."

"And…?" Ben tilted his head fractionally. His eyes remained focused on his papers, checking through them at speed. She persisted. "You might not have known about him if I hadn't put you on his track," she wheedled. At last, he looked up at her. She'd expected hostility after the way they'd parted last time, but to her surprise his expression was wary, if anything.

"We found him; contacted him via his Facebook page. He had moved on to Australia. The Brisbane police got him on Skype for us. He says he saw Lucas at the Lion's Heart that Saturday afternoon around 4 p.m."

"Did they speak?"

"Briefly. According to him, Lucas was looking for someone. He had the impression – but only the impression; he had nothing concrete to back it up – that Lucas was meeting a woman, a girlfriend."

"And you think that was Anna? Because of the text from her phone?"

Ben gave her his *I'm-not-going-to-answer-that* look. She examined his familiar face; his stubborn chin with its five o'clock shadow, his imposing nose and bright eyes; eyes that were narrowing fractionally…

She blinked. "I can't help thinking that the burglary at the Granger house this June figures in all this somehow," she said hurriedly.

"Really?" Ben stretched across his desk and selected a file. He flipped it open, tilting it so she could see. It was the Granger burglary file. She moved in to perch on the edge of his desk.

"So what have we got?" she asked.

Ben flicked up the edge of a page to remind himself, but he seemed to have the pertinent details in his head.

"According to her statement, Mrs Mavis Granger returned home from a walk with her dogs to find the French windows leading to her husband's study broken. The study sticks out in a sort of extension," he explained. "It's a private corner in relation to the rest of the house, not overlooked."

"Mavis Granger called it a crime of opportunity – she said the thief was an amateur who took his chance. Did he get into the rest of the house?"

"No. Just the study. The inner door was locked. Superficial damage, apart from the desk drawers being forced." Ben drew out a photograph of the scene. Papers were scattered on the floor. "Whoever it was didn't take a high-end laptop computer. And there were a couple of expensive pictures on the walls – also untouched."

"Fingerprints?" asked Faith.

"Only household, but most people know to wear gloves."

"Surely not if it was a spur-of-the-moment thing."

Ben shrugged, and she saw a flicker of irritation.

"So, what was taken?" she asked. He handed her a list. Much as Mavis had said; small portable items in silver and gold; a gold Rolex watch; a few heirlooms.

"Did anything ever turn up?"

"No. Apparently Robbery checked the usual pawn and resale sites – but you know that's all just a shot in the dark."

Faith leaned over and picked up the sheaf of crime scene photos. She shuffled through them and stopped at a wider shot of the study showing the floor running up to the French doors.

"What's that on the floor – a silver cup?" She looked more closely. "It's been crushed." She checked the list. There was notation at the bottom. "But it wasn't before. Looks like the thief stamped on it. Why do that?"

"Maybe he got scared and did it in the hurry to get out."

"Makes you wonder."

Ben bent over the pictures on her lap. She could smell the shampoo he used.

"'Chased silver christening cup,'" she read to distract herself, "'circa 1765; engraved to Neil Edward Granger.' The insurance value was £1,000. Looks expensive too – it's the first thing I'd take."

"Good point," said Ben.

From her perch she was looking down on him. He leaned back in his chair, a smile on his face. She looked down at the papers.

"Where was Neil Granger at this time?"

"On a business trip in Norway and Denmark."

"Confirmed?"

"Confirmed."

"Any witnesses?"

"The neighbours are too far away to hear anything. The domestic help had left for the day. The son, Vernon, was up in his room at the opposite end of the house and didn't hear anything."

"Is that feasible?"

Ben nodded. "You should see the house. Mansions of the rich and famous… What?"

Faith stared at the picture in her hands. It showed Neil Granger's trashed desk and behind it, a section of bookshelf. On the shelf, just to the left of where Neil Granger's head would be, were he sitting at that desk, sat a small white sculpture maybe six inches high, a stylized mother and child in flowing lines.

"I've seen this piece before."

"Where?"

She looked into his bright, intelligent eyes, frowning as she tried to make sense of it.

"On the Bagshaw's mantelpiece in The Hollies." She heard a noise in the corridor behind her and looked over her shoulder. Peter had returned with a subdued Sue in tow.

"All done?" asked Faith.

"Yes." Sue wasn't her usual self at all. "Do you mind if we go, Faith?"

"No problem." She got up from her corner of Ben's desk. "I have to get back too. I am due at church."

"I know I am a coward," Sue confessed, as they walked out of the station together. "But I don't want to be here to see them bring Vernon in. He's only a boy. I've known him most of his life."

* * *

Oliver Markham and Fred Partridge had put up the church Christmas tree, lacing it with lights. When they switched it on, it glowed and sparkled to magnificent effect. To one side, Pat and Faith spread straw and set out the great nativity figures around the manger, stringing the star on its web of fine wires.

The others had gone to get their dinner: only Pat and Faith remained in the quiet dimness of the waiting church. Outside in the dusk, a few flakes of snow drifted through the orange glow of the street lamps. Inside the sanctuary breathed contentment and peace.

Pat laid the baby Jesus gently in his crib.

"To be honest, Christmas is not my favourite festival," she admitted.

Faith looked up from tweaking a Wise Man's stiffened robes. "No?"

"Well, it's for families, isn't it? And since Gordon passed…" Pat's deft hands tidied the straw around the baby Jesus. Faith took a risk.

"Pat – what happened with your sister?"

The churchwarden closed her eyes. She swallowed and turned to lift Mary carefully out of the tissue paper packing in her box. "It happened a long time ago. She was… we were very different from one another. We were never close." Pat met Faith's eyes, her expression defensive and sad. "You have to remember, it was the fifties. We had different standards then."

"So what happened?"

"Valerie broke up a perfectly good marriage and she ran off with a married man." Pat's words were bitter. "We never spoke again."

"How sad," said Faith, reaching out to touch the older woman's arm. "Did you ever try?"

Pat saw the hand approaching and flinched. She sniffed, plonking Mary firmly into her spot by the crib, adjusting the figure's position with a jerk. "Her so-called husband tried to get in touch when she fell ill." Pat glanced over. Faith saw the tears in her eyes. "Cancer. Just like Gordon. I was nursing him at the time…"

"So you didn't have a chance to respond."

Pat shook her head. She got up and rummaged in the boxes. "I know there's another shepherd in here somewhere."

"Pat. I am so sorry."

"Yes, well… We make our choices and we must live with the consequences."

"And I hear your sister's son has been in touch?"

Pat bent over one of the boxes. Faith couldn't see her face. "He was going to come and see you?"

Pat turned to her, clasping the shepherd tightly. She controlled her expression into complete composure, but her eyes – her eyes were pure sorrow. Faith felt the sadness rise in her own throat.

"He didn't come," Pat said brusquely, "and I can't blame him." She looked down at the figure in her arms. "Here it is." She knelt down and manoeuvred the figure into place.

The display was complete. The holy family, the kings, the shepherds, the ox and the sheep and a few miscellaneous villagers gathered around the crib where the baby Jesus stretched out his arms to welcome them.

"It is so very hard when the chance to say sorry has gone." Faith spoke quietly. "But this Christmas story, it isn't just about families; it's about every kind of love – a thread of hope that joins us all together. Nothing that has happened – even the bad stuff – is lost or wasted. It all comes in handy in the end, because the chances to express love come again and again. The things we got wrong, things we missed – well, we can grieve about it shut away all alone, or we can keep on trying again; we can go out and put it right again by loving. *And death shall have no dominion.* There is always hope, Pat – there's always another chance. There is. I'm certain of it."

It wasn't a sight she would quickly forget: Pat on her knees, framed against the tableau of the manger, looking straight out at her without defences.

The churchwarden sniffed. She rolled over onto all fours to push herself up. Faith leaned down to give her a hand.

"Joseph has a chip on his nose," said Pat. "I should fetch a tea bag and touch him up."

"What are you doing for Christmas lunch, Pat?"

Pat stiffened. "Mr Marchbanks and I will share a turkey breast. He's very partial to white meat and we never miss the Queen."

Faith hesitated a second, wondering how the Beast might feel about Pat's lordly Blue Persian, Mr Marchbanks. They would just have to manage.

"Come to the vicarage instead. Mr Marchbanks is welcome too. He can have his white meat with us."

Pat looked offended and embarrassed all at once. "I had absolutely no intention of fishing for an invitation," she bristled. "Mr Marchbanks is excellent company. We are both very fond of our routines."

"I know you are. But please come and join us. My sister Ruth is cooking and she's very good at it. Christmas lunch isn't Christmas lunch without loved ones to eat it with."

Pat averted her face. She clasped Faith's arm and squeezed it hard. "Thank you," she whispered, adding graciously as she recovered her equilibrium, "Mr Marchbanks and I accept with pleasure. I shall bring some of my brandy mince pies. They are very good. A family recipe from Gordon's side."

Faith saw Pat safely home across the Green. The snow had stopped falling and the stars shone clear. She returned to the church for one last look before turning off the lights and locking up. The pine smell from the tree permeated the air, reviving that childish thrill of expectation. Faith straightened a prayer cushion or two, and stripped one of its cover when she saw an unsightly muddy stain. She wanted everything perfect for the Mass. On her way toward the vestry, she noticed some of the leaflets for the church book group scattered on the flags and felt a momentary pang of guilt as she stooped to gather them up. She really should read January's novel properly – Marilynne Robinson, wasn't it? – because she'd rather bluffed her way through November's meeting.

As she was stacking the leaflets, she realized that others were hopelessly out of date. The bakery fair was long past, and the Little Worthy Rural Show too.

She scooped them up, then paused.

It might be nothing, of course, but...

The Little Worthy Rural Show.

LWRS.

She cast her mind back to the police station. She couldn't remember exactly, but hadn't that metal plaque, bagged up, battered and inconsequential, read "WRS, 987"?

LWRS, 1987.

She felt the thrill run from her neck down her arms to her fingertips. She fumbled for her phone and located Ben's number.

CHAPTER

19

The following evening, they gathered in the dusk at the bottom of the Green, people from Little Worthy and the surrounding villages, with their lanterns and scarves and excited children. Banjo the donkey was the star of the show. How fortunate that Oliver's wife was small-boned. Ms Whittle gave her permission to ride and, after a wobbly start, Julie Markham looked perfect in Mary's blue robes, sitting rather demurely side saddle with her belly padded and her Joseph hovering solicitously at her side. And how fitting, though surely few people knew, that she carried a new life inside her. Banjo paraded, his ears perked up, with Ms Whittle in a shepherd's cloak following behind.

The procession wound its way in stages around the Green toward the ancient Saxon church. Timothy, Clari's barrister husband, did them proud as Wise Man and narrator, his height and presence and dark skin carrying off the purple and blue onion turban regally. The angels and shepherds, for the most part, remembered their cues, and Timothy's sonorous voice held the crowd spellbound.

It was all going so well, and yet Faith remained distracted. How was Ben getting on? Faith had spoken to him for almost an hour the evening before. His tough façade had vanished when he realized the significance of what she told him. The excitement in his voice, the thrill of the chase nearing its conclusion, had been unmistakeable. But had the search warrant come through? Had they found what they were looking for?

She saw Mavis Granger cross from the church hall where Pat presided over assembling the traditional feast to be offered after the carol singing in the churchyard. The procession straggled through the wicket gate, leading the spectators with their bobbing lanterns. The musicians struck up "Hark the Herald Angels Sing". Mavis was watching alone. Faith went over to stand beside her.

"How are you, Mrs Granger?"

Mavis barely looked at her. She was as immaculately turned out as ever. "They haven't arrested him, you know," she said.

"Vernon?" said Faith.

Mavis glared at her. "Of course *Vernon*! It's all a mistake." She braced her back, her head held high.

"I am sorry. This can't be easy for you."

"This is one of the highlights of the Christmas season in this community," Mavis answered, as if she were instructing a stranger. "The WI president always attends."

"Is your husband, Neil, here with you?"

"Yes, he's with Vernon somewhere."

Faith glimpsed Peter walking into the church hall. And there was Ben, moving toward them through the carolling crowd. Faith's mouth felt suddenly dry. Ben stopped in front of them, his eyes on Mavis.

"Mrs Granger – will you come with me, please? We need to have a word." In the flickering light of the lanterns, Mavis Granger's face was a perfectly painted mask. Only her lips moved.

"Vernon?"

Ben led them across the Green to the church hall. Behind them, the congregation, clustered in the churchyard, was singing "Silent Night". In the main hall the folding tables were laid out with food and drink. The helpers were at the carol singing – all except Pat. She stood, like a statue in the far corner, inconspicuous for once. Ben waved them on into the meeting room at the back.

It was an odd rerun of that first time, when Pat had brought Mavis Granger to the pageant planning meeting. Peter Gray sat where Sue had sat, a notebook open before him. Neil Granger sat near the door and, under the escort of two police constables, on the far side of the table, Vernon sat beside Anna, holding her hand. Ben drew out a chair for Mavis. Her eyes were on her son.

"Mrs Granger, there are some things we need to clear up," Ben began. "Now that we are all here, I want to discuss the burglary at the Old Mill this last June."

Mavis blinked. "Our burglary? What about it?" Peter slid a file toward Ben across the table. He opened it and ran his finger down the list. Faith knew him well enough to know he had it off by heart.

"I was interested in the items that were taken," Ben said. "A gold Rolex man's watch."

"My father's," Mavis said. Ben nodded.

"… an eighteenth-century snuff box with German enamelling; a gold half hunter watch with a nineteen carat Albert."

"Vernon's grandfather's watch."

"Family treasures?"

"Yes," said Mavis.

Ben looked at her for a moment. He folded his hands over the file. "Earlier today we executed a search warrant…"

"Where? By what right?" demanded Neil Granger. Ben held up a hand.

"In a moment, sir." He signalled to one of the constables standing against the wall, who brought him an open cardboard box. Ben dipped his hand in, bringing out plastic evidence bags which he laid out on the table one by one. "My team discovered this enamelled snuff box, and this gold Rolex and this… I believe this is what they call a half hunter pocket watch?"

"The items that were stolen!" Neil Granger said. "Where did you find them?"

Ben was watching Vernon. The boy's face had drained of colour, his lips clamped together. He gripped Anna's hand in his.

"Can you tell your father where we found these, Vernon?" Ben asked.

Mavis looked at her son in horror. Vernon said nothing.

"That Bagshaw boy stole these things," Mavis interrupted. "It was nothing to do with Vernon."

Ben picked another bag from the box. This time the plastic was weighted down with a small white statue. Faith happened to be watching Neil. She saw his face close down, almost as if she were watching a piece of film that had been paused.

"Where did you find that?" Mavis demanded, her brow creasing.

"On Trisha Bagshaw's mantelpiece. Her brother kindly let us have it for a while."

Mavis's frown deepened. She moistened her lips. "I told you Lucas was a thief."

Ben's hand entered the dark mouth of the box. He lifted up another bag. They all leaned forward to see it. It contained a second, identical statue. He laid them side by side.

"Mr Granger, I believe this one is yours?"

Neil cleared his throat. "It's from my study." His wife was staring at him.

Ben poked one of the statues with a finger. "They are not entirely identical. This one – from the Bagshaw home – has an inscription chip in the base. An 'N' and a 'T'." His blue eyes met Neil Granger's brown ones, in casual enquiry. "Can you explain this?" Neil lifted his chin a fraction, either in defiance or to avoid looking at his wife.

"It was a gift."

"To…?"

"Trisha Bagshaw, Lucas's mother. She looked after my mother for many years. Mother was always very fond of her."

"So, just a thank-you gift?"

Mavis's eyes burned.

"Yes," said Neil, as he brushed a couple of the bags containing the gold items on the table with one hand. "But these things – they're different. You found them at the Bagshaw house, you said?"

"No. I didn't. The search warrant wasn't for the Bagshaw home; it was for the Old Mill."

"My home!" Mavis gasped. Ben sat forward, his forearm on the table. Faith noted idly that the hand resting on the table was pointing toward Vernon.

"Do you know where they were found?" he asked the boy.

"In my sock drawer," he answered blankly. Mavis's mouth dropped open.

"Vernon – don't say a word," his father pronounced. He brought out his phone. "I'm calling you a solicitor."

"You just keep out of it!" Vernon's words exploded from his mouth. "You started this – let's just see it finished!" His father was buffeted back by the words; he sat silenced and baffled.

"Vernon!" breathed his mother.

"It's not what you think." Anna spoke up, her curls quivering. "It's not Vernon's fault. You don't understand."

"Then why don't you explain it to us?" Ben invited. Vernon sat up. Anna dropped her head. "Let me get you started," Ben continued calmly. "You were in your room the day of the burglary, Vernon? Your mother had gone for a walk with the dogs…"

"No." The denial was uttered quietly, but all the more shocking for it.

"You weren't in your room?"

"Yes. But she didn't take the dogs for a walk." He swallowed as if the words were blocked in his throat. Anna hugged his arm and spoke up for him.

"We – we were there in V's room that day," she said. "The dogs have their kennel in sight of his window. They were there the whole time." She looked to Mavis. "We thought you were out, but you didn't have the dogs with you. They were there, and when you said there was the break-in – the dogs never barked once."

"When did you find these things?" Faith asked Vernon. She'd said the words before she remembered she was only supposed to be observing; she couldn't reel them back now. His eyes were soft and sad as he looked back at her.

"Last Wednesday. I went looking in her wardrobe for a jumper. Anna was cold. I found them at the back." Faith thought of his anger toward his mother when she saw him at the Civic Service that night.

"What did you think?"

"I didn't know what to think." Vernon was holding back the tears, his eyes red. He addressed his mother. "Then I thought maybe you'd done it so you could blame Lucas – but you never did that – not really."

"Why didn't you say anything?" she asked.

He looked straight at her. "I thought we kept secrets in this family, Mother – isn't that what we do?" He hung his head, staring at the tabletop, blinking back the tears.

"Lucas was a thief," Mavis said stubbornly.

"No. He wasn't," Ben contradicted her. "At least, he didn't take these things."

"He took so much more!" Mavis whispered through gritted teeth. She spoke so softly, maybe only Faith, sitting beside her, heard her.

"What did he take from you, Mavis?" she asked gently. Mavis shook her head, and kept the shake going as if she couldn't stop it.

"Miss Hope," Ben's authoritative voice startled them all. "This last Saturday I believe you sold a particular bunch of flowers." He consulted his notes. "Twisted willow, white narcissus, heather sprigs, pussy willow and red amaryllis. Do you remember it?"

Anna's eyes were huge in her small face. She nodded.

"And do you remember who you sold it to?" Anna looked desperately at Vernon. He sighed and squeezed her hand.

"Yes," she said. "Him." She pointed across the table. "Vernon's dad."

Neil Granger lifted both his hands and ran his fingers over his head in a shocked gesture. He wore old-fashioned cufflinks. Sitting at an angle to him, Faith saw them clearly for the first time: globular silver cufflinks with a familiar infinity twist. She looked over at Ben. He caught her recognition and lifted an eyebrow.

"Do you have Lucas's keys there?" she asked. Silently he looked in the box and brought them out, offering them to her in their plastic wrappings. She spread them out in the bag, separating the pendant fob and stretching the plastic around it so it could be seen. She held it out toward Vernon and Anna.

"Do you recognize this?"

"That was Lucas's mother's pendant," Anna told her.

Vernon barely glanced at it. "And the pattern on it is just like Dad's cufflinks," Vernon interjected, his voice hard and sarcastic. "What could that mean, Mother?"

The wisp of thought that had eluded Faith when she had been talking to Anna in the pig pen rooted and blossomed. Anna didn't work at Mavis's florist shop on Mondays – and it was on a Monday that Lucas's body had been discovered. She had been surprised that evening at the meeting in the church hall that Mavis and Pat had known the identity of the victim at the river. She had assumed, she supposed, that somehow news had spread through Jim and the choir, through Anna, to Mavis. But Monday was Anna's day off.

"You faked the burglary. You trod on the silver cup, because it was his," Faith said. "But you couldn't bear to get rid of the heirlooms. They were family items. So you kept them."

Mavis looked only at her.

"I can't. Please," she whispered. "Not in front of Vernon."

Faith looked over at Ben. "Might he and Anna be escorted to the other room?"

* * *

Ben laid out a sheet of A4 paper like a card in a game. He looked over at Faith.

"This is a photocopy of a page from the *Hampshire Chronicle*," he said.

Faith leaned over and saw the date at the top: "September 4th, 1987."

The top half of the photocopy was a photo of an old man with a white beard holding up a certificate and a walking stick. In the grainy photo, the metal collar was indistinct. A young woman stood beside him, fresh-faced and smiling.

When Faith had first seen the page at the library that afternoon, just after closing time, the face had meant nothing to her. The librarian had been about to go home, but Faith knew her in passing from the genealogy club, of which Pat was an avid member. Faith had persuaded her to give ten minutes of her time.

Looking at the photo now, she realized it was the expression that misled her, more than the actual features. But the caption confirmed it. It was a younger, more hopeful version of Mavis Granger. The article featured Henry Jenner, seventy-nine, victor in the prize ram competition for a record-winning sixth time. Faith turned the photograph over. There was a legend on the back written in a neat, well-formed hand – *Henry Jenner with his granddaughter, Mavis*, listed the winners of the Little Worthy Rural Show.

"Mavis," she began conversationally. "Your grandfather was a record-winning sheep breeder."

Mavis looked temporarily pleased, a little imperious even. "We were all very proud of him and that stick." Her expression darkened. "It's gone now. Sadly it broke."

"When – do you remember?"

"I can't think."

"This year?" Faith pressed.

"Yes – earlier this year. Spring sometime."

"What happened to it?"

Mavis shot Ben a puzzled look under her lashes as if to say, why are you allowing this woman to waste our time?

"Please answer the vicar, Mrs Granger," said Ben.

"I threw the bits away," she said, addressing him pointedly.

"In the rubbish bin?" said Faith. Mavis wrinkled up her face as if this was an absurd line of questioning. For a moment, Faith wondered if they'd got this wrong, but then she remembered all the interrogations she'd sat in on, in the olden days. They fell into two categories, with rarely anything in between: the instant confessions, or the stubborn denials, even in the face of the evidence. Sometimes, she'd thought, they even convinced themselves they were innocent.

"I suppose I gave the bits to the dogs to play with," she answered Faith carelessly. "They enjoy chewing sticks." Faith frowned at the photograph.

"But isn't that a metal presentation collar? I can't imagine that would be good for your dogs' teeth."

"I must have thrown it away," Mavis said, giving her a sour look.

"Seems odd," said Faith. "Didn't it have sentimental value?"

"I'm not a sentimental person," said Mavis, biting off each word.

"Do you often walk down by the river?" Ben asked.

Mavis fluttered her eyelashes. "We walk all over. The boys like a lot of exercise. It keeps me slim."

Ben reached into the box again.

"The reason I ask is because we recovered this by the river." He showed her the twisted metal plaque.

Mavis swallowed, her eyes impassive.

The door to the hall opened and Pat stood in the gap. She was carrying a tray full of mugs of tea and a plate of home-made biscuits.

"So sorry to intrude," she said cheerily, "but I thought you could do with some tea." Peter leaped up from the table to take the tray from her, shooting a panicked look at Faith. Ben was lowering and ominously still.

"Thank you, Mrs Montesque," Peter said hurriedly.

"Pat – if you don't mind…" Faith intervened. But Pat wasn't listening. Her eyes were on the photograph on the table.

"Why Mavis – that's not you, is it? I mean, you look… oh, yes, that's your walking stick!"

Ben's look of anger passed suddenly. "Have you seen Mrs Granger with this stick recently?" he asked, relatively mildly.

"Well, yes. Mavis always walks with it when she has her dogs with her – that's how she controls the big beasts."

"Yes, of course," Mavis responded irritably. "I was just telling Inspector Shorter how I broke it in the spring and I had to throw the pieces away."

"That's not right," Pat said. "You had that stick at the Red Cross fair just at the beginning of this month. I was on the bric-a-brac stall and we were talking about Christmas gifts – don't you remember? You were holding your grandfather's stick then – the one you're so proud of."

"You're mixing things up, Pat," Mavis said tersely.

"I don't mistake things like that," replied Pat stubbornly. "I am very good with dates. I remember, clear as day. You were standing by my stall when one of those brutes growled at me and you tapped him with that stick. You had that stick with you then. I am certain of it."

"You just have to insert yourself centre stage, don't you! I am sorry, inspector, the stick I have been using for months is blond wood. You saw me with it down by the river, the day we met." Mrs Granger threw a glance across to Faith as well, then refocused her charm on Ben. "Mrs Montesque is just making things up. There is a certain rivalry between us."

"No, Mavis. Pat Montesque doesn't make things up." Faith's voice was calm. "If she says she remembers seeing you with that stick at the Red Cross fair, then I believe her." Pat was bristling with offence. Faith got up and piloted her to the door. "Thank you so much for the tea, Pat. It's most welcome. But they'll be coming in from the carol singing any moment. We need you out there."

"You can count on me," Pat said, and closed the door behind her.

Mavis's eyes had once reminded Faith of flat pieces of sky. *Now*, she thought, *they just look blank*. In contrast, sitting there in his fashionable clothes with his well-groomed hands, Neil's face was gaunt and his eyes bewildered. He hardly seemed to comprehend the scene unfolding before him.

"I think you took Anna's phone when she left it on the counter at your florist shop that Saturday," Faith said quietly. "You texted Lucas to come and meet you at the bridge."

A ghost of a smile sketched itself on Mavis's smooth face. She seemed pleased at her own cleverness. Then even that expression faded.

"What were you trying to do?" As she asked the question, Faith remembered that other time in this very room; Pat was exclaiming over Mavis's burglary – *I remember how it upset you. Some stranger coming in, trampling through your home and touching your private things. It's a violation.*

"It must have been so hard to know that your husband had fathered another son with Trisha," Faith said softly. Mavis jerked her head toward her.

"I say!" said Neil Granger. "Is this really—"

"With that cleaner!" said Mavis.

"Why did you have to stage the burglary?" Faith read the flicker in Mavis's face. "You wanted to go through your husband's desk?"

"The drawers were locked." She threw a disdainful glance at her husband. "I wanted to know the truth. You never let me look at the accounts and I am a businesswoman. I am not some ignorant housewife. I tried to pick the locks, but one of them broke so I had to make it look like burglary."

"How long had you known about Lucas?" Neil's voice croaked.

"Since the summer, when Vernon started bringing him to the house. He had your eyes," she told her husband casually. "And then there was that pendant on his keys. He did that deliberately to taunt me!"

"He knew about me?" Neil's question was pathetic.

"Yes. But he hated you," his wife answered with a certain satisfaction. "He told me on the bridge."

"What happened at the bridge?" Faith asked. She wanted to get this over with.

"I only wanted to talk to him. He was confusing Vernon – asking questions, snooping about. *Saying* things about Vernon's father. They got in a fight at the pub. He gave Vernon a black eye! At first I thought it was to do with Anna. You know – jealousy? But it was because Lucas was putting together the pieces. I wanted him to stop – to leave us alone. I had to use Anna's phone. The boy would never have come otherwise."

"Why didn't you just talk?" Neil protested. Mavis flashed a venomous look at her crushed husband.

"He'd worked it out. It wasn't hard, with all the *gifts* you lavished on her, was it? He said he deserved more money because his mother had suffered, and he needed it to take care of some relative."

"So what happened?" Ben prompted.

"I had the boys with me. They didn't like the little oaf. Jam nipped at him and that wretched charwoman's lout kicked him. So I gave him a jolly good whack." Mavis's arm sketched a backhanded swing with something gripped in her right hand. "It certainly took him by surprise." She stopped for a moment, contemplating her words. "I didn't mean to kill him," she said thoughtfully. "But his head bled." She said the words as if she could taste them. "He fell back against the rail. It all seemed to take a very long time. He put up his hand in front of his face and it was covered with blood. He swore at me."

Faith saw in her mind's eye that bridge and the broken rail and the blood and poor Lucas, just a boy caught up in the complications of others' lives.

"Is that why you hit him again?" She was amazed to hear her voice sound so composed.

"He *swore* at me," she repeated. "And he was staring! As if it were my fault! He was the one who destroyed everything! I hit him again so hard the stick broke." She motioned to the metal collar with a dismissive wave of her hand. "I thought I'd scooped up all the pieces, but I didn't realize until later that the collar was missing."

"What did you do with the rest?" asked Ben.

"Burned it," she said.

"Mavis?" said Neil, as if just waking up. "What have you done?"

Galvanized, Mavis Granger lunged toward her husband. "You lied to me for seventeen years. You carried on with that woman while I kept your house." She pointed at Neil's wrists where the globular silver cufflinks glinted. "I remember when you bought those." She met Faith's eyes. She suddenly looked young and vulnerable, a scarred shell of the hopeful young woman in the photograph. "He brought me a gift too that time – a daisy pendant." She stared at the people sitting around the table as if everything she'd done was perfectly rational. "A *daisy*," she repeated bitterly. "Those are his favourite cufflinks – an infinity symbol! He gave the matching pendant to *her*. She wore it in our *house*."

"Mrs Mavis Granger, I am arresting you on suspicion of the murder of Lucas Bagshaw…" Peter was gentle as he got to her feet and put the cuffs on. Mavis hardly noticed. Her eyes were fixed on Faith as if only she understood.

"I only wanted my family back," she said.

CHAPTER

20

The police, the Grangers, the carol singers, everyone had gone. Even Pat had taken her leave, informing Faith that she had invited Adam Bagshaw to join them for lunch at the vicarage, for the poor man shouldn't be alone at Christmas and *the gospel of love is for all our neighbours.* Faith couldn't help but smile. Ruth would panic at having another guest to feed, but knowing her sister, she'd rise to the challenge with aplomb.

She should be thinking about Midnight Mass. They would have to make do without Jim's choir. In light of the past few hours, that seemed such a trivial concern. They would manage. Ruth and Sean and Mother were all waiting for her back at the vicarage. Her sister had texted to say that there was macaroni cheese in the oven – especially selected comfort food; fuel for the long evening ahead. But they would have seen the police cars, and Faith just couldn't face explaining yet.

She kneeled at the altar rail alone in the light of the tree, and prayed. She prayed for Trisha Bagshaw and her beloved son Lucas, and for tortured Mavis Granger and her bewildered son, Vernon, and for Neil Granger, and for Anna too.

After a while, she felt more at ease. She got up and lit a candle for Trisha, and for Lucas. As she did so, she saw, vivid in her memory, the photograph of the loving Trisha between her two boys on the whatnot in the Bagshaws' living room. *Adam will be all right*, she promised. *We'll look out for him.*

On a whim she went out through west door beneath the bell tower, so she could look back at the sparkling tree illuminating the nativity scene with its glow. Outside, the snow glimmered in the dark, and all around the Green the houses were lit as the inhabitants of Little Worthy ate their suppers. As she pulled the door shut, she heard a motorbike draw up on the road. She walked down the path toward the lychgate and there, on the other side, was Jim Postlethwaite wrapped up in his peacoat, an Arab keffiyeh swathed around his neck.

"Hey," he said.

"Hey, you." It was cold out here. She wrapped her arms around herself and shuffled her feet. "I was so sorry to hear about your resignation. You didn't have to do that, you know."

"But you know why I did?"

"Because you were a heroin addict and you served a sentence for it."

"More than that…"

"Your daughter." She had heard the phrase "etched with sorrow", but she'd never seen its application until now, looking at Jim in the light of the street lamp.

"Before that moment, I didn't know the depth of misery you could feel for something you did. I woke up too late. I've tried to become a better person – but there are some things that just can't be mended."

"Mended," she repeated. "Maybe not quite like that, but…" She glanced back at the ancient Saxon church behind them. "This church was built for the God who offers us the chance to begin again. People have worshipped here for nine hundred years, so I think there must be something in it."

He gave her his old crooked smile. "I wanted to see you," he said, "to explain… I was trying to look out for the kids. Lucas and his friends, they invited me for a drink from time to time at the Lion's Heart. I couldn't believe it when I ran into Keepie. I did my best to keep him away from them. I am sorry if I misled you."

"I appreciate the value of discretion…" she echoed. For a second he looked appalled, and then he smiled ruefully. "I was just teasing," she said.

"I'm a bit fragile for that," he said.

"Oh, Jim – I'm sorry."

"By the way, some of the choir will still be here to sing tonight – seven or eight of them, I think. I told them to be here for 10:45. They know the order of service."

"That's wonderful!" She was so touched. "Thank you so much. Will you stay?"

He shook his head. "I'm on my way up to Manchester."

"Tonight?"

"I phoned my wife. She and my daughter, they're staying up there with friends. Ellie says we can spend Christmas together. I want to be there by morning."

"I am so very pleased for you," she said.

"It's a beginning."

"Yes, it is. One day at a time, huh?"

"One day at a time." He looked down at his gloved hands gripping the handlebars. "I wanted to thank you…"

"What for?"

"For seeing the best in me."

"I'm not naive, you know," she grinned. "I am a good judge of character."

He expelled a breath through his nose, and gave a small, self-deprecating smile. He started up his bike.

"Goodbye, Faith Morgan."

"God bless you, Jim Postlethwaite."

Jim's soloist had a clear, golden voice. She sang like an angel from the choir loft in the darkness, heralding the glow of the procession as they carried their candles down the aisle toward the altar and the tree blossomed into light.

> *Once in royal David's city,*
> *Stood a lowly cattle shed,*
> *Where a mother laid her baby,*
> *In a manger for his bed.*

It was a promise of hope that made the hairs stand up on her arms and expanded her heart. Faith looked around at the faces before her: Fred and Pat, the Grays and the Markhams, Sue and her family, Clari and Timothy with theirs, and even her own family – her mum, with Ruth and Sean. It was her first Christmas in St James's, Little Worthy. They'd made it and soon she could sleep.

They had a full house. Everyone was in good voice. And the best Christmas present of all came from Fred, who offered Adam Bagshaw a job at his agricultural supply business. Pat was genial, with Adam by her side holding Mr Marchbanks in his kitty carrier.

"A good attendance for your first Christmas at Little Worthy," she complimented Faith graciously. "I don't think I remember a better turnout, even in Reverend Alistair's day."

Back at the vicarage, Ruth was in her element, rejoicing in the Aga and in having people to cook for and to admire her table settings. Pat got on well with their mother, Marianne, both old ladies fussing over Adam Bagshaw and exclaiming at his skill in fixing Marianne's broken reading glasses.

At four o'clock, and an hour later than planned, they served lunch. Their guests waited in the dining room while Faith and her mother served up side by side in the kitchen. Faith had just filled a dish of roast parsnips when she noticed her mother's anxious expression.

"Your father's late," her mother said. Faith felt the chill spread from the top of her head down her spine. She swallowed.

"Dad's dead, Mum," she said gently. "He's been gone for five years." The confusion in her mother's eyes squeezed Faith's heart. She watched her pull herself together.

"Of course he is, dear. It's this time of year… I don't know what I was thinking. I'd better get these on the table." Her mother made a slightly wobbly turn and carried the dish out of the room. Faith realized she was being watched and turned to see Ruth in the doorway, watching her with an expression of unsettling compassion.

"You've got a visitor, Faith," said her sister. "He won't come in."

"Thanks."

Ben stood at the threshold. She was so pleased to see him she threw her arms around him and hugged him, burying her face in the warm, solid oblivion of his black coat. His strong arms enfolded her. She felt his chin on the top of her head. He was a wall around her, keeping her safe, just for an instant.

Ben moved his head. She felt his lips tickle her ear.

"What's up?"

"Nothing. I'm fine." She stepped away, smiling up at him. Maybe he wouldn't notice the tears in her eyes. "Just pleased to see you. Happy Christmas."

"Right." His eyes began their forensic examination, but then he let it go.

"Will you join us for lunch?"

He lifted his eyebrows in his most saturnine look. "What do you think?"

"No," she said with regret. He fetched a small cardboard box out of his pocket.

"Didn't have time to wrap it, but this is for you. Thanks for the help with the confession. I guess you always had it in you, this priest stuff."

She opened the box. There in a nest of tissue paper was a delicate Christmas tree decoration. She put it on the flat of her palm – a tiny metal boat with bronze foil sails and a little ruby pennant unfurled in the breeze. She could feel the ridiculous grin spread across her face.

He cleared his throat. "Just nonsense, of course."

Faith looked up at him, eyes glowing. Ben shrugged. "Reminded me of that tatty old centrepiece your mother always brought out this time of year."

"I love it." They stood there with time suspended for a moment, just the two of them.

"Got to go," he said at last.

"You're on duty," she finished for him. "Volunteered again?"

"You know me – not my time of year."

She watched him go, hoping that he might at least look back and give her a smile. He didn't.

A CD of Christmas carols was playing in the front room. The sweet melancholy of the melody carried to her above the chatter and laughter of her guests in the dining room.

She crossed the hall to join her family.

If you enjoyed *The Advent of Murder* delve into another of Martha Ockley's *Faith Morgan Mysteries* in...

* * *

THE RELUCTANT DETECTIVE

"COULDN'T RESIST TOUCHING THE BODY, EH?"
OBSERVED BEN.
FAITH WAS DEFIANT. "I HAD TO CHECK FOR
A PULSE."

Faith Morgan may have quit the world of crime, but crime won't let her go. The ex-policewoman has retrained as a priest, disillusioned with a tough police culture and convinced that she can do more good this way.

But now her worlds collide. Searching for the first posting of her new career, she witnesses a sudden and shocking death in a quiet Hampshire village. And of all people, Detective Inspector Ben Shorter, her former colleague and boyfriend, shows up to investigate the crime.

Persuaded to stay on in Little Worthy, she learns surprising details about the victim and starts to piece together a motive for his death. But is she now in danger herself? And what should she do about Ben?

Then a further horrifying event deepens the mystery...